T0361754

Acclaim for
ECHO NOVA

"If I could only use three words to sum up my feelings about Clint Hall's *Echo Nova*, I would say this—what a ride! If any novel ought to be made into a major motion picture, it's this one. A cinematic smash at its finest, every page of *Echo Nova* feels like jumping straight into a Steven Spielberg film, complete with all the thrills and adventure befitting a timeless hero's journey. Dash Keane is a character that keeps you guessing, cheering, and holding your breath all the way to the end. If reversing time were actually possible, I'd read this one for the first time again and again."

—SARA ELLA, award-winning author of the Unblemished trilogy, *Coral*, and The Curious Realities series

"With action, heart, and well-crafted characters, Clint Hall's *Echo Nova* captured my attention and catapulted me from the distant past to a dystopian future while delving into the core of what it means to be human."

—CATHY MCCRUMB, author of the Children of the Consortium series

"*Echo Nova* is truly a fast-paced, exhilarating ride. From dinosaurs to westerns to a hint of an anime love story, this book has managed to weave together some of my favorite things into a truly one-of-a-kind tale that kept my pulse pounding and pages turning. Trust me, this is a must read."

—S.D. GRIMM, author of the Children of the Blood Moon series and *Phoenix Fire*

"An imaginative and vibrant romp through time! Hall takes readers on a perilous journey in *Echo Nova* with high stakes, fast-paced action, and touches of romance and history. The unique take on time travel is refreshing, adding layers of creativity and possibility, and lends itself perfectly to YA audiences who will eat this up."

–E.A. HENDRYX, award-winning author of *Suspended in the Stars*

ECHO NOVA

ECHO NOVA

CLINT HALL

For my sons.

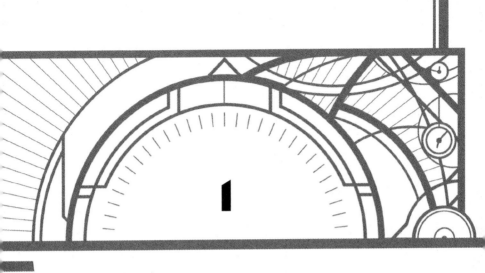

1

"KEEP THE CAMERA ON ME!"

I shout into the disk microphone on my collar as I race toward the edge of the roof, the cold rain pounding against my visor. If I die tonight, I want to make sure it's captured on video.

"Oh, is *that* what I'm supposed to be doing?" Garon's voice buzzes with static in my helmet's embedded earpiece.

The helmet isn't what it used to be. Whoever owned it before me probably tossed it in the dumpster after the statistical display stopped working. At one time, the visor might have shown me the distance to the edge, the wind speed, and the angle at which I should jump.

But through the rainy night, I only see the edge of the roof rushing at me and, beyond that, the lights of the city. I can't see where I'm going to land, but I don't care. All I need is the flashing red dot of Garon's black-market cam hovering in front of me. I pretend the city lights are all shining down on me, waiting for a show.

So I give them one.

My left foot hits the lip of the roof, and I launch myself into the air. This will be the image everyone remembers after the race—the Red Dragon, clad in black leather with stitched flames and a crimson dragon's head painted on his helmet, legs pressed together but arms outstretched like wings, riding the wild night.

But if my gravboots don't activate, it will be the last time anybody sees me alive.

I kick the heels together as I plummet toward the next building.

Nothing happens.

"Uh, Dash . . ." Garon says.

I pound the boots together again, my form forgotten as death stretches out its arms in the shape of a concrete roof, waiting to embrace me.

"C'mon!" I slam the boots against each other.

The energy clicks on seconds before I crash. It's happened before, but never from quite so high.

Still, my body knows what to do. I was born for moments like this, the rush of adrenaline, the reaper's cold breath on the back of my neck. The pulse from the boots feels like a cushion of energy beneath my feet, padding my fall. I pull myself into a ball and roll as I land.

The boots deactivate.

Nothing feels broken, and in a flash, I'm up and running. "Garon, tell me you got that!"

I've heard that the corporations watch race vids to scout talent, that winners sometimes get asked to audition as timestars. Probably just rumors, but it's always in the back of my mind when I compete.

"Nope." Garon gives a nervous laugh. "I decided to cut my losses and move my cam to another racer."

I smile as I jump to the next roof, doing a quick flip over the short distance. "So your camera is way behind me, then?"

"Actually, somebody is about to cross paths with you."

The city lights reflect off a green jumpsuit streaking across a higher roof on my right. I curse the moment I see her. *The*

Serpent. She's beaten me more times than I care to remember, though I'm pretty sure Garon keeps a running tally. I've never seen her—or any of the other racers, for that matter—without her helmet. Rooftop Ralf says it's better for business if we never take them off. It's easier for the fat cats to place their bets and gulp down drinks if they don't have to see our faces when we die.

The Serpent uses her gravboots and repulsor gloves to glide down to a roof ahead of me. Her tech is better than mine, which makes me resent her even more.

But she's a straight runner—no style, no showmanship.

Not like me.

"Think you can catch her?" Garon asks.

I pick up speed. Forget caution. Forget form. The Red Dragon is famous for stunts, but if I lose another race, the gamblers will stop laying credits next to my name.

My boots pound the rooftop as I dodge between antennas and ventilation shafts. The Serpent pauses to look in my direction, a mistake I've never seen her make before. She'll regret that. I gain two steps on her.

She turns and starts to jump for the next building, but her boot slips before she can launch. Her feet slide out from under her, and her back slams against the edge of the roof.

A wave of heat rushes through me as she starts to go over. We're at least ten stories up. If she isn't hit by a gravcar on the way down, the street will finish the job.

Her green glove grasps the roof's edge as I rush toward her, preparing to leap over her body.

Then it happens. The thought of my little brother.

Knox.

I know my kid brother isn't watching. Rooftop races are illegal and broadcast on a short-range pirated signal. The cops don't bust us up unless the money gets big enough to grab their attention. They couldn't care less if a few of us kids from the Dregs kill ourselves to entertain our betters. The people watching are probably screaming for me to blast right past her, a few secretly hoping I'll step on her fingers.

But what if Knox *did* see this? I already know I don't have a choice.

"The others are closing in," Garon says as I skid to a stop at the edge of the roof. If I lose, it's his money, too, but I can tell by his voice he's not trying to talk me out of it. I reach over the ledge.

"What are you doing?" The Serpent clutches my outstretched hand even as her voice conveys disbelief, as if saving her life might somehow be a trick. Can't say I blame her. More than likely, she's from the Dregs too. We don't trust people we don't know, especially when they say they want to help us.

"I have no idea." I pull her up onto the roof as the rain continues to fall. I half expect her to sweep my legs out from under me and take off running, but instead she kneels, chest heaving as she tries to catch her breath.

I take off again. "Garon, how far behind did this put me?" No other racers are in sight, but that means nothing. Rooftop races run from one point of the city to another; racers choose their own route. The only rule—don't touch the ground.

I'm about halfway to the finish point. The others could have easily passed without my seeing them, even if I had been looking.

"You're behind," Garon says.

I leap off the corner of the roof toward a taller building on my right, angling my body. My boots take three diagonal steps up the wall before I launch myself to the left, flipping sideways in the air. I land on another roof below and keep running. "How far behind?"

The pause in his voice tells me the rest. "We'll get 'em next time, Dash."

A wave of anger rushes over me, so hot that I expect the raindrops hitting me to become steam. I don't blame myself, or even the thought of my brother. It's the Serpent's fault for putting herself in a position where I had to save her. If she can't handle the race, she shouldn't be out here.

I sprint toward the next rooftop and jump, catching the lip with my hands and pulling myself up. "Any chance I can catch them?"

"Not unless you . . ." Garon's voice stops, but I know what he was going to say.

Catch the train. It's a crazy idea we've kicked around while shooting baskets on cold nights to avoid going home. We agreed it would be the coolest move ever, if I could pull it off.

We also agreed that it's basically suicide.

"I'm doing it." The adrenaline almost lifts me off my feet as I change direction. I sprint to the other side of the roof, then jump down to the next building. It's a long drop, but not so much that I need my gravboots again. I hit the surface and roll. "Can you track it?"

"Dash, this is a bad idea."

"Garon, I'm doing it." I jog to the edge. If the train were close, I would hear it. I have at least a few moments. "You can either help me time the jump and give me a slim chance to survive, or you can leave me on my own and tell my parents why you brought their son home in a bucket."

Garon is quiet. Maybe he walked away from the controls. Maybe he's finally had enough of me forcing his hand.

But I know better. Garon would never leave me behind. It's his best and worst quality. He's quiet because he's tracking the next skytrain that will come along this route.

"Twenty-three seconds," he says.

The city of Azariah stretches out in front of me—a menagerie of lights and sounds and flying machines. Far below, people hustle through the rain. A few stand still like they have no place to go. I've watched them many times, seen the expression of surrender on their faces, always swearing that would never be me.

The brightest light shines from a screen mounted on the side of the city's tallest building—Dominus Corporation's main offices. On the screen flashes the timenet symbol—a four-pointed star with curved lines pulsing away from it, as if the energy is an echo of the star itself. The symbol precedes every timenet broadcast to remind viewers that they're watching a program set in the past.

The screen shifts to a broadcast on the Dominus Corp. timenet channel from the P-2200 time segment, meaning it's 2200 years behind the present. A news ticker crawls along the bottom of the screen, reporting the same old stuff—Dominus stock is up after opening yet another portal to the past for mining natural resources, a group of exile terrorists have been arrested for trying to hack an Intellenon timenet feed—but my eyes are glued to the show. In this particular series, the timestars are modern athletes sent back to Ancient Rome to train and battle with gladiators. It's one of my favorites; I wish I could sit and watch.

"Ten seconds," Garon says.

I imagine the gamblers screaming at the holoscreen right now at Rooftop Ralf's speakeasy, wondering if I lost my mind. They might be taking bets on whether I'm about to jump off the building and end my miserable life. I wouldn't be the first.

"Five seconds."

I steel myself against the fear trying to creep into my mind. I'm the best rooftop racer this city has ever seen. Even if my record doesn't support it, I know in my gut it's true. The rest of them will see soon enough. They'll cheer for the Red Dragon.

They'll cheer for me.

"Go!" Garon shouts.

I jump, forgetting about form as I stretch out my arms and legs. The skytrain appears around the side of a nearby building like a long, silver eel swimming through the night. I pray that the electromagnets in my gloves work better than my gravboots.

Everything seems to slow down as I fall toward the oncoming

skytrain. The sounds of the city fade away—everything but the hum of the train and the throbbing of my pulse.

I slam onto the train's roof. The breath puffs out of my lungs. My body explodes with pain, but my maggloves activate, and I hold on. My muscles scream at the abuse, but I manage to pull my feet up into a crouch while keeping both palms against the roof surface. I can almost hear the gamblers cheering as I ride the steel beast toward glory. After this, maybe Rooftop Ralf will start taking me to the big-money races. I know he has connections that he doesn't share with us. He says it's for our own good, but I'm tired of everybody else deciding what's best for me.

"Dude!" Garon yells through the earpiece with an enthusiasm I've never heard from him. "That was incred—"

My maggloves deactivate. I cry out as the train slips beneath me, and I tumble backward along the roof.

A raised metal ridge hits me in the shoulder. I grasp it with my fingertips, holding on with every last ounce of strength.

Garon yells through my earpiece, but I can't tell what he's saying over the mechanical roar. The metal ridge carves into my fingers. Why did I do this? I don't want to die. I'm not ready to die. Who will take care of Knox? Who will take care of my parents?

The train whizzes between two buildings. If I had been able to maintain my balance, I could have leaped onto one of the buildings and run to the finish line. As it is, I don't think my fingers would let go even if I wanted.

"There's a stop ahead!" Garon shouts. "Hang on!"

The train slows as it turns a corner, moving away from the finish point, away from my chance at victory.

Within seconds, it stops next to an apartment building. A grated platform extends from its doorway out to the train. I should be happy I'm still alive as I drop onto the grate and make my way into the dim hallway.

But all I can think about is the loss.

ROOFTOP RALF'S PLACE

occupies an abandoned building with a faint chemical smell that gives me a headache. It used to be some type of manufacturing plant until most of the production jobs were moved to the past. Normally any buildings like this in the Dregs are taken over by vagrants and drug addicts, but Ralf carries weight in this neighborhood. People respect him.

A large bar occupies the building's center, surrounded by mounted monitors and several high-top tables made of polished wood that look out of place amidst the rusty steel walls and stained concrete floor, which is littered with torn betting slips. The gamblers don't dare leave an electronic trail. I spot a few red slips—my slips—strewn about, but not nearly as many as I would expect.

More people should have lost money on me tonight. I shake my head as my gaze goes to the light in the window of Ralf's office, which is an elevated room in the corner. The building is empty except for Ralf, so I pull off my helmet and carry it under my arm as I climb the stairs.

The door to Ralf's office is open. He's hunched over a mess of papers on his desk. I make my steps as loud as possible on the metal stairs. Ralf has little reason to fear anybody, but sneaking around in the Dregs can get you shot. There are enough people tweaked out of their minds to put everybody—even the kings of this jungle—on edge.

Still, I'm not sure he hears me. "Ralf?"

"You're out, Dash," Ralf says without turning around.

I freeze. "Out? How can I be out? Did you see what I did? Nobody's ever done anything like that. It would've been the highlight of the year if my tech hadn't shorted out. Maybe we can talk to someone about a sponsorship, you know? So I can get some new—"

Ralf whips around, his face contorted with anger, though his voice remains calm. "There isn't going to be a next time, Dash. I wish I could say I can't believe you did something so stupid as jumping onto a skytrain. The problem is . . . I totally believe it."

I laugh a little. Ralf's right about that. The Red Dragon is fearless. It's part of the brand I've built for myself. I want people to be excited about betting on me, so I do crazy stuff to win races—jumping from the highest places, swinging from cables, whatever I can do to get more attention.

And it's working. At least, I think it's working. The Red Dragon is popular on the underground vidstreams. I wish people knew it was me, but sharing my name is against Ralf's rules.

"It's not a joke, Dash," Ralf says. "I should have seen it coming, but I kept hoping you knew your limits. I'm not going to have your blood on my hands. You're out."

My frustration wraps around my gut like a hot coil. "C'mon, Ralf. You can't seriously be this hypocritical. Everything we do is dangerous. For crying out loud, we're jumping off buildings. Don't pretend like you care about us."

Ralf stands so fast that his chair nearly topples over. His fists are clenched.

My fear dissolves into guilt. I know I crossed the line. Rooftop races are common all over the US. I've never been anywhere other than the Dregs, but I know from the vidstreams that most organizers treat their racers like garbage.

For all his faults, Ralf's never cheated me out of money or even encouraged me to compete. The rumor is he knows that if he doesn't operate the races, somebody worse would fill the role. Rooftop races are actually one of the safer ways that teenagers in the Dregs can earn money. The elite love dropping big credits to see us risk our lives. Ralf does what he can to protect us.

"Ralf, I'm sorry, man." I hold up both palms in a sign of contrition. "But you can't take this away from me because I jumped a train. You and I both know there are no rules out there."

The anger melts off his face. Ralf sinks into his chair. "It's more than the train, Dash. The gamblers don't trust you anymore."

"What? That doesn't make any sense. I just proved that I'll risk my own life to win. Like I said, if my tech hadn't failed—"

"Oh, the skytrain jump was a big hit," Ralf says, "but helping the Serpent . . ."

I feel like I'm going to collapse. "This is because I helped *her*?"

"It cost you the race. Gamblers don't care much for self-sacrifice. They love the spectacle; nobody puts on a better show than you, I'll give you that. But they love winning more. I can't run racers that nobody bets on. You understand that, right?"

I don't respond. I should thank him for everything he's done for me, but I'm too angry. I rush out of his office, down the stairs, and toward the door of the building.

"Dash!" Ralf calls after me.

I look back at him.

Ralf stands at the top of the staircase. "What you did for her . . . that was a really good thing. Don't lose that part of yourself."

An apology begins to form on my lips, but the sound of a door creaking open stops the words in my throat.

A man in a black suit strolls into the building. His dark hair is perfectly styled—a razor-straight part and not a single strand out of place. The suit is tailored for his frame. His shiny, spotless shoes tap on the concrete floor as he approaches.

He smiles, his eyes combing my leather suit with its stitched flames. His eyebrows lift with curiosity, but he flashes a confident smile. "Hello. Aren't you the Red Dragon?" He has the face of a man in his twenties—no lines or wrinkles—but his voice seems much older. He extends his hand to shake mine, revealing a wristwatch with a black leather band, a white metal face, and Roman numerals. I'm surprised that someone so rich would wear something so archaic.

"This is fortuitous," he says. "I've been wanting to meet you."

I return the smile without knowing what I'm doing. "Yes, my name's—"

Ralf's footsteps echo throughout the building as he hurtles down the staircase. "Get out of here, Dash."

I blink at Ralf. "What? Why?"

Ralf reaches the bottom of the stairs, walks over, and grabs my arm. "We'll talk later." He ushers me to the door, then returns to the man in the suit.

My fingers swipe the disk microphone off my collar. "Garon," I whisper into the device, "you better still be listening. Patch the feed from the collar mic through to my earpiece." I'm not wearing my helmet, so I have no idea whether he responds.

I drop the disk on the floor, walk outside, and immediately crouch beside the door. The rain has stopped, but the streets are soaked, leaving a haze of steam rising from the surrounding Dregs and distorting the city lights.

I put my helmet back on. I hear Ralf's voice. "—not sure if any of my racers are ready for this type of thing. Why are you interested anyway?"

"I need new blood," the man in the suit responds. "My other timestars are becoming a bit . . . troublesome."

"Yeah, I saw that your big name got himself into some serious trouble, might even get exiled to P-100. Is that true?"

My skin crawls at the mention of P-100. It's the time segment where the worst criminals are sent to rot, though rumors of other things that happen there are a favorite topic among Dregs kids trying to scare each other.

But I'm still hanging on the word *timestars*. For years, I've dreamt of starring in one of those timenet programs where they send people back into the past to have adventures.

"The investigation is ongoing," the man says as if it's a frivolous detail. "Regardless, it's time to give someone new an opportunity. The public loves that, Ralf. It reminds them that anything is possible, that no matter who you are, you can make a better life. Don't you think that would resonate with your racers?"

A chill runs over my skin. It's like the man is speaking directly to me.

"I'll think about it." Ralf says it as if he doesn't have much of a choice.

"That's all I ask. Tell any interested applicants to be at the platform near the docks at sunrise the day after tomorrow." The suited man's voice grows louder as his steps echo off the floor. He's getting closer, and I doubt he would appreciate being spied on.

I run off into the night, my adrenaline overcoming my weariness from the race. I nearly collide with an old man stumbling down the street.

"Sorry." I sidestep to avoid him.

He reeks of liquor and grumbles words I don't understand. I'm used to seeing men like him. People in the Dregs drink to forget that time is against them, that they'll never ascend to the kind of life that is illuminated on screens and holograms all around. We're born here, time passes us by, and we die here. If we're lucky, we end up no worse than we began.

But as I jog toward home, the pain and soreness from the race long forgotten, one thought fills me with such energy that I feel like I could fly.

This could be my shot.

A timestar.

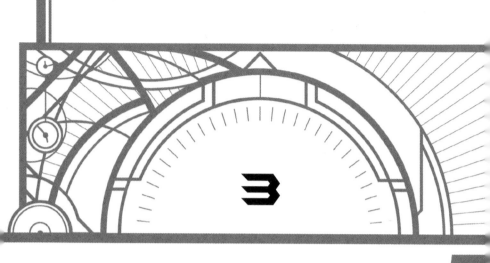

MY PARENTS ARE ASLEEP

by the time I sneak back into our apartment. Like most people in the Dregs, they work long hours at the local factory and only come home to sleep a few hours before going back to work. Even with both of them working double shifts, we can barely afford to feed ourselves after paying rent. It's one of the reasons I spend my nights jumping between rooftops.

Our apartment isn't much more than a steel box divided into a few rooms by thin walls and surrounded by other steel boxes—way too many people crammed into not enough space. My father says there are blessings in the anonymity, but I think he's trying to make the best of a terrible situation.

Besides, my little brother deserves better.

Our apartment's living room is cramped, to say the least. A dingy breakfast bar separates it from our tiny kitchen. A green secondhand couch squeezes next to the folding table where we eat dinner.

When I open the door to our room, Knox sits up in bed. His leg braces lean against the wall next to his pillow.

"Why isn't the holoscreen on?" I whisper as I toss my jacket onto the nightstand and climb into my bed.

"I was waiting for you," Knox says, but I know that isn't the whole truth. He doesn't enjoy the timenet as much as I do, but he never complains when I turn it on. Holoscreens are the sole luxury we have in the Dregs. The government uses them to communicate with people, so it's law that at least one be installed in every room of a home. If there's ever an emergency, instructions appear on the screen, but the orders are always the same—*Stay in your home.* We never mind when that happens. It's not safe to go outside anyway, especially for Knox. I hate that he has to grow up here.

When I touch the control pad on the wall next to my bed, the holoscreen lights up with the timenet's echoing star symbol. The glow reflects off his braces.

"How are they?" I ask, nodding at the metal contraptions.

Knox rocks his head from side to side. "Joints are getting a little loose again."

I nod. The leg braces were a gift from Rooftop Ralf, who despite my best efforts, wouldn't tell me where he got them. They're rusted and rickety, but I'm grateful to have them. Still, it angers me that our society can travel back in time but won't help my little brother put one foot in front of the other.

"I'll tighten them tomorrow." I use the control pad to search through the timenet for videos. There are thousands of choices in the catalog, but I prefer the livestreams. At this time of night, the corporations don't bother to edit the footage, which makes it feel more like you're actually there alongside the timestars.

I flip to the livestream of the gladiator show on the Dominus Corp. channel. Right now, the fighters are eating breakfast before the day's training begins. Most people consider this the boring part, but I could watch it for hours, thinking about how incredible it would be to travel back in time and fight against echoes while millions of real people in the present cheer me on.

"How was the race?" Knox asks. He's not paying attention to the show.

"Eh, it was okay."

Knox offers an empathetic sigh. "You'll win next time."

"Yeah, next time." I keep my eyes glued to the holoscreen. I hate when Knox knows I failed.

"At least you looked good," Knox says. The Red Dragon persona was his idea, and he stitched most of the flames and dragon designs onto my costume. The kid is talented, but he's also arrogant in his skills as a designer.

I love that about him.

"Got that right." I jump from my bed to his, being careful not to land on him. Knox laughs as I put him in a headlock and rub my knuckles on his head. After a few seconds, I let him push me away, and I crash to the floor.

"Oh no!" I say in my best timenet announcer voice. "The Red Dragon is down!"

We're both laughing so hard we can't even hear the holoscreen. Knox grabs his braces and raises them above his head. "The Red Dragon is no more! Long live . . . the Steel Dragon!"

4

"YOU LOST MY DISK MIC?"

Garon grabs a basketball out of his locker and closes the door. He's much taller than me, with an athletic frame and sandy-blond hair.

"C'mon, man. You know I couldn't go back for it." I take a quick look around. The halls of our school are filled with voices as students push past us in droves. Nobody looks like they're paying any attention to our conversation, but I lean closer to Garon and lower my voice anyway. "And I didn't lose it. I know exactly where it is. It's at Ralf's bar. But you heard that conversation. That guy was looking for racers to—"

Garon interrupts me. "Dash, we can't afford another mic unless you win a race. And that's going to be hard to do if you can't compete."

"Forget rooftop racing. Don't you think I should go after . . . whatever this other thing is?"

"You mean chase that small piece of a conversation you overheard when you were eavesdropping? The audition you weren't invited to?"

I shift my weight and adjust the straps of my backpack. "Well . . . maybe I could sneak in?"

Garon stares at me for a second, then walks away. I can't blame him. Getting dropped from the racing circuit hurts both of us. It isn't the first time that partnering with me has cost him time and money. Garon should have turned his back on me months ago. I can't decide if he believes in me or feels sorry for me.

I chase after him, brushing past a few other high schoolers to catch up. I bump shoulders with a guy named Craig. He's not as tall as Garon, but he's much broader, like a Viking who let his body go but held on to his anger. I nearly tumble over.

"Out of my way, dork."

I regain my balance, eyeing Craig for a moment before jogging to catch back up with Garon. "Listen, if this works out, we won't need the races anymore."

"What if we upload the vid anyway?" Garon says, keeping his eyes forward as he walks. It's like he doesn't hear what I'm saying. "People like the Red Dragon, and I got a good angle on that first jump. Maybe we clip it after you land so nobody knows you lost. That might get a handful of views . . . help build the platform . . ."

"C'mon, Garon," I say. "Nobody cares about that." I start to say more, but the words stop in my mouth the moment I see Braelynn Bonner coming toward me with her shining blonde hair, confident smile, and ice-blue eyes that always seem to know the secrets of the universe.

Before I know what's happening, she walks right by.

"Hi, Braelynn." My voice cracks when I say her name.

Braelynn keeps walking as she gazes over her shoulder. She's looking in my direction, but not focusing on me, like she's not sure who called out her name. Still, she smiles. This must happen to her all the time.

"Hi!" she says, throwing a polite response back to whatever faceless admirer tried to get her attention and, of course, failed.

When I turn back around, Garon laughs at me.

I shrug. "Dude, how am I ever going to be world-famous if nobody at this school even knows who I am?"

"Braelynn Bonner is the most untouchable girl in school," Garon points out. "That's not a good measurement for whether anyone knows your name."

"So you think people do know about me?"

Garon shakes his head. "No chance. I just wanted to correct your methods."

A few minutes later, we're outside on the basketball court, a tall chain fence separating us from the rest of the city. Most of the other students are gone, either heading home or to jobs or to wherever else everybody goes after school without inviting us.

Garon starts shooting as soon as we step onto the court, so I take my place under the backboard to rebound. Garon keeps his lips pursed and his gaze focused on the rim as he takes shot after shot. I've known him a long time; this is how he looks when he's thinking.

"You really think this is for real?" Garon asks, then calls out "Bank!" as the ball leaves his hands. The ball ricochets off the backboard and rattles through the chain-link net.

I catch the ball and toss it back to him. "I think it's for real. Anyway, it's worth a shot, right? If Ralf isn't going to let me race, we've got to do something to earn some money." The truth is that Garon could easily catch on with another rooftop racer. Even as a cameraman, he may be more well-known than I am; the guy is an artist as a cinematographer.

But he won't bail on me, and that's a sword that cuts two ways. When I screw up, I'm taking away his income too.

Garon nails another shot. He has a nice touch on the ball. If our school had the money for a basketball team, he'd be a star. As it is, the races are all we've got, and I have more natural athletic talent in that area.

Or maybe I'm just the one who's dumb enough to jump off rooftops.

I let the ball bounce once before I grab it.

"Your turn." Garon starts to walk toward me.

"But you haven't missed yet."

"If you wait for me to miss, you'll never stop rebounding."

I laugh. He's right.

I throw up a shot that clanks off the rim and bounces toward the fence. "Engage practice mode." The sensor in the ball lights up to indicate the command is received. When the ball hits the ground, it spins back in my direction. A couple of bounces later, it's in my hands. I never feel right making Garon chase rebounds on my terrible shots.

"So this audition . . . it has to be related to racing." Garon watches my next shot arc through the air and into the hoop. "Otherwise, why would he talk to Ralf?"

"Maybe he wants some warm bodies to throw into whatever crazy situation he's cooked up."

"But if you're supposed to be down at the docks," Garon says, "I think Dominus Corp. has a lily pad there. Is it possible they'd send you back?"

I freeze in the middle of my shooting form. My mind runs wild. I've been back in time before. Certain time segments have been designated for public use per government mandate, but they're always the most boring times available.

My father says his generation marveled at the ability to be sent back through the timestream to another time platform—called a *lily pad*—in the past. He says walking among the people in the past is a privilege, and he's never used the word *echoes* to describe them like everybody else. He doesn't like the term *lily pad*, either, as actual lily pads are anchored to the same point in a stream of water rather than floating along with the current the way time platforms do. My father used to refer to *lily pad* as "marketing jargon thought up by powerful people who don't fully understand or respect what they were dealing with."

People his age call my generation The Timeless because we

have never known a reality in which people couldn't experience other time periods at will. It isn't a big deal for us to spend an afternoon seeing authentic early American settlers farming and making candles from a distance.

There are more exciting lily pads on the timestream than colonial life, but they're owned by private corporations. Only the super-rich can afford to go to those places. The rest of us experience the excitement on the timenet.

What if I actually got to go to one of those other time periods? I hoist the ball at the rim and miss completely. The ball hits the ground and bounces back toward me, practice mode still activated.

Garon's face lights up. "You know what we should do?"

I catch the ball and shake my head.

"I mean," he amends, "on the small chance that you can even get into whatever this is, and then on the even smaller chance you get sent back in time, we should broadcast it."

I dribble the ball a couple times, frowning at him. "Can we do that?" I have no idea how the timenet works. All I know is it takes a lot of energy to create new lily pads along the timestream, and that those portals move consistently with the speed of time. You can never travel back to the exact same moment until another lily pad comes along.

The good thing is that because the speed of time is consistent, any timestream ripples we create by changing the past never catch up to the present, meaning the corporations who own those time segments can do whatever they want. There are a few regulations, one being that corporations are mandated to broadcast programs from the past so the public can benefit from the technology that generates so much profit. The programs are supposed to be educational, but that doesn't seem to be strictly enforced.

Not that I'm complaining. I'm much more interested in the action.

We learned in school that sending signals through time requires far less energy than sending physical matter, but I assume that it takes more equipment than Garon and I could get our hands on.

I keep dribbling as I play with the idea in my mind. "You can't really broadcast me from the past, can you?"

"No, but I can record you, as long as you don't break the cam. I've got one we could mount on your helmet. It's old tech, but it should do the job. Everything will be shot from your perspective. When you get back, we can upload it."

A thrill surges through my body. A good underground time video is the type of thing that could really catch people's attention, especially if they know it's me. *Maybe Braelynn Bonner will see it.* There's a dance coming up in a few weeks. The last guy she dated was a street fighter who posted a vid of his best knockouts and got national attention.

I take another shot, and I know the ball is going in the second it leaves my fingers. Everything about my form clicks perfectly. The ball swishes through the net.

"Let's do it," I declare. "What do we have to lose?"

5

THE MORNING MIST COLLECTS

on my helmet's visor as I sprint through the maze of warehouses near the docks. A dreary fog hangs over the Dregs this morning. My boots pound against the wet pavement with rapid splashes. It took longer than expected to get here, and now I'm late. I've probably missed my opportunity, but I still have to try.

This part of the city always feels haunted. Most manufacturing and shipping are now done in past time periods; businesses prefer cheap echo labor, and most lily pads are large enough to move large quantities of materials through time at once.

As a result, the manufacturing and shipping industries have been decimated. Moving around the docks feels like I've gone back in time already. Nothing here has been updated in decades. Many of the workers moved to the past so they could hold on to their jobs. They're not considered echoes, but they're paid as if they were and live at the whim of the corporations. It's an option I've considered once I get out of school, although I hate thinking about it. I'm determined to have a better life than that. After all, the future is the one thing that isn't certain.

But nowadays, I guess the past is no longer certain either.

I turn a corner and see the Dominus Corporation logo on

a massive building in front of me. I've stared at it a thousand times on the timenet—the word *Dominus* in all capital letters, leaning forward as if moving ahead through time. Knox has always admired the logo. He even copied the idea when he created my Red Dragon outfit. Everything he's made for me sports a red *K* for Keane, our last name, somewhere on the material. But instead of leaning forward, the *K* tilts back.

I touch the red *K* on my chest as I straighten and march toward the door. The exterior of the warehouse is solid metal and has no windows. Other than the massive Dominus logo, the look of it is entirely unremarkable.

The man at the door is so large he would dwarf Garon. He wears full armor—a dark, slate gray that covers his entire body with thick black fabric between the joints to allow for mobility. His helmet hides his face, which makes me think he might not be a "he" at all, although I'm more worried about the rifle in his hands.

Be cool. Profiting from less-than-legal activities has taught me the value of acting like I know what I'm doing. My fingers touch the side of my helmet, activating the tiny camera Garon installed last night. If I'm going to die here, maybe someone will find it. At least people will know I went out trying to do something great.

As I walk toward the door, the guard steps in front of me.

"This is a restricted area." It's a man in there after all, though the communicator in his helmet digitizes his voice enough that I can't tell his age. Doubtless, by now he's tried to access my own helmet for personal data about me, but he won't find anything. Sometimes it's good to have gear that was pulled out of dumpsters.

I lift my chin. "I'm here for the job."

"You're late," the guard says.

"Then you should probably let me through." I reach for the door.

The guard seizes my wrist, his grip enhanced by the suit. Pain shoots up my arm, but I don't show it.

"What's your name?" the guard demands.

"Red Dragon."

"Your *real* name."

"What's *your* real name? I was told to be here for the job. How would I be here unless I was invited? Your boss wanted me to come, but they were supposed to send a transport, which—as you can see—they didn't. But I came anyway. I'm trying to do what I was hired to do, and if you're—"

"Yes, sir," the guard says, still holding my arm as he cocks his head to the side, looking in a different direction.

Is he still talking to me? I don't see anybody else around.

"Yes, sir," the guard says again, and I realize that he's getting a transmission inside his helmet.

My heart drops to my stomach. Of course. Dominus Corp. must have cameras everywhere in an installation like this. They've probably been tracking me since I came within a mile of this place. The only question is why they didn't stop me sooner.

This was a stupid idea, and worse, I don't know how to erase this footage from the camera. At least nobody but Garon will see my failure.

The guard lets go of me, opens the door, and stands aside. "Go right in, sir. They're expecting you."

The words almost knock me off my feet, but my adrenaline pushes me through the door before I realize what's happening. Why would Dominus Corp. expect me? Do they know me from the races? Maybe that's why the man in the suit came to Ralf's office.

Yes. I decide to go with that explanation. It gives me the confidence I need to move forward.

Inside the warehouse, a narrow hallway leads to a large open room. The center of the room is dominated by a metal platform the size of a football field and raised a few feet off the ground. On the other side of the room, a wall of computers and workstations occupy the space, filled with men and women wearing dark-blue bodysuits with Dominus logos and hacking away at the keyboards.

"The Red Dragon!" A woman rushes toward me. "We didn't think you were going to make it." She has short brown hair and wears a white lab coat over her bodysuit. I see a few more white coats scattered throughout the room. I assume the white coats are time scientists who oversee the process of sending people back, though the people dressed in all blue seem to be doing the actual work.

I consider apologizing for being late before realizing that's not what a real timestar would do. I'm not going to lie about them not sending a transport again. She seems like the type who might know whether that's true. Then again, she *does* seem to think I belong here. I need to keep that going.

"Are you ready to send me back?" I ask, taking a risk that this is indeed a time jump.

The woman stares at me briefly, as if studying me. "How old are you?"

"Nineteen." I'm glad I'm wearing a helmet. Otherwise, she might see the lie in my face.

She gestures to the platform. "Stand in the middle. The temporal- and geographic-relocation coordinates are set. We'll get you there as fast as we can."

I walk to the middle of the platform with as much confidence as I can muster. Every eye is on me. For a room filled with people, it's quiet. My boots seem to thunder across the platform.

"Don't screw this up, Keane," I whisper to myself.

A grid of inactive energy lines runs across the black platform. I'm unsure where the exact center of the platform is located, and I break into a sweat beneath my suit as I wonder whether that's a common thing that an experienced timestar would know.

A few steps ahead of me, the energy lines light up, outlining a small square.

The center.

I hold my breath and step into the square.

The woman's voice echoes throughout the room. "Prepare for time jump." She's using some type of voice amplification. I look around but can't see where she's standing.

It's been years since I've gone back in time. I've never done it alone, but I remember the school field trips. Our whole class stood on the platform and held hands. When we were little, some kids would get scared, but as we got older, the whole thing became almost dull.

But standing here with all these people staring at me isn't boring.

It's exhilarating.

I kneel on one knee in the center of the square and drop my head, hoping it looks as dramatic in real life as it does in my imagination. "Ready."

The lily pad hums to life, energy surging from the sides of the platform to the small square that surrounds me. The lights reach straight up, creating glowing walls on all sides of me. There is no countdown, no instructions from the Dominus employees, nothing but light all around, enveloping me. When I was a kid, I closed my eyes during this part because I was afraid. Now I close them because, even through my visor, it's so bright.

I can tell the instant I'm traveling through the timestream. All sound disappears. My body suddenly feels perfectly still, as if the ground I had been standing on before—while I thought it stable at the time—had actually been shaking. It's like someone has pressed pause on everything.

The first sound that returns is my own breath. My eyes are still closed, but I can tell the bright light is fading. If I had better gear, my helmet might be outfitted with temporal technology that would give me accurate readings up to the nanosecond of exactly where I was in the timestream.

As it is, I have to open my eyes to find out.

At first, the platform looks exactly like the one I was standing on before. I wonder if I went anywhere at all. Maybe this was some elaborate prank, a hidden camera show to make me look even more like an idiot.

That idea fades as I realize this platform is much smaller. There is a wall to my left, filled with computer stations, but the faces are different. Though there are several people in blue Dominus bodysuits, the woman in the white coat is nowhere to be seen.

I stand as a man approaches. A red scarf rings his neck, and his white button-down shirt is stained with sweat. Dust covers his brown pants and boots. I can tell he hasn't shaved in days, and his tanned, weathered skin suggests that he spends most of his time in the sun. It reminds me I'm not in the Dregs anymore, where the smog makes the sun about as rare as having spare credits in your account.

"The Red Dragon?" the man scoffs. Muscles bulge beneath his shirt, but he limps like someone who has seen more than his fair share of adventures.

"That's me."

"Myrtrym told me to keep an eye out for you." He extends his hand, but it feels more like a duty than a friendly gesture. "My name is Cooper."

Myrtrym? Maybe that's the man in the suit? I try to etch the name in my memory. When I grip Cooper's hand, we both shake firmly.

"So what am I doing here?" The question is a risk, but I have to know.

"Better if I show you," is his reply.

He leads me outside, and I find that I'm on the edge of a cliff. The rising sun casts a golden glow over a beautiful, lush valley. The air is warm and smells unlike anything I've experienced in a long time. *It smells like life*, I realize—leaves, wind, even animals. I remove the helmet, keeping the camera facing forward to take in the setting. Garon would never let me live it down if I didn't capture this on video.

Vegetation fills the golden valley. A steady river flows through the center of it, broken up by mossy rocks and tiny islands with vibrant green copses. Large jutting rocks tower in the distance. The scene is overwhelming, and I realize I haven't felt so clean, so dry in a very long time. No wonder people pay small fortunes to visit the past, to get away from the pollution and the artificial smell that fills the air in our time. I could spend weeks . . . no, years here.

"When are we?" I ask, forgetting myself for a moment, being more Dashiell Keane and less Red Dragon.

"The Cretaceous period," Cooper says without an ounce of suspicion in his voice.

The moment he says it, the entire valley appears to come alive. Objects I thought were trees along the river begin to move—a herd of brontosauruses walks next to the water, some drinking while others nip at the trees. In the distance, what I previously thought was a flock of birds is a group of pterodactyls gliding down from the distant rock formations, probably in search of morning fish.

"You've been here before, right?" Cooper asks.

The question shakes me from my serenity. I have to keep my mind on what I'm doing. After all, the camera is rolling. "Nope, but I'm ready to get started."

"That's good, cause you're way behind." Cooper pulls a circular device from his pocket and thumbs a button on the side. A holographic map of the area appears above his hand. From the look of it, the building behind us is the only man-made structure in the vicinity. Everything else is undeveloped.

"We're here." Cooper places his finger on the square designating the building. It turns bright green. "And your objective is here." He touches a point on the other side of the river—a grove of trees between the water and the rock formations. The area blinks red.

I nod. "And what exactly is my objective?"

Cooper pushes another button, and the hologram shifts from a map to an egg. It's dark brown with yellow striations.

"Is that a brontosaurus egg?" I put my finger on the hologram and rotate the image of the egg.

Cooper laughs. "Not exactly."

My blood runs cold. I've seen enough timenet to know this period has a lot more creatures lurking around than those gentle giants nibbling leaves by the river. Maybe it's better I don't know what laid this egg. There's no way I'm turning back.

"Can't say I'm into the idea of stealing babies," I say, although I've already made up my mind to do it.

"Your peace of mind isn't my endeavor, junior," Cooper says, "but if it makes you feel better, we've found evidence of a disease affecting the embryos. Surmise we can introduce a cure to the ecosystem. If the egg is infected, I can treat it, but not out there. I need it in my lab."

"And what do I get out of this?"

He scrunches his eyebrows. "You don't know?"

My breath stops. That was a mistake. What kind of legitimate competitor would risk his life in the Cretaceous period when he didn't know the prize?

I shoot him the best smile I can manage. "Never asked. The ride is enough for me, but my people insisted I find out before I do this for you."

Cooper snorts. "You can tell your . . . *people* . . . that it's more credits than you ever got bouncing across rooftops in your pajamas."

"Works for me." I put on my helmet, wondering if Cooper knows that none of my tech works. My gravboots probably have no charge left. If this is a Dominus operation, I'm sure Cooper has some of the best stuff available, but I don't ask for anything. A real timestar wouldn't need to request better gear. Cooper cocks his head to the side and hands me the map device. "The trail to our right will take you down to the water, but you better hurry. Your competition is way ahead of you."

My hand touches the red *K* logo over my heart as I run toward the trail. The adrenaline fuels my steps, replacing fear with a spirit of adventure–the Red Dragon sprinting into a valley filled with dinosaurs.

The path slopes downward into the trees. My boots kick up dirt as I run through the forest, pushing myself so fast that I feel like I could lose my balance at any moment.

But I won't. I know this feeling well from racing across rooftops. I'm not thinking about the danger, the camera, the allure of fame, or the specter of failure.

There is only the run. I'm alive when I run.

The sunlight greets me as I emerge from the trees at the bottom of the path. The brontosauruses continue to eat and drink along the other side of the river. Some have waded into the water to escape the heat. If they see me, they don't seem to care. Still, I creep along the edge of the river, watching the pterodactyls in the sky and casting occasional glances behind me. If this is a popular watering hole, more dinosaurs are likely to be around.

When I reach the place where I need to cross, I ease into the water. Knox may scold me for this later; I'm not sure whether this outfit is waterproof, but if the credits are as big as Cooper says, I'll be able to make it up to him.

The sun warms my back as I move through the river. After a few steps, the water rises to my chest, the current causing me to move on a diagonal path. I've never been in water this deep. There's nowhere to swim in the Dregs. My friends and I have dared each other to jump off the docks, but nobody ever did. Even if we could swim, the polluted water would make us sick.

My arms float along the surface and though my boots can

still touch the bottom, I pick up both feet, letting the current carry me a short distance downstream before I slam my boots back down onto the rocks of the riverbed. I grin, then do it again, this time using my arms to swim forward.

The movement works, though clumsily. I'm still upright, taking long, slow steps that are almost like jumping through the water, using my arms to propel myself forward. I pull off my helmet and hold it up with one arm as I dip my head below the surface. The current pushes cool water over my face and plays in my hair. When I come up again, I feel clean, invigorated, as if a layer of grime has been washed off my skin.

I should stay here. The idea sends a thrill over my soul. Something about this untamed place resonates with me, satisfying a hunger I hadn't realized was there, buried deep in my heart. I'm already learning how to swim; I'm sure I could pick up whatever other skills I need to survive.

But I can't stay. Garon is counting on me. And so is Knox.

Besides, what I've captured on camera is already enough for a great timestream vid. People at school will love it. I don't want to miss that. I put my helmet back on.

My steps get shorter as the bottom of the river slopes up near the other side. The pterodactyls are gone. Downstream, a mother triceratops watches one of her babies bounding into the water.

The rocks give way to grass as I move out of the river and into another grove of trees. I have to be close. "What I wouldn't give for a visor with a working bioscanner." I say it loud so people viewing this vid later will know I'm at a disadvantage.

I crouch and move into the trees, looking for signs of a nest. The woods grow thick around me. I don't see any of the other racers anywhere nearby. I wonder if we were all given the same objective. If Cooper needs eggs for study, maybe he sent us to different nests to maximize his return.

I scan for a few minutes before I see it—a circular arrangement of sticks and mud at least ten feet wide. If I wasn't looking for it, I might have mistaken the egg for a rock. It's not as big as I expected. I won't be able to palm it, but I should be able to carry it under one arm as I run. I remember the triceratops in the river and the enormous horns on its head. I know it's an herbivore and wouldn't normally attack me, but if I'm stealing a baby, that's a different story. That's assuming this egg belongs to a triceratops, and not something . . . worse.

After one last glance around, I scurry to the nest, scoop up the egg, and start back toward the water, this time moving slowly so as not to make noise.

Then I hear it.

The roar behind me sounds like a jet engine. The ground shakes as something approaches.

And it's coming fast.

I break into a mad sprint, no longer trying to be quiet as I dodge trees, bounce off rocks, and slide beneath fallen trunks. The beast roars again, louder. Trees snap behind me with deafening cracks, but it doesn't sound as if it's gaining on me. It's fighting its way through the forest, which means my smaller size is an advantage.

For now.

I race up the side of a massive boulder and jump toward a tree. My foot lands in the joint between a large branch and the trunk, then I thrust myself forward. I grab a limb of the next tree with my free hand, swing, and let go, sailing through the air.

I roll when I hit the ground, then bounce up, still cradling the egg. The river must be close; the trees are thinning out. That means the mother will run faster too. A bloodcurdling roar confirms it. The ground trembles as if ripping apart. I nearly topple over tangled roots that grab at me from the forest floor, but I keep moving forward.

Almost there. The river appears ahead of me. The dirt changes to rock beneath my feet. A group of small dinosaurs drinks at the edge of the water. They whip their heads around, but they're not looking at me. One of them screeches out a warning, and they all run in the opposite direction.

There's no time to swim, but I spot a path of wet rocks leading across the river. No way I can make it to the other side without slipping, but if I try to swim, I'm dead.

I turn for a split second, not because I need to see what's chasing me, but because the *camera* needs to see it. My audience needs a good show.

The dinosaur explodes out of the trees, sending leaves and birds flying into the air. It's far larger than the triceratops and runs on its hind legs. A row of large spikes extends down its back. Vicious teeth fill a long, narrow mouth, and huge claws protrude from its two front arms.

"That should do it." I turn my head back as I hit the edge of the river and jump to the first rock. My foot slips a little, but I push off toward another rock. If my gravboots worked, I wouldn't even have to touch them.

The dinosaur crashes into the river behind me, surging forward, fighting against the current. It roars again, thrashing through the water.

I come to a small island in the center of the river. A long curvy branch snakes off the side. I run up the branch, balancing on the wet bark. When it starts to give way beneath me, I try to take one last step before I jump.

My foot falters. The egg flies from my hands as I flail.

I crash into the river. Rushing water thunders in my ears. My body swivels, and I slam into a large rock, the water pinning me against it.

The dinosaur towers over me, but its gaze is on something else. The egg.

I look to my right. The top of the egg bobs above the water line. It rolls around the rock and starts to float downstream.

My boots find the riverbed, and I push myself up, climbing

over the rock. The dinosaur strikes, its mouth missing me by inches.

When I reach the top of the rock, I jump off and crash into the water, wrapping my arms around the egg. The instant it's in my hands, the dinosaur's head slams into my side like a wrecking ball.

The force of it lifts me out of the water, and pain shoots through my body as I hurtle through the air.

I land on my back along the bank of the river, the egg clutched to my chest. I don't think it's broken, but I don't have time to look. I scramble up the bank toward the trees. The dinosaur lurches forward. No way I can outrun her up the path.

Blood seeps from everywhere—the gashes in the side of my jumpsuit, the tears in the fabric at my knees. I try to run, but my left leg falters. I must have broken something in the tumble. I can hardly stand.

The dinosaur roars as she closes in, sensing the kill at hand. Water cascades off her teeth, and hot breath pushes over me. Why is she taking so long?

Then it hits me. She wants to kill me but doesn't want to hurt the egg. I grab a sharp rock nearby and turn around to face the dinosaur, egg in one hand and rock in the other. The dinosaur moves forward.

I raise the rock and bring it down as if I'm going to strike the egg, stopping an inch from the shell.

The dinosaur freezes.

"I don't want to do it." I know she doesn't understand me, though I can see fury in her eyes.

The dinosaur lowers her head, and her eyes focus on something behind me.

I look over my shoulder and see Cooper sauntering down the path, a knowing grin on his face. He carries a green box like a suitcase in his left hand.

"Easy, Stella," he says.

The dinosaur shakes her head and makes a large huffing sound. "I said easy." Cooper takes the egg from me, kneels down, and places it on the box. A hologram appears around the egg, creating hundreds of flashing numbers and symbols in the air. Before I know what's happening, the hologram disappears. Cooper takes the egg off the box and goes toward the dinosaur. He sets it on the ground in front of her.

The dinosaur takes a last look at me before picking up the egg between her teeth. She turns her massive body around and stomps off across the river.

"I thought you couldn't scan the egg out here?" I say, my hand clutching my side.

"Am I the only person telling lies today?" He points a finger at my wound. "We better get you patched up. You're lucky that wasn't worse."

My side throbs and I'm getting dizzy. The adrenaline is wearing off, and the realization of how close I came to death pours in.

But before the moment passes, I need to do one more thing.

I pull off the helmet and point the camera at my face, doing my best to give a confident smile without looking directly into the lens. After all, that *was* one of the best races I ever ran.

"Did I win?" I ask, then reposition the camera so it's pointing at Cooper.

If he knows I'm recording, he doesn't acknowledge it. "That remains to be seen. Follow me."

He helps me up the path and into a small medical facility attached to the building with the time platform. The latest technology fills the room, a stark contrast to the prehistoric era around me.

The scans reveal some bone bruising but nothing broken. After several painful injections, I'm lying in a reclined chair while a robotic arm grafts new skin onto the side of my torso. If not for the numbing agents, the pain would be unbearable. Instead, it feels warm and tingly.

Cooper stands on the other side of the small room, studying the readings from the egg.

"So that dinosaur knows you?" I turn off the camera. Nobody needs to see me getting stitched up.

He doesn't turn around. "I've been here for decades. I imprinted on a lot of the specimens in this area at birth."

"You've been doing this kind of research for *decades*?" A surprising envy wells up inside of me. This place is alluring, even with predators the size of small buildings wandering around. It's so different than the present.

Cooper glances at me. "Not always research. I used to be . . . someone else."

My breath catches as I realize why he looks so familiar. How did I not see it before? This is *Cameron Cooper*. When I was a kid, he was my favorite timestar. "You're the dino-rider?"

Cooper goes back to his work. "Not for a long time."

A thousand images pour into my mind. *The dino-rider. The most hardcore PhD on the timenet.* I remember how he used to look, sitting on the back of a triceratops, binoculars in one hand as he held the reins in the other. His was a survival show, a way for people of the present to witness real dinosaurs. But after they had all been seen, the show got kind of boring, and it was canceled. I still remember the final episode—Cameron Cooper gliding into the sunset on the back of a pterodactyl. The story was that he had known the creature since its birth and that it trusted him.

"So what happened?" I ask, again noticing the limp in his leg. I can't imagine that he couldn't fix that if he wanted. Dominus Corp. has unbelievable technology and resources. "You were one of the best timestars on the net."

"I was *the* best," he states. "But the same thing happened that always happens. People got tired of seeing me connect with dinosaurs. Ratings dropped. They wanted me to do things differently."

"Different how?"

He leans against the computer station and crosses his arms. "Let's say I reached my limit of what I was willing to do for an audience, so I fell out of favor."

A shiver runs over my skin. Does he mean he fell out of favor with the audience or with Dominus Corp.? What did they want him to do? And why wouldn't he do it? The questions stop in my throat. I don't want to get on Cooper's bad side. I have no idea how to work this equipment or get back home. "So you're here by yourself?"

"I made a deal. I get to stay here and study these species. They use my work to make their timenet programming more exciting. And, for the most part, they leave me be."

"But don't you have family, friends?" I ask. "You know, in the present?"

Cooper scoffs. "I did, once, but spending my time riding dinosaurs in the past wasn't exactly conducive to fostering meaningful relationships. I'm where I want to be. Pretty sure I'm where everybody else wants me to be too."

The skin grafts are almost complete. A redness stretches across the flesh on my side, but if I hadn't seen it, I would never have known I got slashed by a prehistoric monster. The new skin feels a little tougher than normal. Maybe it takes a while to break it in.

"There weren't any other racers here, were there?" I ask.

Cooper gives me a long look, as if he's evaluating me. After a few seconds, he lets out a sigh, like there was something he was hoping to see in me but didn't. My heart sinks. If he's working with Dominus Corp., that means this was my shot and I blew it.

"Does it really matter?" he asks.

"No," I say as the grafting machine deactivates, and I pull my tattered jacket back on. At least my red *K* logo is still in place. "I guess it doesn't."

I gather my equipment, and Cooper takes me back into

the room with the lily pad. I don't ask about the credits. The mission was to return with the egg. I failed the moment he had to save my life.

The Dominus employees watch as I take my spot in the center of the platform. I wait for Cooper to say more, but he just stares at me until the blinding light washes it all away.

When I reach the present, I'm quickly escorted outside by Dominus' guards, still in full armor. The same cold rain and fog from this morning blanket the Dregs. Hours have passed here while I was in the past running from dinosaurs, but it doesn't seem like it. I'm already longing for the warm sun of the prehistoric valley.

It's the weekend, so I make my way over to Garon's house to drop off the camera. He asks how the trial went, but I'm sure my face tells him all he needs to know. The rest he can learn from the vid.

I leave his apartment and make the long trek back home, stashing my Red Dragon outfit behind a nearby dumpster, where I hid a change of clothes. I decide to keep wearing the jacket. After getting kicked off the rooftop-racing circuit and blowing my timestar audition, there's no reason for me to hide the fact that I'm the Red Dragon anymore.

Besides, it's not like anybody will care.

When I walk through the door of our apartment, Knox is busy at his sewing station. No sign of my parents, which means they must be at work. At least I don't have to lie about where I've been. I hate lying.

Knox's machine is so loud that I'm not sure he hears me as I hurry into our room, flop onto the bed, and try to forget that I wasted the best shot I will ever have at changing my life.

Our lives.

I sleep for hours, and when I wake, dusk is settling over the city. I throw on my jacket and sneak up to the roof.

This is my favorite spot, sitting and facing the sunset, an

orange haze that fades into the deep gray of the darkening sky. But my eyes are on the moon. I could stare at it for hours. It feels like an escape, somehow, to be here in the Dregs and still see something so far away from my reality. Our history teacher taught us that mankind once believed we would go into outer space and create colonies on other planets or moons. The discovery of time travel rendered that type of space exploration unnecessary; we gain more land and resources far easier by going back into the timestream, as many corporations have chosen to do.

It always seemed disappointing to me, even now, that we no longer look beyond our own world. The speed of time is constant, so we can go back in the past and change whatever we want without impacting the present. In that way, I suppose, we are exploring new frontiers with the new ways we choose to live out the past.

But still, it's going back, not forward, and not to new places.

As I have on many evenings, I watch the moon and pretend it's a distant planet. A place where anything is possible, a place I could reach someday.

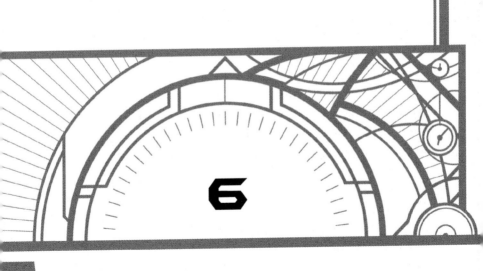

6

WHEN KNOX AND I WALK OUT

of the apartment on Monday morning, I pull the zipper of my Red Dragon jacket all the way up and bury my face in the collar to keep the cold away. I spent all day yesterday wondering if Garon had seen the vid, but I couldn't build up the courage to ask.

My parents leave for work before Knox and I wake up, so there's nobody to see us off in the mornings, which is fine by me. The less I see them, the less time they have to ask me questions. They work long hours, and it's not that I don't appreciate it–I would love to help out more–but they seem dead set against everything I do to try to make a better life for myself. For *all* of us.

Knox and I shuffle down the sidewalk, passing rows of run-down apartment buildings. Every so often a convenience store or a cheap restaurant breaks the monotony, but there isn't much else in the Dregs. The rain has stopped, but the sky remains overcast. Knox's leg braces make a rhythmic clop against the sidewalk. I walk slowly so he can keep up.

"How are they feeling today?" I ask. To take my mind off the vid, I spent a couple of hours yesterday adjusting the braces while Knox repaired my jacket.

He grins at me. "Better than ever."

I smile back, but I doubt that he's telling the truth, since like most of our things, his braces are basically junk that nobody else would want. It's better than him not being able to walk, I guess.

But today, every clank of his braces on the pavement, every squeak from a rusty joint, reminds me of my failure. If I had gotten that egg back to Cooper, I might have been able to buy him real medical equipment.

"Hey, Red Dragon!" somebody calls from across the street.

I drop my head deeper into my jacket, pushing my nose behind the zipper. I'm surprised someone recognized the jacket, but no way am I looking to see who was calling after me. The last thing I want right now is to be teased. "Sorry, Knox, but can we walk a little faster?"

"Uh, sure," Knox says. "Watch this." My little brother takes off at a jog, faster than I've ever seen him move. His legs wobble as he goes.

I rush after him, certain he'll crash at any moment. Sure enough, just before I reach him, he takes an awkward step and starts to tip over. I grab him, my heart pounding in my chest.

But Knox only laughs. "Did you see that? That was awesome."

I shake my head but can't wipe the smile off my face. "You really scared me."

"That? Just getting warmed up. If you keep improving my braces, pretty soon I'll be rooftop racing right next to you. Actually, I'll be way in front of you."

"No doubt. But for now, maybe we should take it—"

"Red Dragon!" This time the call comes from a man in a business suit on the other side of the street who looks to be in his midtwenties. He's walking in the other direction but pumps his fist at me. "Great run!"

"Uh, thanks." I wave. *Great run?*

"Who was that guy?" Knox asks.

"No idea. C'mon, let's get to school."

For the rest of the walk, I can't shake the feeling that people are staring. I feel like I'm catching eyes with everyone on the street. A few have a look of recognition when they see me. Each time, I turn my head away and walk faster until I remember that Knox can't keep up. *Maybe I'm being paranoid.*

But when we get to school, everything changes.

Students mob us the moment we walk through the outer gate. At first, I can't even tell what they're talking about. All of the voices jumble together.

". . . best vid I've seen in a long . . ."

". . . really Cameron Cooper? I thought he was . . ."

". . . Red Dragon, man. I always thought that . . ."

". . . going back soon? I think you should go to . . ."

". . . not sure about you stealing that egg. I heard Dominus uses them for . . ."

Students push in on us from all sides, trying to get my attention. My heart races, and I pull Knox close, afraid they're going to knock him over.

"Give him some room, people!" Garon's voice rings out to my left somewhere. He's a head taller than the other students, so I spot him right away. He pushes his way to Knox and me.

"Garon, what's happening?" I say.

"I switched your life to 'on,'" he says with a big smile.

"What does that mean?"

"I posted the vid, Dash, and it blew up. That's what's happening."

Garon clears a path through the other students as Knox and I make our way into the school. I'm nervous until we drop Knox off at his first class. People continue to crowd us in the hall.

And for the first time, I let myself enjoy it.

Girls throw their arms around me, telling me they were so worried when they saw the vid, that they were certain that dinosaur was about to rip me apart. Of course, they didn't stop watching either. They use their own hovercams to take vids of themselves with me that they will post on the feeds. Some pretend they're dinosaurs about to bite me, then run off laughing.

A few guys glare at me sideways, but most are congratulatory. I'm getting fist bumps and high fives from some of the street fighters. The smart kids lob questions at me about the dinosaurs. I shrug and stutter out some version of "I was running too fast to really notice." They eat it up. After all, that's what the Red Dragon does.

He runs.

I don't get a chance to speak with Garon until the bell rings for first period and the halls start to clear. We've both got phys ed first period, so we hustle to the gym, get changed, and start shooting baskets in a corner of the gym. After another round of congrats from other students, we get a few minutes to talk.

"I knew it was good," Garon tells me. "But I didn't think this would happen. When I uploaded it to the vidstream, I just shared it with a few people. I guess it caught on."

"You posted the whole thing?" I ask while taking a shot. The ball hits the back of the rim and goes in.

"Nah." Garon bounces the ball back to me. "I took out the part where you nearly got cut in half. And that stuff with Cooper. Basically, the vid looks like you made it across the river and into the compound on your own."

I shake my head and nail another shot. Garon is the best, and what's better, there's nobody I would trust more with the truth about my failure, except maybe Knox. People in the Dregs look out for each other, but that goes double for Garon and me.

He checks his hand device. "Your views are blowing up."

"You mean *your* views. It's your vid, Garon. You made me look good."

"But you're the star."

I stop before taking another shot and instead go over to him. "I might be on camera, but we're in this together. Any attention

I get, I'll do everything I can to help you."

The rest of the day goes by in a mixture of blurs through the hallway and endless class periods. I catch Braelynn Bonner looking at me during history class, but when I wave at her, she snaps her head back to her notes. My entire body feels like it's on fire when that happens. I'm not sure whether it's nerves or excitement, but I'm glad she's not looking anymore because my cheeks are probably beet red. I'm going to have to learn to deal with this better.

By the end of the day, my excitement morphs into anxiety. People have said their congratulations, posted their vids, and given their high fives. As I walk the hallway to the place by the water fountain where I always meet Knox at the end of the day, it seems most of the students have moved on and are leaving me alone. Could that really be possible? It's been less than a day. Am I old news?

Knox leans against the wall, waiting for me. For the first time, I realize that I'm exhausted. I've been "on" all day, talking to people, trying to look like a star. I can't stop thinking about two things: getting my little brother home and what my next vid will be so I can recapture everybody's attention.

"Ready to go?" I ask Knox.

"Yeah, let's get out of here."

We walk down the hall and into the courtyard outside the school. As always, other students hang around—some shooting on the outdoor hoops, others circled together talking, laughing, play fighting. I hear a couple shouts of "Red Dragon!" as we approach the gate, but I try to focus on Knox.

"What should we do for dinner tonight?" I ask. "Mom and Dad are probably working late, so I was thinking we could celebrate and . . ." My words trail off as something in the air catches my attention.

A shiny black gravcar flies toward us from down the street, shimmering in the late afternoon sun as a blue glow emanates beneath it. Gravcars aren't uncommon in the Dregs. Nobody that lives here can afford one, but they pass through from time to time on their way to better parts of the city.

But I've never seen one so nice.

The other students gawk as the gravcar approaches the gate, slows down, and descends. What could a car like that possibly be doing here?

Knox and I stand motionless as the car lands about twenty feet in front of us. The rear door opens.

I recognize the man as soon as he steps out. He's in a different suit than he wore in Ralf's office, but he's every bit as polished. He removes his black sunglasses to reveal green eyes.

"Dashiell Keane?" He says my name as if it's a question, but I have little doubt he knows exactly who I am.

I give a quick nod, but I'm not sure I meant to do it. It's more like a reflex, like I'm outside my body, watching it do things.

"My name is Myrtrym." He walks to me with his hand forward, wearing the same watch he wore in Ralf's office.

I shake his hand. His skin is much smoother than Cooper's. "Nice to meet you, sir."

"Please," he says with a smile, "call me Myrtrym."

"Okay, Mr. Myrtrym," I say, knowing it's not exactly the same, but I'm not comfortable being any less formal than that.

"And you must be Knox." He reaches a hand toward my little brother. "I'm a big fan of your work."

Knox shakes his hand with a perplexed look on his face. "You are?"

"Of course," Mr. Myrtrym says, then points at the red *K* on my jacket. "This is you, right?"

Knox is beaming. "It is."

"Extraordinary," Mr. Myrtrym says. "You two are a talented pair."

The other students have quieted down, and they're all staring.

Mr. Myrtrym's gaze flicks past us to them. "I guess I've made a show of myself here. My apologies."

"It's okay," I say and mean it because in my mind, I'm thrilled. An extremely well-dressed man in the nicest gravcar I've ever seen is shaking my hand in front of everyone, and it has to be because of my vid. Hopefully someone is taking pictures.

"Listen," Mr. Myrtrym says, "can I give you guys a lift home? I'd like to talk to you about some things."

"Seriously?" I've never been in a gravcar. The closest I've ever gotten is riding the public skytrains that snake throughout the city.

I start to accept, then hesitate. I'm pretty sure my parents are at work, but if either of them is home, they're going to go ballistic, especially my father. He's always on me about drawing too much attention. Riding home in a flying car is the exact opposite of everything he stands for.

Knox leans against the fence rail, balancing himself on his braces. By the end of the day, he's always exhausted, and the walk home takes a long time for him.

"Seriously," Mr. Myrtrym answers. "But no pressure. I know the gravcar is a bit much. My job rather requires that I have it."

"Your job?" I ask.

He nods. "I work for Dominus Corp."

"Doing what?"

"Tell you what," he proposes. "I'll walk you back to your house and tell you all about it." He motions to his bodyguard to follow.

I look at Knox again. He deserves better than this. "No. Let's take the gravcar."

Mr. Myrtrym nods his approval. "Excellent."

Thirty seconds later, Knox and I are sitting in the most comfortable black leather seats I could ever imagine, drinking sparkling water as the gravcar lifts into the sky. Mr. Myrtrym sits facing us, sipping his own water. The partition is behind him, blocking our view of the driver, though I've heard that some gravcars are automated.

"It's a short ride," Mr. Myrtrym says. "So I'll get to the point. Among other things, I'm in charge of programming for Dominus

Corporation's timenet broadcasts."

My heart races, but I lean back in the chair. Part of me can't believe it, but the other part knows I need to play this as cool as possible.

"What you did with those dinosaurs," Mr. Myrtrym says. "That was seriously impressive, especially considering that you had absolutely no tech. Where did you train?"

My brow creases. "Train?"

"Yes, for rooftop racing. I know it wasn't Ralf who trained you, but you had to learn those moves somewhere. Whoever taught you must have been expensive."

Knox and I look at each other, trying not to laugh. "No," I manage to say, "never had any training other than growing up in the Dregs."

"Extraordinary," Mr. Myrtrym remarks. "You're a natural then. *The Red Dragon*. Was that moniker your idea, Knox?"

It was, but I know he won't take the credit he deserves.

"Yes," I say. "He came up with the name, and we built the persona together, mostly because we had a lot of red fabric to use."

Mr. Myrtrym sets his water in the cup holder at his side. "Well, my programming board loves it. We'd like to use your face more. Not just the Red Dragon, but *Dash Keane . . . The Red Dragon*. You see the difference?"

"I do." And I love it. Through the tinted windows, I see that we're getting close to home. If I weren't so concerned with keeping my composure, I would beg him to circle the block a few times.

"You're a superstar, Dash." Mr. Myrtrym leans forward. "We would like to offer you a chance to be one of our timestars."

"What kind of chance?" Knox asks.

Mr. Myrtrym nods. "Direct. I like that. Ultimately, it's always up to the audience, isn't it? That's the great thing about this world. No matter what we try to give them, the audience decides what it wants. I've seen vids of your races. You understand the importance of showmanship. Dominus can provide a platform to show the world what you can do. If the people like what they see, and if the metrics are good enough, we will make you a very lucrative offer."

The gravcar lands in front of our apartment building. My head is swimming. Everything I've ever wanted is right before me. "I'm not sure what my parents will say."

Mr. Myrtrym looks thoughtful. "I don't mean any disrespect to your parents, but if I'm not mistaken, you're of legal age to emancipate yourself, provided you have viable options to support your own living. Our lawyers could help, if you chose to pursue this option."

He's right. I am at the legal age, but Knox isn't. He's a few years away, and my parents would never allow him to go with me.

But if I can pull this off, I could give them money to get him treatment. And when he's old enough, I can get him a job. Timestars are known for keeping an entourage. If I make a name for myself, I can bring on Knox as my wardrobe designer and Garon as my cameraman.

No, not *if* I make a name for myself. *When* I make a name for myself.

The door to the gravcar opens on its own.

"Thanks for the ride." Knox gives me a quick look as he makes his way out.

"Think about it, Dash," Mr. Myrtrym says as I follow my little brother out of the gravcar. Myrtrym hands me a rectangular piece of glass. It's about the size of my palm and has a white tint to it. "You can use this to communicate with me."

I shove the piece of glass into my side jacket pocket. I want to ask more, but I can already hear my father yelling from the door of our building.

7

I STAND IN THE MIDDLE OF

our living room, silent as my parents lecture me, mostly because talking won't do me any good.

"Of course we saw the video!" My father stands in front of me with hands outstretched, shaking with anger. "*Everyone* saw it! Do you have any idea how dangerous that could be for—"

"What were you thinking?" my mother asks. She steps between us and shoots my father a look, an unspoken message. After a moment, he flops onto the couch and buries his face in his hands.

My mother sighs and looks back at me, her eyes glistening with tears. "Do you even care that you could have easily died out there?"

"I'm dying here already, Mom." The tension builds in my stomach. I'm starting to sweat.

"What is that supposed to mean?" she demands.

"This life!" The anger erupts out of me like a volcano. I couldn't stop it if I wanted. It's almost like reciting lines from a play. I've been sitting on these words for way too long. If I don't say it now, the rage will tear me apart inside. "What is my life even about? What's the best possible thing I could hope for?

If something doesn't change—doesn't *drastically* change—I'm going to wind up in the factory like both of you."

Saying it out loud makes me cringe, but the fury doesn't subside. After all, it's the truth. I've seen my life heading in that direction for years, and despite my best efforts, I've been powerless to change it. Sometimes it seems like my parents are trying to keep me from succeeding.

Still, the guilt gnaws at me. "I know you both work hard, and I appreciate it. But I want something better. I know everybody says that, but I have a chance to make it happen. You're my parents." I plead, "Don't you want that for me?"

My father draws in a deep breath like he's about to match my explosion with one of his own. Instead, he just releases a huge sigh. "You have no idea what you're doing. These people, these corporations . . ."

"I know how it works, Dad. Mr. Myrtrym was clear. They're driven by profits. I have to earn my spot or I'm out. But I can deliver. I can be a real timestar. Dominus Corp. must see it, too, or they wouldn't waste their time and money giving me a shot."

My mother sits next to my father and takes his hand. Her eyes are on me, somber. "Dash, you don't understand the world yet. I know you think you do, but there's so much you don't know."

I stand a little straighter, making myself taller. I'm not letting them win. Not this time. "I love you both. I really do, but this might be my one chance. And I can't pass it up."

I don't wait for my parents to respond. I storm into my room and slam the door. Knox sits on the bed and watches as I toss my jacket onto the nightstand and flop onto my mattress.

"Dash?"

I raise my head enough to look at him out of the corner of my eye. I grunt a response.

"What you did out there," he says, "Well . . . it scared me too."

His words cut straight to my heart. I can't deal with this right now. Maybe I should sneak up to the roof. Though it's my favorite place to think, the last thing I need is to give my parents more ammunition against me, so instead I reach over and turn out the light.

I roll to the other side of the bed and hit the power button for the holoscreen. The timenet star shines bright, then the Dominus Corp. channel comes on, playing a show about comedians who sneak into fancy parties in the Victorian era and do silly things, seeing if they can get the echoes to play along. It's a good show, but I'm not paying attention. Knox's words keep bouncing around in my head.

"Hey, Knox."

"Yeah, Dash?"

"Sorry you were scared."

"It's okay." The light of the holoscreen reflects off his face.

I pull myself up so I'm leaning on my elbow. "It was pretty cool though, right?"

"Yeah," Knox says with an easy smile. "Extremely cool."

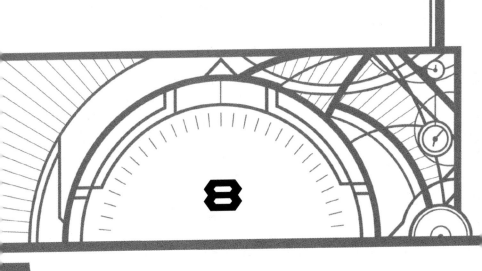

A FLASHING LIGHT WAKES

me from my sleep. I had been dreaming I was back with the dinosaurs. Cameron Cooper was nowhere around, and I had no mission. Instead, I floated down the river in a canoe, carving through the valley while the sun rose in the east. All the dinosaurs were there, even the mother with the vicious teeth, but none chased me. Most didn't appear to notice me at all, like I was another natural part of the ecosystem. The sensation put me at ease. I understood why Cooper preferred living there.

At first, I thought the flashing light was a signal coming from farther down the river. It intensified until I realized I was in bed back in the Dregs, back in my actual life. None of it was real.

At least, not this time.

The holoscreen is off, which means the light is coming from somewhere else. I raise my head and see my side jacket pocket glowing on my nightstand.

The glass card that Mr. Myrtrym gave me.

I reach over to the nightstand, trying not to wake Knox. He stirs a bit and mumbles words I don't understand, then rolls onto his other side.

My fingers pull the smooth rectangle from the pocket. I hide it under my covers to get a closer look without the bright light shining in the room.

The card shows text in simple black letters on a white background.

Time, once lost, cannot be regained.

It's a quote from Dr. Suvea, a scientist most people credit with the invention of travel through the timestream. We learned about it in school. A lot of people say the discovery saved humanity. Going back in time meant we could harvest natural resources to bring back to the present, avoiding a worldwide energy crisis.

Dr. Suvea died not long after the discovery. This quote is the first thing that comes up whenever anybody mentions his name. It means that even though we can go back to previous time periods, we can't stop time itself. The stream continues to flow. The present keeps moving forward, and most importantly, we continue to age.

I stare at the words and think about my day at school. This morning, I was everything. Everybody wanted their moment with me, but hours later, I was old news. When I walk in tomorrow morning, my adventure vid will most likely be forgotten. What if that was the greatest moment of my life and it's already gone? What if, in five years, Garon and I are on our lunch break from the factory, sitting and reminiscing about the morning our vid ruled the high school and regretting the fact that our lives are over?

The text on the card changes. *We would like to bring you in for a meeting. To accept, double tap the glass. - Myrtrym*

I know I should take my time responding, maybe sleep on it, but what more is there to think about? This is my chance to be great.

My finger taps the glass twice.

The white screen shifts to green in confirmation.

My life is about to change.

9

I WALK OUT MY FRONT DOOR

with Knox the next morning, expecting to find a gravcar waiting to fly me to my new life.

When it isn't there, my heart drops.

Did I miss my chance? The idea is crushing, but then I remember that Knox has no idea what happened last night. I've decided not to tell him. If Dominus does come get me sometime today, my parents will ask him later if he knew what I was doing. I don't want him to lie. I hate secrets, but I hate lies even more.

I'm not sure how well I can hide it from him, so I'm grateful when he starts the walk by asking questions about the dinosaurs and Cooper. The conversation carries us all the way to school.

And that's when I see the gravcar outside the gate. Mr. Myrtrym steps out of the car door.

"It's him," Knox whispers.

The students gather around the chain-link fence again, all watching Mr. Myrtrym with a collective look of amazement. Normally they would call out stupid jokes and rude comments. After all, we're kids from the Dregs. The "us versus them" mentality runs deep. We pride ourselves on being tougher, smarter, more capable than the rich people driving through our neighborhood. Maybe it's true, or maybe it isn't. I can never decide which would scare us more.

But none of them say a word to Myrtrym. The way they stare at him reminds me of when our elementary class visited a zoo— it's like he's some other species on exhibit.

Garon runs out of the gate toward us, his attention alternating between me and the gravcar.

Knox stops and tugs my arm. "He's here for you, isn't he?"

I take a breath. "Mom and Dad won't understand, but I hope you do. I have to do this."

There is a pause, then he says, "I know." He looks down at his braces. I'm afraid he's going to tear up. I'm not sure I could handle that.

But Knox just nods. He's stronger than I am.

"I promise I'll visit as much as I can." I give my little brother a tight hug.

The bell rings.

I let him go. "Alright, Knox. Get to class," I say. "I'll call you soon, okay?"

"Good luck." Knox ducks his head and makes his way into the school, moving faster than usual. Garon dodges him as he jogs up to me.

Mr. Myrtrym approaches as well. "Good morning, Dash. Are you ready?"

I should be, but the thought of my little brother makes me hesitate. Garon takes Knox's place at my right side.

"Let me show you something." Mr. Myrtrym pulls another piece of glass from his pocket, slightly larger than the card he gave me yesterday. A video appears. A young girl—she can't be more than eight years old—runs through a park, plays on monkey bars, and climbs a ladder into a wooden fort. At first glance, she looks like any other child. But as I watch her, I notice faint lines of energy running through her white blouse and pink pants.

"Her name is Katya," Mr. Myrtrym says. "Her condition was similar to Knox's. A lot of doctors said it was hopeless, but Dominus' healthcare tech division recruits the best. The bodysuit fits her like a second layer of skin."

"It lets her move around like anybody else." My eyes are glued to the video. If not for the energy lines, I never would have noticed anything different about her.

"More than that," Mr. Myrtrym declares. "It's constantly collecting data about her body. We use that data to further refine her treatments. The more she plays, the more we learn. In a couple of years, Katya won't even need the bodysuit."

The vid stops. Mr. Myrtrym catches my attention with his eyes. "Dash, you understand this treatment is expensive. We can't do it for everybody, even as much as we'd like to. But you have a chance to earn enough."

The vid is paused. The little girl is frozen on the glass card in midjump as if time has stopped for her, but I keep thinking about how Knox would look running around on the playground. Really running, like his older brother.

"Can I have a moment to think about it?"

"Of course." Mr. Myrtrym climbs back into the car and closes the door.

Garon and I take a few steps away. He leans over to me. "You sure you want to do this?"

The question surprises me. "This is everything we wanted, isn't it? I mean, you helped get me into this. I can't turn back now."

"I know. But it's all happening so fast."

The idea that he might be jealous blows through my mind for half a second, followed by a pang of guilt.

"I have to do this," I tell him. "And I promise, as soon as I can, I'll send for you."

"I know." He cracks a smile. "Nobody else can make you look as good on camera as I can."

Garon follows me back to the car. I raise my hand to knock on the window, but the door opens before I get the chance.

Mr. Myrtrym waits inside. Two women sit next to him, one on either side, both with hair the same shade of red that I wear on my jacket.

"Good luck," Garon says as I get into the gravcar. He shuts the door behind me.

10

"DO I NEED TO BE DRESSED
better for this?" I tug on my Red Dragon jacket. I've never been as proud of something I've owned as I am of this jacket, but the other people in the car are all wearing more formal stuff.

Mr. Myrtrym sips from a glass of sparkling water. "No need to worry about that. We'll make sure you're properly attired."

One of the women moves from her place next to Mr. Myrtrym and sits next to me. She's wearing a black blazer with a matching skirt and a red blouse. Her skin smells like cinnamon. She runs a hand over my jacket. "This jacket is incredible, by the way. Myrtrym tells me your brother made it for you?"

"That's right." I point to the red *K* logo over my heart. "He brands everything he makes with that."

Her fingertips trace the red K. "Love it. Feels very . . . authentic."

"So where are we going anyway?" I shift a little in my seat, leaning away from her touch. A quick look out the window tells me we've left the Dregs. The gravcar soars above the city of Azariah, picking up speed. Only the tallest buildings reach higher than we are at the moment.

"Back to the docks." Mr. Myrtrym raises his glass as if

making a toast. "The stage of your former glory."

"The Cretaceous period?" Excitement rises within me. I've hardly been able to stop thinking about the valley.

The woman next to me laughs. "Not exactly. Tell me, Dashiell Keane, have you ever been to Paris?"

I almost snort in her face. Do these people know where I grew up? Except for the occasional school field trip, I've never left my neighborhood.

"No," I say, trying to sound nonchalant. "I haven't, Miss . . . ?"

"Call me Ramona," she says.

I can't quite place her age, probably a few years older than me. "Ramona . . . ?"

"Just Ramona. We're not formal here. Let me introduce you to my colleague, Esmerelda." Ramona gestures to the other woman still sitting next to Mr. Myrtrym.

Esmerelda smiles at me, and suddenly I don't remember the names or faces of any girls at my school who—until a few days ago—couldn't seem to remember my name either.

Within a few moments, we're back at the Dominus facility near the docks. When the gravcar lands, several armored guards wait for us. One opens the door.

Mr. Myrtrym smiles at me like I'm the most important person in the world. "Go ahead, Dash."

As I step out of the gravcar, the guards snap to attention. The sound of boots knocking together is almost intimidating. Each guard holds a rifle in their hands. I'm not complaining about the reception, but I'm not sure it's necessary. There's nobody else around.

Mr. Myrtrym leads us inside the facility and to the center of the lily pad. Dominus time scientists offer pleasantries as we pass by. Mr. Myrtrym gives no directions. Everyone seems to know exactly what they're supposed to do.

He orchestrated all of this for me. The realization makes me puff out my chest as I stand and wait for the platform to activate.

"Do you ever get nervous before going back?" Ramona asks me. "I always get a little nervous."

I grin and lie. "No, not really."

The platform lights up, and we're transported back in time. When the light fades, we're in another large room. I see all the standard time-displacement equipment—the platform, the monitors, a crew of scientists and Dominus employees.

The room is filled with pillars and archways leading in every direction. There are no windows, but a large fireplace occupies one of the walls. The ceiling and pillars are brick, but the floor is made of stone.

"Welcome to P-500." Mr. Myrtrym holds out his arms like an old circus ringmaster. "This is La Conciergerie."

We step off the lily pad and take a long walk through the echoing archways until a staircase appears on our right.

"This way." Ramona leads me up the stairs and down another hallway lined with paintings and sculptures, the old-fashioned kind that don't move. She stops at a wooden door and pulls me inside.

The room is exquisite. The furniture looks straight out of a museum—everything is polished wood and golden flourishes. A massive painting adorns the wall over the bed, an image of my home city of Azariah, but painted in the warm tones and crowded style of a time long before my own.

Clothes are neatly laid out on the bed. There's a black coat, a white shirt, a red vest—my shade of red, of course—and a long piece of lace fabric that I have no idea how I'm supposed to wear.

I hold the black pants up so Ramona can see them. "These aren't long enough. They'll only go down to my knees." I hope she knows I'm joking.

She claps her hands, and the door opens. An older man walks into the room, wearing a black tunic and matching pants. He's well-groomed, with salt-and-pepper hair and a beard.

I smile and extend my hand. "Hi, I'm Dash."

He looks at me and shrugs. Ramona only laughs as she leaves the room. I try a few times to talk to the man I assume is a butler. He responds in French, of which I don't know a word. I get the distinct feeling he understands most of what I'm saying but is pretending he doesn't.

The experience is a little unsettling. I've never had this close of an encounter with an echo. I know he isn't real. The government decreed years ago that people in the past are just residual energy in the timestream. I could punch him in the face, and in the authority of the present, it would be no different than hitting a rock. This man is the property of whatever corporation owns this particular segment of time, which I assume is Dominus.

Regardless, he seems kind. Though for all I know he's mocking me in his own language.

The butler doesn't seem at all perplexed by my modern clothes. Maybe he's dealt with other people from the present. It's possible he's a real person who's been employed to work in the past, but I doubt it. He feels like a part of this place in a way that I'm not.

I manage to get into the pants and shirt with no problem. The butler wraps the lace fabric around my neck like a tie. He buttons my red vest and helps me pull on the black coat. The final touch is a white wig with long curls that reach my shoulders.

Soon I'm dressed and ready. The butler leads me back through the palace and outside, where the sun is setting. Lanterns light the streets.

Mr. Myrtrym, Ramona, and Esmerelda are waiting when I walk outside, each dressed in the fashion of the time period. I know from timenet programs that corporations go to great lengths to maintain authenticity in certain time periods. People pay lots of money to travel back in time; they don't want to see gravcars and other present-world technologies. Usually there are a handful of people—echoes and real people from the present—who are aware that time travelers walk among them. But for the most part, the goal is that nobody knows who we are or where we're from.

"You look great." Mr. Myrtrym reaches out to shake my hand. He wears clothes similar to mine, though his colors are Dominus blue. Ramona and Esmerelda both wear gowns that are my shade of red. I appreciate the gesture.

I shake his hand heartily. "So do you, Mr. Myrtrym. Thanks for this."

"You haven't seen anything yet."

We start down the street. When we reach the river, we turn and stroll along the water until we come to a bridge. As we cross, the light from the streetlamps and surrounding homes reflects off the river in dancing ripples. Ramona points out Notre Dame cathedral, which looms on the other side of the river. I almost ask where the Eiffel Tower is located, but I assume it either isn't in this area of Paris or hasn't been built yet. I decide to keep my mouth shut.

We arrive at a restaurant named La Tour D'Argent, where we're ushered inside and led to a table overlooking the river. A server fills my glass with wine, and no one says a word as I take a sip. My friends and I have managed to get our hands on alcohol before, but it never tasted like this.

The conversation is mostly casual. Mr. Myrtrym tells me this place was named one of the best restaurants in time, a distinction I had no idea even existed, though I'm not surprised. Most corporations' timenet feeds include cooking programs set in the past. Shows where people are embedded in historical kitchens, but Mr. Myrtrym says Dominus has decided not to do that with this particular restaurant.

"Some things should be kept . . ." he pauses, staring at his wine glass as if there are words floating inside it and he's deciding which one to choose, "must be kept untouched, don't you think?"

"Sure, I could see that," I say as a plate of duck and vegetables is set in front of me.

"Any changes we allow here are thoroughly considered." Mr. Myrtrym cuts into his meat. "Because of the popularity of this restaurant, we have visitors from all over the world."

"Even other corporations?" I ask, then take a bite. It's greasy but rich.

Mr. Myrtrym points his fork at me. "Especially other corporations, though not tonight, Dash. I can tell you the name of every person in this restaurant right now. Do you know why?"

I shake my head and take another bite, trying not to show my astonishment at the meal. It's real food, not like the prepackaged stuff they sell in the Dregs. These vegetables were grown in the ground and harvested by hands, not processed in some factory.

"Because of your audition vid, every corporation knows your name, and right now they're having conversations about how they can sign you to work for them. If you want, you could have ten of these dinners in the next week."

I try to mask my excitement. I've spent so many nights lying in bed, wide awake and thinking of the day when people like these would bring me to places like this and try to convince me to work with them.

And now it's really happening.

"But I think you know that," Mr. Myrtrym goes on. "And I think you know that Dominus can do more for you than any other corporation. We own the best time segments, but that's not why our ratings are the highest. Do you know why our vidstreams are the most popular on the timenet?"

I take a drink of wine. "You have the best timestars."

"And why is that?" Mr. Myrtrym asks.

I straighten up a little in my chair. "Because you recruit the best?"

Mr. Myrtrym chuckles. "Maybe that's true, but it's a lot more than spotting raw talent."

Esmerelda leans forward. "We develop the best."

"You have talent," Ramona chimes in. "We've never seen anyone run like you. The moves you make, the way you take risks, it's an art. Plus, your natural agility is off the charts, and believe me, we have the best charts."

"But you need more," Mr. Myrtrym adds.

I sit back. More? Are they saying I'm not good enough? Sweat breaks out on my forehead.

"We're talking about a full image-development program." Esmerelda lets the words soak in.

"What?" I ask in a joking tone, trying to keep things light, clinging to my confidence. "Am I not good-looking enough?" I pretend to brush off my suit. All of a sudden, I feel ridiculous wearing it.

Ramona smiles at me. "You are very good-looking. We're talking micro-adjustments here. Your vid is extremely popular. Dominus wants to build off that, so we need you to still look like you. But maybe a slightly improved version."

"It's not so different than makeup, really," Esmerelda says. "Tiny facial modifications, a few millimeters here and there, pigment alterations, hair follicle implants. Even your close friends won't be able to tell what we've done. People will find you more appealing, but they won't know exactly what changed."

"Okay," I say slowly. "That doesn't sound like a big deal."

"Well, it's only the beginning," Ramona responds.

"Really? What else?"

Ramona begins to answer, but Mr. Myrtrym stops her. "We'll help you improve physically and mentally. Also, serious tech upgrades."

I straighten again as a smile spreads across my face. Faulty tech has always limited my potential. With better gravboots and basic optic technology, I could do things people have never seen. "I'm listening."

Mr. Myrtrym finishes his glass of wine. "There will be plenty of time for all that. Let's have some fun. What do you say?"

A lot of food is still on my plate, but Mr. Myrtrym doesn't wait for me to respond. He stands, and the rest of us follow suit. He leads us out of the restaurant, and I realize that when you have his type of power, things like waiting for the bill don't exist.

We walk briskly through the night streets of Paris. When we reach the palace, Ramona and Esmerelda part ways with us, explaining that they have more work to do in this time period.

After they leave, Mr. Myrtrym takes me back to the lily pad. He doesn't tell me where we're going, and I don't ask. The surprise seems like more fun. After all, I just traveled back in time for *dinner*. The next stop can only get better.

We stand in the center of the platform. The lights come up, and when they fade away, the archways are replaced by an ultramodern room. The walls are white, and the floor is black marble, spotlessly clean. The time scientists greet us as Mr. Myrtrym leads me into a dressing room with black leather couches and a mirror. An array of clothes hangs on a rack against the far wall.

"Pick out what you like," says Mr. Myrtrym. "I'll be back in a few minutes." He closes the door.

My spirit lights up as I approach the rack. *Cowboy stuff. Awesome.* There are options in white, black, and shades of brown. I rifle through them, eventually choosing black pants, a white shirt, and a black vest with a red star sewn into the chest. The star reminds me of the *K* that Knox stitches onto my outfits. I select a black hat with a red band wrapped around the place where the crown meets the brim.

I sit on the couch, pulling on a pair of black boots with

shimmering silver spurs when Mr. Myrtrym says, "Don't forget these."

He stands in the doorway, dressed in a dark blue suit with a matching hat and black boots. A gold chain attaches to his center shirt button and runs to his vest pocket, holding what I assume to be a watch. I didn't even hear the door open. *How long has he been there?*

He hands me a black leather belt. A gun holster is attached to one side, holding a revolver.

"Whoa." I immediately stand and put on the belt. "Is it loaded?"

"I'm afraid not. I don't think you're ready for that." He slaps me on the shoulder and nods toward the mirror. "But it completes the look, don't you think?"

I take a glance and grin. "Oh, yeah, it definitely does." I do my best quick draw, remembering the Old West timestars I loved as a kid. Those men and women were lightning fast, but I fumble as I try to pull the gun from the holster. Good thing it's not loaded. Dominus probably wouldn't appreciate me firing a gun in their dressing room.

I follow Mr. Myrtrym out of the room, down a short hallway, and up a staircase that's shrouded in darkness. When we get to the top, a trap door slides away above us. A thin layer of dust wafts down from the opening.

When we emerge from the stairs, we're in a barn surrounded by horses. Mr. Myrtrym points to where a farmhand, a young boy covered in freckles, is holding the reins of a black horse. "That one's yours."

I look at the horse. "I don't know how to ride one of those things."

"Don't worry." Mr. Myrtrym hauls himself onto the saddle of a white-speckled horse. "That one's not real. We manufacture them for guests so they can get the full experience of this time segment without taking lessons."

The horse is remarkably lifelike. It twitches as I approach, knocking at flies with its tail. I run my fingers over its fur for a few seconds before climbing onto the saddle, which is softer than I expected. The material feels like a gel that molds to my body.

I give the horse a slight kick. Nothing happens.

"Use your voice," the farmhand says.

"What do I say?"

"Whatever you want."

I take hold of the reins. "Okay . . . uh . . . go?"

The horse trots forward. I've never been on a real one before, but I think it's supposed to be bumpier than this as we go along. I wonder if Dominus installed shock absorbers somewhere inside this thing.

"You look good up there," Mr. Myrtrym remarks.

I let go of the reins and thump my chest. "Like a real gunslinger, huh?"

"Close, but not quite authentic," he says. "We'll train you to ride a real one. The audience will respond to that much better."

"Is yours real?" I ask. "Do you know how to ride?"

He shakes his head. "Never needed to learn." He looks at me. "I'm not the timestar. You are."

We leave the barn and ride across the plains, rocky cliffs in the distance but miles upon miles of flat land in front of us. The midday sun beats down on me. Maybe black clothes were a bad choice, but the wind from riding such a fast horse keeps me comfortable. Besides, nobody said being a timestar would be easy.

The horse runs smoothly. Even when we reach a high speed, the gentle, rhythmic bouncing lulls me into a type of serenity. I pretend the horse is real and wonder what I should name him.

I still haven't picked a name by the time we ride up to a small town that seems to have sprung up in the middle of nowhere. As we trot down the main street, I wonder whether Dominus had a hand in crafting the buildings. The saloon, the hotel, the bank—they all look too perfect for the period, like stylized versions of how an audience would want an 1800s western town to look, rather than how it should.

A handful of people mill about the town, most sneaking glances at us. A young boy beside his mother points his finger at me, but she quickly scolds him for it.

"You stand out," Mr. Myrtrym says. "That's a good thing. Some people have that quality about them."

I am pleased by his words. I had assumed it had something to do with our clothes or maybe the fact that we're strangers.

"So what are we doing here?" My eyes are scanning the area, and I'm thinking about all the trouble I could get into in a place like this.

"You'll see," Mr. Myrtrym replies.

We are now on the other side of the town, where a crowd gathers around a circular wooden fence. A grandstand has been erected next to the ring, and I see a small booth with a sign that reads: "Admission 5 Cents."

"Is this a rodeo?" I ask, excitement tingeing my voice.

Mr. Myrtrym smiles. "I thought you might like that."

We tie up our horses and enter the rodeo, breezing right past the admission booth. The man at the booth begins to speak but stops when he catches sight of Mr. Myrtrym. The look of recognition is unmistakable as he tips his hat toward us. "Your seats are ready, Mr. Myrtrym."

Moments later, we sit surrounded by cheering people as cowboys take turns attempting to stay atop enraged bulls. It's as thrilling as I'd hoped, but I can't stop looking around. The people here are definitely watching us. Do they know we don't belong?

A gasp from the crowd snaps my attention back to the arena. One of the riders lies in the dirt in the center of the ring, blood pouring from his side as a bull is distracted by other men, trying to draw it back into a pen.

I look at Mr. Myrtrym. "We have to help him." I jump out of my seat and start forward. I have no idea what I can do. Maybe we can get him back to the time platform and get him some medical attention. Maybe they have a skin-graft machine in that Dominus facility.

Mr. Myrtrym grasps my arm firmly. "Sit down, Dash."

I pull against his grip on instinct before thinking better of it. Others are rushing toward the man in the arena, one carrying what appears to be a doctor's bag.

"But we could help him," I protest.

"It's not a man, Dash," Mr. Myrtrym reminds me. "None of this is real. If you're going to be a timestar, you have to remember that. The man down there died hundreds of years ago. All of this is a reflection of energy enduring in the timestream."

I can't even see the man anymore through the crowd around him. "He seemed real to me. He bled like a real man. Did you know this was going to happen?"

Mr. Myrtrym frowns. "There was a chance it wouldn't. Records from this time aren't always the most accurate, plus we've had other people visiting the period, interacting with the echoes. It was possible that the ripples caused by our presence would alter this outcome, though the timestream does have a remarkable way of undoing the changes."

He's talking about the self-correcting time phenomenon. It's a theory that smart people often discuss on the few holoscreen programs that my parents do watch. Most time scientists believe that—given enough time and without additional unnatural intervention—the timestream reverts back to the way it was supposed to be, regardless of what we've done to change it. The amount of time it needs to repair itself depends on how much everything has changed, and there are specific points in time that seem to be somehow very significant. I heard one woman say that echoes will sometimes alter their behavior in radical ways to make up for significant changes. In one experiment, time scientists allowed the assassination of a would-be warlord decades before he took power. A few years later, someone else rose to power and committed the exact same atrocities. The timestream self-corrected.

"You brought me here to see him die?" My voice shakes a little. I notice the stands are almost cleared.

"I understand it's not easy," he says. "It goes against our human instinct. Echoes seem real. We can talk to them, touch them. But they're not real, Dash."

I know he's right. I've seen echoes die on timenet programs since I was a child, but seeing it in person is very different.

"Don't worry," Mr. Myrtrym assures me. "We're going to set you up to be a hero. Any echoes you kill will strike you as evil anyway."

I nod, grateful that I'll be portrayed as a hero.

But it doesn't settle the uneasy feeling in my stomach.

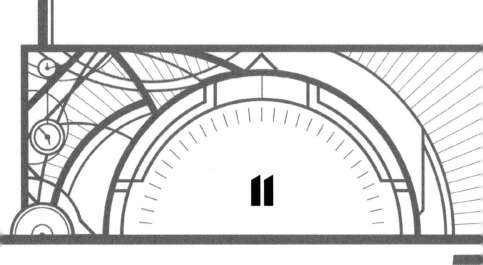

BY THE TIME WE RETURN

to the present, night has fallen over the Dregs. The lily pads move at the same speed along the timestream; if an hour passes in the past, an hour passes in the present, which means I've been gone all day.

Mr. Myrtrym puts me in his gravcar and instructs the driver to take me home. As I settle into the car, he hands me another glass card and tells me to contact him when I've made a decision. I spend the entire ride home fighting the temptation to accept his offer immediately.

The instant the gravcar lands in front of our apartment, my father bursts out the door of our apartment building. I try to keep my head high as I climb out of the car, reminding myself that this had to happen sooner or later.

"Where have you been?" my father yells as the gravcar pulls away. My mother stands behind him. Knox peeks at us from the doorway.

"Are you sure you want to know?" I ask. I've never felt this bold in front of my parents, but I have options now. Dominus wants me to be their new timestar. I hoped my parents would be at work tonight so I could think it over before making my decision, maybe talk about it with Knox.

I can see now that's not going to happen.

"This has to stop, Dash." I might've expected my mom to be emotional, but she's not. She has a way of compartmentalizing her feelings at times, pulling a blank expression over her face. It's how I know she's either really sad or really angry. "You don't know what you're getting into."

"I know it's dangerous, Mom."

"You have no idea how dangerous." My father grits his teeth. He is nearly shaking with anger. My mother places her hand on his shoulder, and his tension deteriorates into a defeated expression. "I know I can't stop you," he says.

"That's right." I pull the glass card from my pocket. "You can't stop me. My one regret is that I can't take Knox with me."

I tap the card. It blinks green.

The gravcar returns seconds later. I'm amazed it got back so fast. I don't even take the time to say goodbye to my parents as I climb into the gravcar. They will understand soon enough, when they see me on the timenet.

The partition is down, revealing a human driver—a man with gray hair and a grizzled face. "Where to?"

"I don't even know," I realize. "I should probably call Mr. Myrtrym and ask him where I should go."

"Hang on." The driver puts a finger to a small device in his ear. "Okay," he says after a few seconds. "We'll be there soon."

He looks back at me. "You're going to like this. Just enjoy the ride."

Minutes later, we land in front of a high-rise building in the nicest part of the city—an area I've never seen except on the holoscreen.

A man dressed like a 1950s bellhop opens my gravcar door from the outside. "Mr. Keane," he says. "Welcome home."

I step out of the gravcar feeling ten feet tall. *Welcome home.* I spend about two seconds wondering if Mr. Myrtrym arranged this last minute, or if he knew I would contact him so soon.

The inside of the building is a polished wood decor with plants arranged throughout the room. The plants look real, but as we walk to the short marble staircase that leads to the elevator, I touch one of the ferns. My finger passes through like it's made of mist. I take a second look at the bellhop. Is he a hologram as well? He appeared to open the door to the gravcar, but those doors can also open themselves. It's hard to tell what's real, but I'm not concerned about it. Besides, it would be awkward to touch his suit to see if it was tangible.

We step into the elevator, and the bellhop pushes the button for the top floor. The doors open a few minutes later, into a fully furnished apartment. Wooden walls. Marble floors. Dark leather furniture. A massive holoscreen hangs on the far wall. Outside, I see white lounge chairs arranged along a balcony with a private pool. Beyond that, the lights of the city.

The bellhop follows me into the apartment. "Your home features the latest in Dominus Corporation technology. Simply ask for whatever you want, and it will be presented to you. Your bedroom is to your right. You will find a full wardrobe of clothes in the closet. To your left—"

I hold up a hand to interrupt him. "Thanks. I don't mean to be rude, but I'd rather explore the place on my own."

The bellhop smiles and gives a slight bow. "Of course, sir."

He departs, and I watch the holoscreen for a moment, which is broadcasting an ancient Aztec game similar to basketball. I recognize it but can't remember the name. All I know is that the losers are sometimes killed. The picture is crystal clear.

"Music," I say. "Something upbeat."

Electronic beats play over speakers I can't see, energizing me to the point that I think I'm going to explode. *I'm here. I've arrived.* The bass pounds as I run from one room to the next. The first thing I find is a gym with a variety of workout equipment, including a VR simulator with a full haptic suit and optics. I should use it soon. I'm a timestar now, so I've got to stay in shape.

The kitchen is stocked with food. I've never seen so much fresh fruit in my life. Growing up in the Dregs, everything we ate came from a can or a box. I grab a banana off the counter and eat it as I continue wandering around. The bedroom lights activate, casting a dim glow when I step through the door. The wooden wall on the other side of the room seems to disappear, revealing another spectacular view of the city. I walk over and press my hand against the clear glass. Outside are two more chairs and a small table.

"How do I open this door?" I ask.

The door slides open.

It's cold out, but I step onto the balcony to take in the view. Warm air pushes over me. I look up to see an array of red glowing rods heating the balcony.

I stretch out my hands like I'm taking the city in my arms. Millions of lights flicker in the windows of buildings before me. Out there, people are probably ending their days in front of holoscreens, seeking escape from their lives, wanting to be taken on adventures.

Soon, they'll be watching me. Maybe I should let them know I'm coming.

I let out a whoop of pure joy.

A BEEPING ALARM WAKES

me the next morning. I'm not sure what time it is since, for all the luxuries in my apartment, I can't find any clocks. I didn't sleep well, anyway. My brain couldn't turn itself off all night, thinking about what today would bring.

I take a long, hot shower, hoping it will help me calm down and pull my thoughts together, but my mind is still racing. After the shower, I walk into the closet and find my Red Dragon jacket draped over what appears to be a dark gray mannequin torso. A single light mounted in the ceiling shines down on the jacket like a spotlight. I'm not sure how it got there. I fell asleep with the jacket on the nightstand.

I pull on a pair of jeans and a black T-shirt I find in the closet, then throw on my jacket. The jacket smells clean. I can't wait to tell Garon I have a housekeeper.

I don't see gravboots in my closet—or any wearable tech, for that matter. But there is a pair of sneakers that fit perfectly. They're black with my shade of red.

When I walk into the kitchen, I find a steaming cup of coffee waiting on the breakfast bar next to a plate of eggs and bacon, and bowl of oatmeal with strawberries. Real strawberries. I've never actually tasted one. It looks delicious, though I can't help but wonder who made the meal and when.

"Hello?" I call out but receive no answer. "Is somebody here?" I assumed they'd be watching me, but the idea of a stranger sneaking in while I was sleeping is unnerving. Maybe this is what it's like to be rich.

I'm almost too nervous to eat, but I do it anyway. If I'm going to be tired, at least I won't be hungry. After I eat, I leave the dishes on the bar and take the elevator to the lobby.

A gravcar waits outside with the same driver as the day before. I nod, say "Good morning," and step into the car. The driver says nothing, for which I'm grateful. I'm sure Mr. Myrtrym has already told him where I need to be and when.

Besides, I say stupid things when I'm nervous, so it's probably better if I don't speak at all.

The driver drops me off in the business district of the city. "Dominus headquarters," he says as the door opens. I step out, and the door shuts behind me. The sun glints off the windows as the driver pulls away.

Dominus Headquarters is intimidating. It's much bigger than the high-rise apartment building where I'm staying. A fountain sits out front with a huge Dominus logo carved from real stone, which is impressive. Holograms are easy, but when people make art out of actual physical materials, they're showing off.

People hustle by on both sides of the street, most of them having conversations on various devices. One woman's face is surrounded by holograms of people all talking over each other as she walks.

Farther down the block, other buildings are covered with company logos I recognize from the timenet—Elite Enterprises shows a lot of sports programming, The Fine Arts Collective is a snooty boutique channel, and Intellenon Corporation is mostly educational content. I guess those companies are my competition now.

Let the games begin.

When I walk inside the Dominus building, a man behind the marble front desk immediately stands up. He's a few years older than me, but his shiny hair and perfect complexion suggest a wealthy upbringing. He's probably fresh out of some fancy university. "Good morning, Mr. Keane."

"Hi." I put my hands on the desk and lean forward. "I'm . . . not sure where I'm supposed to go."

"Not to worry," he says, walking out from behind the desk. "That's my job. If you'll follow me, please."

Minutes later, I'm in an elevator that seems to be going up forever, trying to decide whether I'm supposed to make conversation with this guy. I can't help but wonder how many other would-be timestars have taken this elevator ride with him.

"So, uh, have you worked here long?" I ask.

"Longer than most people our age."

Before I can ask him what he means by that, the elevator doors open into a huge boardroom. People in suits surround a large black table. Mr. Myrtrym stands at the other end. A window dominates the far wall. I would have expected a view of the city, but instead, the window reveals dinosaurs moving through a forest, mountains looming in the distance.

"Welcome," Mr. Myrtrym greets me, then notices that I'm gawking at the window. "Oh, yes, you've already seen this time period. Let's switch to something else." The view changes to an ocean. Large wooden ships sail across the sparkling blue. The heads of the ships are carved with images that look like fairy-tale creatures. Men wearing furs and leathers fill the boats.

"You're a warrior, right?" Mr. Myrtrym says. "These Vikings are on their way to a raid. Or maybe that's too distracting. Let's try Babylon."

The window changes again, and I'm looking at a gorgeous shot of a white, tiered palace. Trees, bushes, vines, and flowers hang from the walls. A waterfall streams down each layer of the palace into a pool at the bottom. Even the sky looks like something an artist would have painted—with the perfect amount of clouds in shades of blue, purple, and white. Mr. Myrtrym is showing off for me.

And it's working.

"Please have a seat, Dash." I sit, but Mr. Myrtrym remains standing. "No reason to belabor this. I would introduce you to everyone around the table, but what's the point? You'll forget their names and jobs the moment I say them. We're all eager to get started, so . . ." he gestures to the table with both hands, "this is the team."

Men and women of various ages smile at me.

I give a quick wave.

"In front of you is a contract," Mr. Myrtrym says as a digital document appears on the table before me. The Dominus logo is on the top left corner. The echoing star of the timenet is in the top right. My eyes linger on it.

"It's an employment agreement," Mr. Myrtrym informs me. "You may have a lawyer review it if you like, but I assure you it's all very standard. We are contracting you for a trial period with certain incentives and the opportunity for a longer-term agreement based on the viewer ratings of your performance. In the unlikely event that you win the Suvea Award while this contract is in effect, you will be rewarded with a significant bonus and other incentives. You'll see all of this outlined on page two."

The Suvea Award. Corporations give it out every year to the timestar with the best ratings. I'd be thrilled just to have a steady slot on the timenet. Winning the Suvea would be beyond my wildest dreams.

I run my hand over the document and the virtual page flips to show another page crammed with columns and numbers. If I took the time to read it, I'm confident that I could understand it, but there's another matter I'm far more concerned about.

"When does Knox get his treatment?"

The people at the table look at each other and begin to murmur.

Mr. Myrtrym cocks his head. "Treatment?"

"You showed me that video of the little girl in the biosuit or whatever. It was treating her disease. When does Knox get that? What page is that on?"

Mr. Myrtrym pauses, then waves his hand. "Give us the room."

The people clear out fast, watching me as they exit. The smiles are gone, and I wonder if I've blown everything.

Mr. Myrtrym sits on the table. "I get your concern, I do."

"I thought if I signed, Knox would get treated."

"I said you would get the opportunity to have him treated," Mr. Myrtrym clarifies. "And that's what this is. Look at those numbers. That type of care is expensive, and I can't convince a room full of suits to spend that kind of money out of charity. You have to earn it. And you can. This is your chance to make enough money so that Knox can live a better life. You can make enough so that your entire family will never have to worry about finances ever again."

My mind flashes back to Cameron Cooper telling me he lost touch with his family, that he prefers to be left alone with the dinosaurs. No matter how much peace I felt there, I can't let that become my story. I can't let my family down, even if my parents don't understand what I'm doing.

Still, I would feel better with a guarantee that Knox would get some benefit out of this agreement. Maybe I could walk down the street and try the other corporations. Maybe I could start a bidding war and drive up my price, at least enough to have Knox covered.

"Dash," Mr. Myrtrym leans forward, "I stuck my neck out for you here. We've got a full list of other candidates brimming with talent. On paper, many of them are far more qualified than you."

The time window changes again. It's sectioned off into five different video screens. Each screen shows a guy or a girl around my age. One is blowing away the competition in a track meet. Another bench presses so much weight it looks like the bar might snap in half. A few are in different time periods doing things like fencing and bare-knuckle boxing.

"But I chose you," Mr. Myrtrym continues, "because I think you're a star. It's all right there in front of you. The question is, do you believe in yourself? Do you know you have what it takes? If you don't know that in your bones, you will absolutely fail. If that's the case, do us all a favor and don't sign. You can walk away right now with no hard feelings. I'll even let you stay at the apartment until you figure out your next move."

Then he gives me a quick smile. "But I don't think that's the case. You've got what it takes, and you know it. Am I right?" Mr. Myrtrym taps his finger on the signature line and hands me a stylus.

I pause. Not because I'm doubting my abilities, but because I'm wondering what my signature should look like on the contract. Soon, I'll be signing autographs all the time.

13

"IS IT GOING TO HURT?" I ASK

as the chair leans back. Bright lights shine down on me, but I'm too nervous to close my eyes. I keep reminding myself that I signed up for this.

A team of doctors surrounds me. The man in charge has tanned skin, dark hair, and an athletic build that's evident even beneath his green scrubs. He introduced himself as Dr. Saini.

"Well," Dr. Saini says, "I'm not sure if physical pain is the proper description. There will be discomfort, but the others complained more about severe disorientation throughout the process."

Another doctor sticks a needle in my arm. I try not to think about it. I'm not the biggest fan of shots.

"The others?" I ask. "How many times have you done this?"

"Enough," Dr. Saini states. "There were lots of trials, but we've done several successful procedures now."

I begin to feel the tendrils of sleep. My vision doubles.

"Trails?" I say, then realize it's the wrong word. "Trials? What trials?"

Dr. Saini is somehow standing on my other side, his hair now covered by a green cap. He laughs. "This conversation started hours ago, but don't worry about them. They're monsters . . . P minus 100 . . . never coming back . . ."

"What?" I try to shake the heavy sleepiness away, but it doesn't work. A throbbing pain comes over me, blacking out my vision.

When the light returns, I'm hovering in a different world. Floating mountains appear in front of me, full of trees and moss. Stone archways crisscross in the sky, connecting the mountains. I will myself forward, flying toward the arches, looking at the strange creatures moving between the rocks. In the distance, I hear a roar not unlike the dinosaurs.

It grows louder and louder, coming up from behind me. I try to turn and see what's approaching, but my body won't respond. Panic sweeps through me. I'm in a dream and can't wake up, but the roar grows louder, and the air becomes so hot I think I may combust.

"No!" My head jerks up. I'm still in the chair, doctors all around me. I look down and see that my chest is split open. Human surgeons and robot arms pierce my skin with steel fingers. I'm hit with blinding pain.

"Up the dosage," a voice says. "He's coming out."

I try to scream, but the sound doesn't come. I feel my consciousness fading away.

The cycle seems to go on for an eternity—slipping in and out of strange worlds, never feeling like I have my feet on the ground, like I'm fully in control. The pain endures, rising and falling in unpredictable patterns. More than once, I believe I will die, that my heart will give out or my brain will explode.

Then, it ends.

I open my eyes to find that I'm in a hospital room, lying in a bed that is tilted forward so that I'm almost standing. Mr. Myrtrym stands in front of me, Ramona and Esmerelda at his sides. The pain is gone.

"What . . ." I start to ask, then think of a better question.

"How long have I been out?" I would believe him if he said a couple of hours. I would also believe him if he said a month.

"Long enough," is Mr. Myrtrym's reply.

My head feels like there's a thick cloud inside of it. I keep waiting for the pain to return, but it doesn't come.

"I feel . . ." I test my arms, my fingers. My eyes widen. "I feel great."

Ramona chuckles. "You should. Waking up is the last stage. You're fully healed."

"How is that possible?" Energy pulses through my muscles. I'm ready to sprint out of this room and take on the world.

"We employ the best," Mr. Myrtrym says. "You've received genetically modified regeneration cells, among many other things."

I step forward off the inclined bed. I wear hospital scrubs, but my feet are bare. Ramona motions me to a mirror in the corner of the room. "Take off your shirt."

I do as I'm told. There are no scars on my chest, just rippling muscles like I've never seen. Rooftop racing kept me fit, but nothing like this. My chest and biceps bulge. My abs are clearly defined, almost like somebody drew them on me.

"The enhancements are head to toe." Ramona stands behind me, looking at my reflection in the mirror. "It goes beyond your muscles. Your hearing and vision have also been improved."

"Really?" I squint. "Everything looks the same."

"Your brain will need time to adjust to the changes," Mr. Myrtrym says. "The reason you're not seeing better yet is that you're not convinced you can see better. It'll come. The neural implants will allow you to acquire new skills at an accelerated rate."

I take a deep breath, studying my appearance in the mirror. My skin is slightly darker, and my eyes look different somehow, though I can't quite put my finger on it. My hair too.

I can't deny that it looks better, but a twinge of fear nips at the back of my thoughts. I can never go back to who I was before.

And I wonder what else they might have put inside me.

14

"IT'S IMPORTANT FOR REDEVELOPING
your neural pathways, fine motor skills, all that good stuff," Ramona says as we walk toward the front door of the Dominus building.

"Okay." I scratch the back of my head, grateful that I'm not in hospital scrubs anymore. Ramona gave back my jacket, which I wear over a white shirt with jeans and sneakers. "So you want me to grab a cup of coffee from the place down the street? Don't you have coffee here?"

"It's not about the coffee," Ramona says. "It's about practicing with your neural and physical enhancements. You need fresh air, sunlight. You need to brush past people on the street. If you don't want coffee, get juice." Her face lights up. "Smoothie! There's a fantastic place three blocks down. Grab me one too. Tropical Sunshine, but substitute blueberries for the banana. Thanks!" She nearly pushes me out the door.

I pause for a moment on the sidewalk, almost afraid to move. My legs feel unsteady but pulsing with energy. It reminds me of a VR simulation I tried one time in which I drove a starship through outer space. The ship was extremely fast, but I couldn't figure out how to steer and kept crashing into asteroids and stars. That's what my body feels like—lots of power, little control.

Here goes nothing. I try to take a step, but my muscles are so much stronger that I surge forward and collide with a middle-aged man in a suit, knocking him over. I apologize profusely as I help him up.

At first, he scowls at me, but when we make eye contact, the anger dissolves from his face. "Hey, no problem," he says. "Have a good day."

Have a good day? I didn't expect to hear that. Being ignored is nothing new to me. People from this part of society are rare in the Dregs, but when they come around, they would rather spit on us than look at us. If we get in their way, they unleash a stream of curses. I can't imagine one of them telling me to have a good day.

As I walk down the block—growing steadier with every step—every person I pass smiles at me. I can't help but smile back. *What is happening?*

Soon, I'm weaving my way through the crowded sidewalk with ease. When I come to the first intersection, I feel like I could jump across the street, but I wait for the signal.

"Nice day," I say to the woman standing beside me on the corner.

"It is." She runs her fingers through her brown hair, then turns and whispers to her friend. They both laugh to themselves.

By the time I reach the juice bar, I feel like a new person. The girl behind the counter raises her eyebrows at me. "What can I get you?"

"Hi!" I put my elbows on the counter. "Can I get two Tropical Sunshines, both with blueberries instead of bananas?"

"Of course." She turns to a young guy in a sleeveless T-shirt standing behind her. "Mark, can you get that?"

He nods. The girl turns back to me. "So who's the other one for?" she asks over the whir of the blender.

"Uh, just a friend. I guess she's a co-worker."

"Co-worker?" she asks. "What do you do?"

How is this my life now? "I work for Dominus Corp. I'm going to be on the timenet."

Her face lights up. "Really? You're a timestar?"

"Yeah, I guess so."

The co-worker sets the drinks on the counter, and the girl picks one up. "You're sure one of these isn't for a girlfriend?"

"Positive."

"Good." She grabs a pen, scribbles her name and number on the side of the cup, and hands me the smoothies.

"How much do I owe you?" I hope that Dominus has transferred some credits to my account.

She shrugs and flashes me a smile that reveals her dimples. "Give me a call sometime, and we'll talk about it."

When I get back to the Dominus building, it's like I'm walking on air.

15

THE FOURTH TIME CONLEY,

my costume designer, pokes me with a needle, I'm convinced Ramona has put him up to it.

"Alright, that time was on purpose for sure." I twist around, pretending to be angry. It's tough because I already like the guy.

"Hold still," Conley orders. "Or I'll keep sticking you until you bleed out, and then we'll have to find a new diamond in the rough." He's got short-cropped hair, dark skin, and wears glasses that constantly have digital lines running across the lenses that I assume are for designing. Despite the physical differences, he reminds me a lot of Knox, which makes me feel guilty. It's weird having somebody else put my outfit together.

"Diamond in the rough?" I shoot a glance at Ramona. "Doesn't this guy know I'm the Red Dragon? Didn't you tell him?"

Ramona's in full-on business mode as she studies the black clothes that Conley measures for me. "We might downplay the Red Dragon thing a bit," she remarks without making eye contact with me.

"Downplay it?" I drop the sarcasm and try to hold still as I protest. "What are you talking about? I've been crafting that persona for years. That's my character."

"Is that what you really want?" Ramona asks. "Think about it. The Red Dragon is a faceless entity. That's why you pulled off your helmet after the dinosaur thing, right? So people could see your face. The Red Dragon could be anyone, which means you could be replaced. Wouldn't you rather people know your name?"

She's got a point, but I always had a lot of fun with the Red Dragon. Knox and I came up with it together, and Garon helped refine the idea. We even had a fake backstory where I was an alien from a planet created by a great cosmic dragon and I came here to take over this world for his glory.

Ramona comes nearer. "Look in the mirror. We didn't do all that work on your face so you could hide it."

I catch my reflection in the mirror and think of the people on the street and the counter girl at the smoothie shop. If nobody sees my face, they won't know I'm a timestar.

"Alright." I run my hands over the black robes covering my body. "This looks good, but it's pretty thick. I'm not sure my jacket will fit over it."

Conley's mouth drops open, and he looks at Ramona. "Jacket?"

"About the jacket . . ." Ramona says.

"C'mon, Ramona!" I hop down off the pedestal. "I always wear that jacket. It's the first thing my brother made for me."

Ramona shakes her head. "It doesn't fit. We're not doing the fish-out-of-water story. You need to wear clothes from the time period."

"But it's my jacket. That's my signature. Especially that red stripe. People will remember my video, right? The jacket ties my story together."

"Don't worry about that," she says. "We've already rebranded that vid with the Dominus logo and placed your new head in the video."

"My new head?"

"If somebody hasn't seen the original, they would never know you were ever wearing a helmet."

I wonder if Garon got paid for any of that. I make a mental note to ask Mr. Myrtrym later.

"Besides," Conley interjects through the pins he holds between his teeth, "we are keeping that shade of red. It will be incorporated into all your costumes."

"And what about my brother's logo? The red K?"

Ramona and Conley exchange glances.

She relents. "Fine."

"Good," I say, relieved. "Thank you. It's important to me." I step back on the pedestal so Conley can resume his work. "Where am I going anyway?"

"You'll find out soon enough," Ramona says.

16

AS THE LIGHTS FADE AROUND
me, I kneel with my hand on the katana at my side, the folds
of my black robes hanging over the matching red sheath and
sword handle. A microcam buzzes around my head. This will
be the first image people see of me, the first scene of my timenet
program. I want to look heroic but humble.

I raise my head and peer into the camera, looking into the
homes of millions.

Mr. Myrtrym's voice buzzes in the device in my left ear.
"Let's do that again. Smile this time."

My head jerks back in disbelief. "Again? I thought this
was live!"

He laughs. "Live? No. Every new timestar needs the benefit
of an edit. We won't interfere too much because it's important
you look natural. But this is the first shot. We need to get
it right."

I thought it felt right. I look at the time scientists managing
the equipment. A few of them are snickering at me.

"Okay," I say. "So what do I do?"

"Kneel and bow your head again; that part was good. When
you look up, smile like you know this is going to be easy."

"Is it going to be easy?"

"No. This training will be one of the hardest and most painful times of your life, but we're trying to make this a fun show."

"Got it." I resume my original position. The lights come up for a few seconds, then fade to create the illusion that I've just traveled through time.

Smile, I tell myself. *Nail the smile.* I think about Knox watching. He'll be so excited. When I look up into the camera, I imagine I'm staring right at him. *Look at what I'm doing, Knox. We made it.*

"Perfect," Mr. Myrtrym pronounces. "Now, go outside. You'll find a horse waiting for you. It's not real, but we'll edit the footage so the audience can't tell. The machine knows where to take you."

When I step outside, the scenery stops my breath. In front of me, a snow-capped mountain pierces the blue sky like a giant rising from a blanket of clouds. I realize I'm also on a mountain, though one not quite as tall. The air warms my face. The rising sun paints the surrounding bushes in deep orange.

A saddled black horse waits for me, as still as a statue, even when I climb onto its back.

I give it a slight kick. When nothing happens, I remember the voice commands.

"Let's go."

The horse comes to life and starts toward a trail leading down the side of the mountain. I can't see the camera anymore, but it must be around here somewhere.

"A little faster," I say, but the horse keeps its pace. I kick again. The horse stops and regards me as if saying *no, we won't be going any faster.* Perhaps it's programmed for specific speeds on certain terrains. I hope Dominus won't use this footage of me being sassed by a fake horse.

I give in. "Fine, do it your way. Let's walk."

The trail winds down into the clouds, so thick that I lose

sight of the ground. The horse maintains a steady walk until the fog clears and the trail levels off into a forest.

"How about now? Can we run now?"

And the horse breaks into a full sprint. I nearly topple out of the saddle. I think I hear Mr. Myrtrym laughing in my ear, but the sound is lost in the wind as we gain speed. My legs squeeze the horse's sides, and I manage to stay on.

This is amazing. My blood rushes and my heart pounds as we gallop through the woods. For a fleeting moment, I wonder how I look on camera–the young warrior riding valiantly toward his destiny. But the thought disappears in the joy of the moment, the rush of riding a creature made of thunder and wind.

Soon we come upon a lake. The snow-capped mountain reappears, a titan welcoming me into its realm.

Or perhaps warning me.

My horse turns and follows a path around the lake. Though I'm enjoying the ride, I settle into the saddle, deciding it's probably wise to retain my strength. "Let's slow down."

The horse does as I ask.

A building of deep red waits for me on the other side of the lake. It has three tiers, each with a roof that slants up at the corners, and a tall spire at the top. A stone staircase leads up to the building.

Mr. Myrtrym's voice buzzes in my ear. "Your training begins in that pagoda."

"Pagoda." I say it out loud so I will remember it better, which triggers a question I hadn't thought of before. "Do any of the echoes there speak English? How will I understand them?"

"Your neural implants include translations and conversions for all known languages throughout history. To you, it will sound like everybody is speaking English."

"And when I respond?"

"You'll think you're speaking English, but what comes out of your mouth will be the appropriate language for that region and time period. The translations are triggered by auditory clues, so make sure you let them speak first."

"Sounds easy enough."

My horse and I come around the final bend of the path and approach the stone staircase.

"Don't speak to me anymore unless you have to," Mr. Myrtrym advises. "It ruins the shot, and we'll only get one chance at the footage once you start interacting with the echoes. They're expecting you."

"Who told them I was coming?"

"We control the emperor. He informed the samurai who oversees this region of your arrival."

"Samurai?"

"Yes, samurai. Alright, you're on. This is where it all begins. Godspeed."

The horse stops at the bottom of the staircase. I climb out of the saddle and pause to run my fingers over the coarse hair of its neck. I know it's not a living creature—nothing here is real—but I don't want to think about it as a machine, not after the thrill of that ride. It was almost like rooftop racing.

The horse chews grass at the base of the steps like a real animal. Maybe it knows we're filming, or perhaps it's controlled by someone at Dominus.

Regardless, I'm disappointed that I probably won't see it again.

I pat it a couple of times on its back. "Thanks for bringing me here, my friend."

After a deep breath, I start up the steps, my boots tapping on the stone. They're not gravboots, not yet. Dominus has decided to keep things more traditional, at least on the surface. The one exception is the sword on my side, which I'm told was made using modern techniques that prevent the blade from ever going dull. Dominus gave me a few hours to train with it before sending me here. My neural implants helped me learn the techniques much faster. By the end of the session, I felt like I could hold my own in a sword fight, so long as my opponent wasn't too skilled and didn't have my enhancements.

I guess I'll find out soon whether that's true.

When I reach the top step, two men in deep-blue robes stand at attention. Their black hair is pulled back in buns.

They step in front of me as I approach the pagoda. Behind them lies a stone courtyard. Sculptures of dragons, tigers, birds, and fish stand vigil. A stream runs through the center, snaking between the statues and plants.

"I . . ." I start to say before remembering what Mr. Myrtrym told me about language. *They have to speak first.*

One of the men eyes the katana on my side. His gaze returns to me, a stern expression telling me all I need to know. My weapon is not allowed past this point.

Surrendering my sword so soon strikes me as strange. Then a possibility occurs to me. Maybe Dominus wants to start my story with an action sequence? Maybe these men aren't echoes, but machines like the horse. If that's the case, they might be programmed to lose a fight to me. I don't think Dominus wants its new timestar getting whipped in his first episode.

I pause to see if Mr. Myrtrym will provide some direction, but he stays quiet. *I guess I have to make this decision alone.* I reluctantly remove the katana and hand it over.

One of the men receives the sword with two hands and a slight bow before turning to walk toward the pagoda. I follow close behind, stepping over the narrow stream as orange-and-white fish swim beneath me.

The walls inside the pagoda are made from dark wood. Green pillars reach from the floor to the ceiling, and there is a scent in the air like burning flowers. A raised platform is in the center of the room, on which stands a samurai dressed in all black. The samurai's mask is shimmering gold beneath a black helm, and on the forehead is a golden emblem that looks like horns. He would be a good head taller than me even if he were on the floor. Standing on the platform, he towers over me. His mask tilts down as I approach. I can see nothing but his eyes. *Please say something so I can talk to you.*

The samurai removes his mask. Long black hair tumbles from the back of the helmet as I look upon a face I didn't expect.

A woman.

I kneel before her and bow my head in what I hope is a sign of respect.

One of the men brings her my sword, still in its red sheath. She draws the sword and studies the blade. Can she see that the steel isn't from her time? Can she see that I'm not from her time?

The samurai returns the sword to the sheath and tosses it at me.

My hand snaps up to catch it. I hold the sword in front of me, uncertain how to react.

The samurai frowns as if unimpressed. She walks toward a door in the back of the room.

I look at the two men, hoping for some clue as to what I'm supposed to do. For crying out loud, why won't somebody talk?

The samurai stops at the door, looks at me, and motions with her hand for me to follow.

She leads me outside to the back of the pagoda, into another courtyard filled with trees that all have winding trunks. Red petals flood their branches, creating a canopy so thick that it blocks out the sunlight, creating a red glow beneath. The petals cover the ground as well.

We walk through the fiery orchard, a cool breeze lifting petals into the air.

The samurai stops. So do I.

The wind increases. The petals swirl around us like a red storm.

The woman eyes the sword in my hands, then pretends to draw her sword. She thrusts up her hand as if she's swinging an invisible blade.

I nod my understanding and move into a ready stance with my knees bent. I draw my sword, wondering if the cameras can see me through the petals. I grip the handle with both hands. My focus locks onto a single petal floating in front of me, a red fairy dancing on the wind.

My sword swipes up in a beautiful arc, and the blade slices through the center of the petal. I kneel and thrust the sword back into the sheath before the two halves of the petal touch the ground.

I stand, face the samurai, and bow my head. It's all I can do not to smile. Even I wasn't sure I could pull that off.

But the samurai wears a stony expression, no sign of being pleased with my demonstration. It's as if she's trying to determine what I am and why I'm here. Fear creeps into my mind. What if she doesn't like what she finds?

The samurai pulls her sword with one hand, spins toward me, and swings toward my face.

The blade stops a whisper away from my lips.

My breath catches. Every muscle freezes.

A petal sits at the end of her blade, its sides lying against the steel as if it were embracing the sword.

My mouth drops. Her speed, her turn, the arc of the blade—it's almost supernatural. She caught the petal without making the slightest tear. It would never have occurred to me to try such a thing.

The samurai returns the blade to the sheath on her side, which I now see is decorated with red petals. She steps toward me.

"Control." She speaks with an accent different than mine, but I can clearly understand her. "You destroyed a beautiful piece of creation that posed no threat to you. Why? To impress me? You must learn control, when to yield. Do you understand?"

I can finally speak now. But instead, I only nod.

"My name is Shimizu Kaida," the samurai says. "Welcome to my home, Dashiell Keane. Your training has begun."

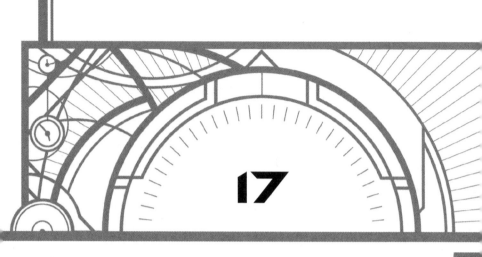

17

"IT WAS INCREDIBLE." I PACE
the room given to me by Shimizu Kaida. The walls look like
paper lined in bamboo, so I try to keep my voice down. The
bed lies on the floor, a candle on a nearby table, a rug, and
not much else. Mr. Myrtrym buzzed my earpiece as soon as I
stepped inside, my body ready to collapse onto the bed. But my
mind was excited to speak to someone about the experience.

"Shimizu's skill is unbelievable," I say breathlessly, mostly
because I've been talking so fast about the day.

"It's Kaida, actually," Mr. Myrtrym says into my left ear.
"In Japanese, the family name comes first, followed by the
individual name. And yes, her prowess is legendary. The local
villages call her the Lightning Sword."

"Because she's so fast," I say, remembering the petal at the
end of her blade. Her blade came close to my face many times
today—I actually heard her steel singing in the wind, but she
never cut me. The sword went where she wanted it to go and
nowhere else.

"No," Mr. Myrtrym corrects me. "In her younger days, she
was quite the warrior, as I'm sure you can imagine. There was
a battle against the army of a samurai-turned-warlord that took

place during a terrible storm. The other soldiers said it was so dark and rainy that they could hardly see. But every time the lightning struck, they saw a flash of Kaida, taking down another enemy."

The Lightning Sword. I'm jealous of that nickname. I love being the Red Dragon, but now that Dominus is pushing my real name, maybe I can have multiple nicknames as well. Maybe I could challenge her for it, but I don't think that would end well for me.

"How long will I be here?" I sit at the foot of the bed, trying to settle down. "I have a lot to learn from her."

"We'll see," Mr. Myrtrym replies. "Your implants should accelerate the process. Combined with your physical enhancements, you will be a formidable opponent very soon. Training will make for one good episode, but not much more. I know you enjoy this, but if you stay too long, the audience will lose interest."

I thank Mr. Myrtrym again for the opportunity and finally stretch out on the bed. Sleep comes in seconds.

One of Kaida's students wakes me the next morning. He still hasn't bothered to mention his name, but he tells me I'm going for a walk. I've seen enough of these shows to know this will be more than a stroll.

I meet Shimizu Kaida in the courtyard, and she leads me into the woods behind the pagoda, saying nothing. After a brisk walk through the trees, we emerge at the base of the snow-capped mountain. Kaida never breaks stride as she makes her way up the side.

We climb for what seems like hours until we reach the place where the snow begins near the summit of the mountain. The climb is rigorous to say the least, though my experience as a rooftop racer serves me well. Heights don't bother me, and I know how to rebound off surfaces, how to use my fingertips to grasp at ledges and support my weight.

But I doubt I could have done this without my enhancements. It makes me realize how much more punishment I can take now.

We tromp through the snow, approaching the peak. Kaida holds up her hand for me to stop.

"Remove your clothes." It's the first thing she's said all day. "All but your *fundoshi*."

I do as I'm told.

The freezing air bites at my exposed skin, turning it red and dry. It's like thousands of needles stabbing me all at once.

Shimizu Kaida walks in circles around me. "Close your eyes."

I do.

"Where is your mind right now?" she asks, her voice continuing to move around me.

I struggle for the correct answer, trying to focus through the pain, trying to put my consciousness somewhere else. "Home . . . uh . . . the pagoda?"

"No," she says. "Your mind should be here. Have you ever experienced anything like you're experiencing now?"

"No, sensei."

"Then why should you miss this?" Her voice gets closer but still circles me. "Focus on the pain. Experience everything that is happening to you right now. This moment is all you have. The next moment could bring your death. After all, Dashiell Keane, time is undefeated in its endless war against man."

Soon my skin feels very hot, like I'm covered in sweat. My arms and legs feel like dead limbs that have been nailed to my torso. I fight to remain standing. My mind drifts into feverish visions. The mountain and snow—even Kaida—slip in and out of my consciousness. But I'm also seeing my parents, my brother, other things. I'm late for an exam at school, and I haven't studied.

I'm racing along a rooftop, stopping again to help the Serpent before thinking better of it and running away. She screams as she falls.

Then darkness.

When consciousness returns, I'm in my bed at the pagoda, sweating through thin white clothes that cover my body. One of the students kneels next to my bed and holds a cup of water to my lips.

"The cameras," I rasp, forgetting myself for a moment. What did they see? Have I failed again?

"You lasted very long," the student assures me. At least, I assume he's a student, but he could be a servant. It never occurred to me to ask. Maybe I should feel guilty about that, but these are echoes. They aren't real.

"Far longer than we would have wagered. You are very strong."

"That's good." I close my eyes and lean my head back. I must have passed out, which means Shimizu Kaida carried me here.

I wonder if they'll show that on the timenet.

The next several days are spent training in unarmed combat, which Kaida says will be crucial to mastering the sword. I do everything she asks. Her attitude toward me seems to have changed; perhaps the mountain earned me some respect. Even though she's an echo, her opinion matters to me. After all, she is the Lightning Sword.

Despite the constant bruises and the overwhelming amount

of time spent on my back, unarmed combat training is like a drug. My body has never done anything like this, and the rate at which I improve is intoxicating. Rooftop racing always came naturally. I never worked at it as hard as I should have. This training is not quite so intuitive, but as I begin to understand the techniques, it feels as if I'm unlocking mystical secrets that give me power.

Within a couple weeks, I can hold my own sparring against Kaida's other students, both of them still nameless. My enhanced speed and strength cover my mistakes, though I focus on trying to correct my errors. When I do, placing my foot in the proper place during a block to allow maximum power and speed on a counter, for example, the experience is exhilarating.

Once I can defeat each student in single unarmed combat, Shimizu Kaida begins setting them both against me simultaneously. I end the first few days bloodied and bruised but inspired by the few short moments in which I hold them both off.

At dusk, when the training is over and dinner has been eaten, Shimizu Kaida disappears into the trees behind the pagoda. She never tells me where she's going, never invites me along, nor does she tell me to stay at the pagoda. The first couple of weeks, I assume this is my time to stay in bed and rest my battered body.

But soon my curiosity gets the best of me, and I limp behind her as she walks into the woods. Kaida never slows down for me, although I'm sure she knows I'm following her. Several times I get lost along the trail, eventually stumbling back to the pagoda long after darkness falls and finding her already returned.

One day, I wise up enough to skip dinner and leave the pagoda ahead of her, covering as much of the trail as I know. I wait for her there in the trees. As the sky turns shades of orange and purple, and I can see the outline of the moon in the distance, she arrives. Kaida says nothing, nor does she look at me as she walks past.

I follow her through the trees to discover a small hill that sits next to the mountain like a pupil at its teacher's feet. She climbs to the crest of the hill, where she stares at the sky for a few moments, then breaks into a series of movements. It looks like fighting in slow motion, practicing against invisible enemies in a kind of dance. The first night, I do nothing but sit and watch, amazed by her fluidity and grace.

On the second night, I mimic her movements as best I can. It's more difficult, somehow, than learning the unarmed combat. I am like a child learning to walk on unsteady legs. My body creaks and jerks in unnatural ways as I venture to capture the motions.

I try for several nights in a row, never seeming to improve in my ability to recreate her motions. Despite my enhancements, my technique feels off. It's frustrating that I can master combat so quickly in the training courtyard but have such a hard time with this. I consider quitting several times. The practice doesn't seem relevant to my timestar development.

But I keep going. Something about it speaks to me.

One night, when Kaida's halfway through the ritual—I have every subtle motion memorized, though I still can't replicate it to my satisfaction—she pauses. Her back is to me, her eyes fixed on a bird arcing through the air. "Stop trying so hard. This is not about your body. This is about connecting your soul to the energy around you. Close your eyes and breathe."

So I do. I allow it to flow through me, trying to imagine a new energy pushing its way through me, allowing the movements to come in ways that feel not perfect, but true. I know I am making mistakes, but as I let go, a type of joy grows inside me. Soon I stop mimicking and break into movements that seem like they're not my own, but of something else, something guiding me. It reminds me of running with the dinosaurs.

The experience changes the way that I train against Kaida's other students. Combat now appears to move slower, and I start trying new techniques against them. At first I seem to regress, losing each fight within seconds.

But the more I go up to the hill and close my eyes, the more I discover new ideas, new actions and responses I might've never thought possible.

A day arrives when I defeat both her students by combining my enhanced speed and strength with techniques I have developed in the kata. It's the first time my victory was never in doubt.

The next day, Kaida puts the sword back in my hand.

18

I'M WEEKS INTO SWORD TRAINING

before I see a building other than the pagoda. At Mr. Myrtrym's suggestion, I decide to take a horse into the fishing village on the other side of the mountain. Kaida has taught me to ride when I haven't been working on combat, and when I tell Kaida I'm leaving for the day, she doesn't protest. My sensei seems to know I have directions coming from somewhere else, orders neither of us should ignore.

The village is a couple of hours away by horseback, a ride I enjoy. The horse is a dark-brown mare with a black mane, black tail, and a dash of white between her eyes. It has a name that doesn't translate to English. After a brief conversation with Kaida, I understand that it essentially means "a powerful serenity."

As I ride the creature around the mountain, I understand why it received its moniker. The robotic horse was thrilling, but riding atop a real animal—which sweats when we reach full speed, and breathes in determined huffs—is another experience altogether. I keep reminding myself that this is not the present, that none of this is reality. But maybe I like forgetting.

When I ride into the village, people swarm the streets in

some type of festival. The smell of roasting fish and the sound of music drift through the air. Children run through the dirt streets, laughing and playing. Many of them wield sticks like swords, pretending to be samurai. I smile. *I guess I'm pretending too.* I'm not wearing any armor today, but my sword is at my side, just in case. Several villagers stare at me as I go by.

A large audience gathers in front of a stage at the center of town, applauding a group of performers wearing robes of various colors. The performers bow, smile, and clear the platform. I stand in the back to spectate from a distance.

A woman glides onstage, taking graceful steps as the gentle breeze caresses her shimmering blue robes. Music begins to play, and the woman starts to dance, making long, sweeping movements with her arms and legs. With the billowing of her robes, she looks like a summer storm come to life. I can't take my eyes off her. Even at a distance, her expression grabs hold of me. There's innocence in it, a purity that matches the idea of flowing water, which I assume she is trying to portray. She has long, dark hair and a smile that makes her look as if she knows everything about me and still accepts me. As she dances, the light reveals streaks of deep red in her hair, like flames in the night. Freckles dot her face.

The dancer falters as she attempts a twirl. The music stops. The audience falls silent as the dancer collects herself. I feel bad for her. This isn't a huge audience, but I imagine the pressure of performance can be staggering.

She doesn't start her routine over entirely but goes back a few moves, attempting to work her way into the twirl again. Despite her obvious muscle tone, the maneuver seems difficult—her arms arced to look like a moon over the water, one leg rising like a wave as she twirls on the other foot. Every time, she fails. It's heartbreaking to see the sadness on her face.

I'm so focused on her that I almost don't notice the other dancer moving onstage. He appears as if out of nowhere. Judging by the collective gasp of the audience, I'm not the only person who didn't notice him until he stepped to the foreground. His robes of red and black are a stark contrast to hers. He wears a red mask with the twisted face of a demon, though he dances beautifully. His movements are strong, confident, deliberate.

The woman watches the demon dance, his robes flowing like dragon wings as he mesmerizes her. After a few moments, he offers her his hand.

And though I know it's not real, even for the echoes, my blood runs cold. I almost scream out the words. *Don't do it.*

She takes the demon's hand, and he dances with her, teaching her to move like she has never moved before. Her innocent smile disappears, her eyes fill with determination that soon grows into a mad rage. She tries the twirl again and executes it perfectly.

The crowd cheers. I clap so hard that my hands hurt.

But she doesn't pause to take in the moment. She continues to dance, making bigger and bigger movements, leaping high into the air. The dancer does the twirl again, and again the crowd cheers. The demon's mask flashes in the darkness behind her.

When she does the twirl a third time, the crowd cheers a little less. She stares at the audience, her mouth agape as if she can't understand our weakened response. She does the twirl faster. The cheers are lesser still. The demon looks on. Something tugs on my heart.

The dancer grits her teeth. Tears pour down her face. She does the twirl over and over, her form beginning to falter. People no longer applaud.

When she drops to her knees, her chest heaving and her breath so loud that I hear it even at the back of the crowd, it is both tragic and a relief. The performance was captivating, but I would never want to see it again.

The demon moves forward from the shadows, dancing and

twirling until he hovers over her, covering her with his black robes until she is gone, and the music stops.

Again, the audience is silent. My breath catches in my throat. The music changes to an upbeat tune. I shake my head a little, trying to regain my composure. It feels like someone has pulled me out of a nightmare.

Both dancers pop up. A cheer erupts from the audience. The demon removes his mask to reveal that, of course, he wasn't a demon at all, but a handsome young man who looks every bit as innocent now as she does. The girl's smile returns, which is the greatest relief of all, and the main reason I clap so hard. *What is wrong with me? She's an echo. They're all echoes.*

I look around for any cameras hovering nearby, hoping somebody recorded that performance. She might have just upstaged me on my own show, and it was so good that I wouldn't care.

The dancers make their way offstage, and another group comes up, four women who begin a synchronized performance to a new piece of music. They're very good, but I can't stop thinking about the girl in blue. I have to meet her.

The stage is so very small, it seems to be the kind of thing that was constructed in a day. I walk around the crowd to find a dressing area behind the stage with tables, chairs, and some freestanding partitions for costume changes. The girl in blue stands talking with a man who looks a bit older. He wears robes of black and green and has his hair pulled up in a tight bun.

My heart sinks. I turn and start to walk away. This was stupid idea, anyway. What would I have even said to her? I should find some food and enjoy my day off.

But the girl's voice stops me from leaving.

"No," she says. "I'm not kabuki."

I spin around and head toward them. The man grips her by her wrists, his face deep red. He spits as he yells at her. "Stupid girl! You dare deny me?"

He draws back a hand. I'm about to grab his wrist when she strikes his neck so fast that I almost miss it, like a cobra. She pulls back into a ready position, but there is no need. The man coughs and chokes as he stumbles away from her.

My smile is equal parts amusement and disbelief as I start toward her. Maybe she isn't so innocent after all. "That was—"

She throws a jab at me. "Get back!"

I sidestep the blow. She misses my face, but not by much. I dance away from her, raising a hand. "Whoa. Easy, champ. I didn't mean to—"

"You men are disgusting." Her blue robes arc through the air as she whirls around and stalks away.

"Hey!" I jog after her. "I'm sorry. I only wanted to say hello."

"Sure." She doesn't turn around but keeps walking. "That's how bad things always start . . . with *hello*."

I slow. It's not right to chase her. If she wants me to leave her alone, that's fine. The last thing I want is to make her feel threatened. "That's how the good things start as well," I say loudly. "By talking, right?"

She looks at me over her shoulder, eyebrow lifting a little.

"I came around to tell you that I thought your dance was beautiful. I saw that man harassing you, and I wanted to help."

"I don't need your help," she retorts.

"I noticed. Where did you learn that move? That was an impressive strike."

"I'm even better with a sword."

"I'd like to see that." And I mean it.

"You might not."

But I'm curious. "Seriously, where'd you learn how to fight?"

"The same place I learned how to dance."

Her words remind me of the kata practice with Shimizu Kaida, how it changed the way I approach my training. "Well, you seem very skilled at both. Your performance was like nothing I've ever seen, and I've seen a lot. I wanted to ask your name, but I'm sorry I bothered you." I walk away before I make things any worse.

"Stop," she calls after me.

I turn around.

"You're *him*, aren't you?"

I scrunch my eyebrows, ready to ask what she means, but then I get a better idea. "Yes, I like to think that I am . . . *him*." I flash a smile, hoping that she appreciates the humor.

The roll of her eyes is followed by a laugh, and I almost run away because I'm not sure this exchange can get any better than this exact moment, the look on her face and the knowledge that I made her smile.

"Most men think that they are *him* in some way or another, I suppose," she says. "What I meant was that you're the foreigner who has been training with Shimizu Kaida, aren't you?"

"You know Shimizu Kaida?"

"Very well. This village owes her a great deal."

"She's a wonderful fighter, an incredible sensei."

"She's much more than that," the dancer says.

That response makes me feel like an idiot. Of course she is more than that. Kaida is a sensei to me, but it's not surprising that her life goes well beyond destroying enemies and coaching timestars like me to do so as well. I can only assume it was Kaida who taught this girl not only to dance, but also to defend herself from demons in the shadows.

"What's your name?" I dare to step forward.

"What's *your* name?" she responds. Her eyes look me up and down so fast I'm not sure she meant to do it. Chills run over my skin. I can't believe I'm so nervous.

I give a slight bow. "My name is Dashiell Keane, but most of my friends call me Dash. You see, in my culture, our family name comes—"

"Yes," she says wryly. "I am aware of the difference, Dashiell."

"It's only fair that you tell me your name now."

She moves back into a fighting stance. "Are you willing to fight me for it?"

"No way. I know when I'm outmatched. I need your name so I can tell Shimizu Kaida that I want to fight more like you do."

She smiles. "Ryoko. Kobayashi Ryoko."

"Pleased to meet you," I say. "But don't let me keep you, if you need to get back to the stage."

"I am pleased to meet you as well, and I am in no rush. The rest of my troupe will be performing for hours."

A daring thought runs through my mind, a question that I would probably be too terrified to ask in the present. But since this is not reality, I go for it. "Then will you show me around the village? After all, I'm a foreigner."

Ryoko pauses as if considering it. Her silence seems to last forever.

She walks away and my spirits drop. Hopefully Dominus will edit this part out, so millions of people don't witness me getting rejected.

Her voice floats back. "Aren't you coming?"

I perk up with a smile, nod, and jog after her.

Ryoko leads me around her village, telling me about her people. Like most who live here, she and her family are farmers. This festival is to celebrate the harvest. When I ask about the man who attacked her, she grimaces. "I learned a long time ago to take care of myself. When pushed, people will always look out for their own best interest above all else."

I frown a little at that answer but decide not to press the matter further.

Torches and cook-fires come to life as we walk through the festival. We traverse in a large circle around the village, never getting so far that other people can't see us. I assume Ryoko doesn't trust me, and I can't blame her. She asks about my family and where I'm from. I keep my answers vague, telling her I'm here to earn money to buy medicine for my brother. I tell her no lies, but it's not the whole truth either.

I turn the questions back to her. She tells me her family has been here for generations, that most of her ancestors are buried close to the farm. But when I ask whether she visits them, Ryoko responds with a shake of her head that tells me I've gone too far. "Life is so wonderful," she says. "I don't like to think about death. I miss them, but they're gone."

Later in the evening, we sit at the edge of a pond as the moonlight sparkles across the water. The music continues to drift across the night air, but the voices grow quieter as the festival comes to an end.

"I'm afraid I need to get back," I say, standing and stretching. "Tomorrow will be another tough day. I'm dreading the morning."

"Are you really?" she says, cocking her head. "Do you dread your workday?"

"Don't you? I mean, today you got to be a dancer, but tomorrow, you'll get back to your daily work right?"

Ryoko smiles. "I have no reason to dread the rising sun, Dashiell Keane."

"Can I walk you to your home?" I ask, hoping she doesn't get the wrong idea. It's not that I'm not attracted to her; Ryoko may be the most captivating girl I've ever met. But I would never cheapen this night by trying to put any moves on her.

"That isn't necessary," she answers. "I am very safe here."

"Well, can I see you again?" I ask.

Ryoko looks away. "I'm not sure if that is a good idea. You will have to let me think about it."

It's not the answer I hoped to hear. I'm not sure how much longer I will be in this time period. Dominus Corp. will probably move me soon to keep the show interesting.

But I don't try to dissuade her. Instead, I thank her for showing me around the village.

Minutes later, I'm riding my horse back toward the pagoda. I try to focus on the trail, but my thoughts keep running back to Ryoko. I'm a little depressed that she didn't give me permission to see her again.

Stop being ridiculous, Dash. I'm at the beginning of my journey; there is so much in front of me. Ryoko was incredible, but I need to stay focused.

Besides, I tell myself as my horse trots along, the silhouette of the pagoda looming against the night sky, *she's only an echo.*

19

"THEY CAME AS COWARDS

in the night," Kaida says from across the table. I kneel on a pillow, the morning light pushing in from the window and warming my back. One of her students sits next to me.

"We received word this morning," Kaida says. "Sato Akinari led the attack. They waited until the festival ended, then started burning homes. Many villagers were killed. I sent a message to the emperor. I trust his soldiers will arrive here soon."

"Akinari is a samurai?" I choke the words out, but my mind is on Ryoko. Is she still alive?

Kaida frowns. "I will not give him the honor of calling him samurai; he lost that long ago when he turned against our emperor. But in the coming battle, you would do well to treat him as one. He is a worthy"—she corrects herself—"he is a skilled opponent."

"But why?" I ask. "What does he gain from attacking a farming village?"

"There have been uprisings around the region," Kaida informs me. "Attempts to shake the people's confidence in the emperor's protection." She looks down, her face tenses as if she's fighting to retain her composure. "And Akinari holds a vendetta against me. He wants to draw me out."

"Is he still there?"

Kaida nods.

I stand. "Then let's give him what he wants."

Preparing for battle takes longer than I would have thought, but eventually I am astride my horse, my powerful serenity, racing along the path to the village. A small contingent of the emperor's warriors rides alongside us. Kaida is in front of me, dressed in the same armor she wore on the day I met her, looking every bit as intimidating. Despite the constant beatings I receive in training, I have come to think of Shimizu Kaida as a caring, wise mentor.

But in the armor, she's someone different. *The Lightning Sword.* I'm glad she's on my side.

The morning mist creates a fog on the battlefield, rolling in off the pond where Ryoko and I sat last night, talking of our hopes and other careless things. Maybe it will rain today.

Maybe we will bring a storm.

Akinari's horde waits for us in the mist, many of them wearing masks of dark blue. Some sit astride horses, others are on foot. The village lies behind them, and I realize that it isn't clouds that choked away the light this morning. It's the smoke of burning homes, and judging by the stench in the air, other things burned as well.

I want to explode into the battle—blast the strategy, the cameras, and death's dark hand if it creeps across the timestream to claim me. If Ryoko is alive, I will fight through them to get to her. If she is dead, the first chapter of my timestar story will be a bloody one.

"Hold," Kaida says.

My horse bucks, snorting as if it shares my rage.

"You're seeing what I'm seeing, right, sensei?" I ask. "You smell what I smell?"

"No fire burns hotter than mine," Kaida says through her

mask. "But there is no great justice in a quick and pointless death."

I remember vids of ancient battles. They often began with leaders from each side meeting in the center of the field. "Don't tell me we're going to negotiate with them."

"No," she responds. "We will not be negotiating."

Silence falls over the battlefield. I know nothing about my enemy except they have wrought destruction in the night, that they might have destroyed something very beautiful.

"Will you attack us, cowards?" I shout into the fog. "Or is it not dark enough? Do you only fight those who can't see you coming? Your reckoning is upon you. The Red Dragon and the Lightning Sword have come!" I know I should have kept quiet. These aren't my men to lead. But I am a timestar after all. And even if the warriors at my back don't know it, I have fans to entertain.

Our soldiers shout in unison behind us, not words, but loud grunts of intimidation. On the other side of the battlefield, an enemy samurai steps forward. On his helm, two steel horns arc high above his head, giving him the look of a silver bull.

Akinari.

"Attack," Kaida commands.

Our force charges into battle. The enemy comes upon us like a wave, and I realize that although this moment is not real in a legal sense, since it's merely an echo of the past, I could very well die today.

I draw my sword.

Both forces collide in a mass of clanging steel and shouts. I target an echo riding toward me, readying his sword. I slash while avoiding his blow, and the smell of blood hits the air with a red mist.

It's not real. It's not real. I remind myself repeatedly as I ride outside the battle and circle back. Many of the warriors have been unhorsed by the first charge and now fight with swords on foot.

I jump from the saddle and run into the fray, my sword held

high. It's hard to tell one side from the other in the chaos, but I search for Kaida as I slash my way through the carnage. The enemy fighters are skilled, but I'm faster and stronger. I crash blades with one enemy, and his sword shatters. Disbelief flashes in his eyes before I sever his leg with a fast downward slash.

Kaida appears in the middle of the battle, facing off against Akinari. Their swords slice again and again, neither gaining an upper hand. An enemy charges at Kaida's back.

"Sensei!" I run toward her, vaulting over bodies, knowing I can't reach her in time.

Kaida kicks the bull backward, then whirls around to block the attack of the other warrior. She knocks his sword away and slashes him across the chest. He falls.

The bull regains his footing and lunges toward her.

I leap forward, ramming my shoulder into Akinari, and his blade hits Kaida's side. She grunts in pain and drops.

I roll to my feet. The bull is still standing.

"Demon!" Akinari calls out at me.

The hatred burns inside of me, but I hear my sensei's voice. "Control," she shouts, coughing up blood. Her students dash to her side, swords ready to defend their master.

Control. I remember our kata as I flip the sword in my hand and approach Akinari. Blood streaks down my face, but it's not my own. I am more than a timestar today. I am warrior.

The bull strikes at me, but I deflect the blow. I doubt he's fought anybody as fast as me. I remember what was said to me about my implants. My greatest limitation is my belief in my own abilities.

The bull brings a powerful overhand slash. I sidestep, imagining that I am a shadow, a phantom that his blade could never touch. I cut the back of his knee, my sword a blur.

Akinari crumbles and tries to parry with a weak swipe. I block the attack and target his hand. He cries out as my sword finds its mark. His weapon clangs on the ground. I slice through his armor and into his chest, creating a sash of blood.

Around me, the fighting has stopped. Men and women from both sides writhe and moan on the ground. Kaida is still alive, her two students at her side.

"Finish him off," Mr. Myrtrym says in my left ear. I forgot he was there.

I look at the smoldering village, then raise my sword. My focus locks onto the thin slice of flesh between Akinari's mask and his armor. I strike.

"Dash!"

My blade stops at the bull's neck, leaving only a red kiss on his skin. My head snaps up.

Ryoko stands in the distance, her blue dress stained with blood and dust. She heads toward me.

My attention returns to the bull. I remember the swirling petals behind the pagoda. This beast is nothing beautiful, but I'm not sure I can do this.

Not with her watching.

I straighten my posture and remove my sword from his neck. "Surrender. You're defeated. You will face the emperor's justice."

The bull removes his mask with a bloody hand. Sweaty hair streaks across Akinari's face, hatred brimming in his eyes. "Look upon me, young warrior," he says, "and see that my blood is real." The bull pulls a short sword from a sheath at his side.

My muscles tense, and I prepare to deflect his strike, but Akinari plunges the blade into his own gut. Blood floods from the wound, creating a dark pool in the dirt. Life disappears from his eyes, and he falls forward.

I can't take my eyes off his body. *Residual energy. That's all he is.* But something inside me aches. This man did exist in time. How would he have died if I'd never come here?

And why did he call me a demon?

THE ELEVATOR DOOR OPENS

into the board room at Dominus Corporation's main office. I step out wearing my jacket, jeans, and sneakers. After so many weeks in ancient Japan, it feels strange to be back in my old clothes.

The same faces all occupy the same spots. Mr. Myrtrym stands at the far side of the table. In the time window behind him, men in the desert are dragging stones up the side of a pyramid under construction.

I smile as I take my seat, but the faces at the table show no emotions. No nods, no frowns, nothing. The call to return home had been unexpected. I had just finished helping Ryoko settle in at the pagoda after ensuring my sensei's wounds would heal. Ryoko's family was killed in the attack and her home destroyed. Given the circumstances, she was holding up well, but I hated to leave her in such a difficult time. At least with Kaida, I know she's safe.

My heart races as Mr. Myrtrym takes a deep breath, releases it, and looks at me. "Dash . . ." He shakes his head. Then he winks at me. "The ratings are incredible."

Smiles appear around the table.

"Really?" I say eagerly.

"Every metric we have," Mr. Myrtrym replies. "Not just views, which are sky-high for a new timestar, but also audience engagement. People smile when you're onscreen. Are more alert. We're getting solid auditory data as well."

"Oh," I say. "What does that mean?"

"They're rooting for you," a woman on my right says. She has short brown hair and wears a white suit with blue trim. "And not just in combat. They were pulling for you when you took a walk with the echo during the festival."

"Nice move, there," a man interjects. He's bald and has a nose like a beak. "We thought that the festival would be extra fluff to ground the audience in the time period and make you look like a man of the people by sharing their food, enjoying their simple entertainment. The whole thing turned into a great segment."

"Plus, that ending," trumpets a short man with dark hair and a beard sitting near Mr. Myrtrym. "When you fought the ronin samurai who destroyed her village, it was perfect. Our data tells us that many viewers were actually crying. Keep that up, and one day you'll hold a Suvea Award."

"Thank you." I still feel a little uneasy. "So, you're happy with my performance?"

The mood in the room shifts. Some of them exchange glances.

Mr. Myrtrym speaks up, eyes leveled on me. "That samurai. You did hear me when I directed you to finish him, didn't you?"

My muscles tighten, but I'm not going to lie. "I did."

Mr. Myrtrym's jaw tics, but the tension is gone a moment later. He walks around the table to me. "Dash, I understand this is a difficult transition. It's one thing to see it on the holoscreen; it's very different when you're face-to-face with echoes. The energy feels very real—I think it's the smell. You never get that at home, and as humans, we pick up on it. I've spent enough time in the past that my senses know the difference. Echoes don't smell human to me anymore. You'll get there eventually."

The woman in the white suit slides her chair over so Mr. Myrtrym can lean against the table in front of me. "I know it's hard, but we've all got a job to do. Every person in this room is committed to making you the biggest timestar ever, but you understand that the timenet is a very small piece of what we do. Most of our business is importing fuels and materials from the past. It's how we solved the global energy crisis and famines. As our hero, you're a symbol of the great things that Dominus Corp. is doing in the world. That includes vanquishing evil. The hero is supposed to destroy the villain."

"But I beat him," I protest. "Isn't that enough?"

Mr. Myrtrym's face suddenly beams as if with pride. "Yes, you did!" He throws a playful punch at me. He's not being aggressive, but it still sets my nerves on end.

"It *was* incredible." Mr. Myrtrym hops off the table and strides to the other side of the room. "The Red Dragon. You were fast, Dash, maybe even faster than the Lightning Sword. Honestly, it was better than we could have hoped."

He faces me. "But it's all about the story. You must complete the narrative. To do that, you have to remember the echoes are no more real than a memory. They're characters in a story."

Mr. Myrtrym leans forward, both hands on the table. "Fortunately, we can spin this as part of your development. The audience loves seeing a hero learn, make mistakes, get better, level up. This shows you're not there yet. That's good."

His demeanor changes. "But those same mistakes won't be tolerated forever."

The words hang in the air. The message is clear. I may be popular, but I need Dominus more than they need me.

Mr. Myrtrym raps his knuckles twice on the table and straightens. "Enough of that. We're giving you a couple of days off before sending you to the next time period. We won't tell you where you're going yet. We want it to be a surprise."

"Sounds good to me." I stand, relieved that for the time being, I appear to be in the good graces of Mr. Myrtrym and Dominus Corp. That means Knox still has a shot at getting his treatment, and I still have a chance of becoming a career timestar.

"How will you spend the time off?" Mr. Myrtrym inquires. "Your apartment is ready for you, of course, and we can arrange whatever entertainment you like. Our one condition is you stay in the present. It helps you remember what's real. But there's a lot to do—the theater, a concert, or maybe lie on the beach for a few days. I'm sure you could find a date for yourself. Your vids are very popular."

An idea pops into my mind, something I've been dying to do ever since this opportunity first came to me. "I don't think any of that will be necessary, but I may need a small favor."

"Name it."

I grin. "Could somebody lend me a suit?"

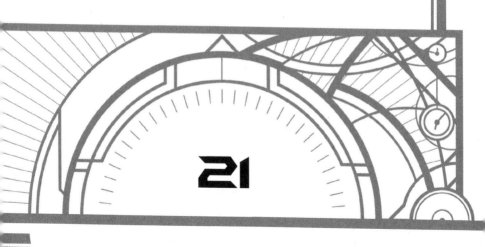

21

"YOU FIRST," I SAY TO GARON,
indicating the door of the gravcar. He sits in the seat across from me, wearing a black suit and red tie that matches my own.

"Seriously?" he asks. Outside, people mill around the car, looking in the tinted windows and trying to see who's inside. "But they're all waiting for you, Dash."

"Maybe." I grin at him. "But none of this would have happened without you. Soon they'll know your name as well as mine. We're a team. Us against the world. You might as well get used to the crowds."

"Works for me." Garon runs both hands over his jacket. Dominus had our suits custom-tailored on short notice. Garon looks better in his than I do in mine. I never feel right without my Red Dragon jacket, though the suit is by far the most expensive fabric I've ever worn.

When Garon opens the door, the screams and shouts of students pour into the car. A steady pulse of dance music comes from inside the school.

I follow Garon out as Dominus guards hold back the crowd. The kids from school are all dressed in their best. The few that have suits probably borrowed them from their fathers. My dad doesn't even own one. It makes me realize how lucky I am.

A lot of them call out my name as we wind through the crowd. "Hey, we're just here for the dance," I tell nobody and everybody, a broad smile on my face. Their voices smash together, but I keep hearing the words *samurai, Ryoko,* and *incredible.*

When we step into the school gym, I have to admit that, for kids from the Dregs, my classmates have outdone themselves. Sparkling lights cover the floor, the walls, and the ceiling along with light beams bursting with various colors. It looks like people are dancing in space amongst stars and nebulae. They're all holograms, I know, but with the music and the excitement in the air, I lose myself in the fantasy.

Garon and I grip hands and bump chests.

"Thanks for this, buddy," he says in my ear.

"No, thank you," I respond. "Let's go grab some—"

My words are cut off as someone tugs on my jacket. I've never seen the girl before, but I don't know how I missed her. Her blonde hair glitters in the lights. She has a sweet smile and a small stud in the side of her nose.

She pulls on my jacket again. "Dance with me."

I'm not dumb enough to argue.

The next hour flies by in a blur of people and music. Electricity courses through me as I bob back and forth to the music. Girls ask me to dance. Guys bump fists with me in congratulations. I wish the cameras were on me so I could capture this moment. This is what fame feels like. *I could get used to it.*

When my throat gets dry from dancing and yelling over the music so Garon can hear me, I wander off the dance floor toward the refreshment table. A girl at the table fills a cup and hands it to me. I thank her and turn to look for Garon.

That's when I see her—Braelynn Bonner checking me out from the other side of the dance floor. She wears a black dress that accentuates her form, but it's her shoes that catch my attention. They're red . . . *my* shade of red. She smiles at me as if she knows I just noticed.

Here we go. I finish my drink and make my way over to her. As I cross the dance floor, a few people stop me and tell me how much they enjoy my vidstream. They loved the way I defeated those echoes and hope to see me do it again soon. I thank them and take a couple of pictures, making Braelynn wait on me like I've always waited on her.

When I reach the other side of the dance floor, Braelynn's still there, swaying back and forth to the music.

"Hi, Dash." She clutches a drink in one hand.

"Hi, Braelynn. I like your shoes."

She giggles. "I thought you would. I really like your show."

A hot, tingling rush of emotion almost knocks me over. *Keep it together, Dash.* "Yeah? That's cool."

She gives a little smile. "I was kind of jealous of that echo," she says. "What was her name? Ryata?"

"Ryoko." The correction blurts out of my mouth, and I realize I almost yelled, like I was scolding her for getting the name wrong. "At least, I think it was Ryoko," I say with a shrug, trying to sound more casual. It makes me feel a little like a jerk. *She isn't real. She isn't real.*

Braelynn steps closer. "That was heroic the way you saved her village."

"He didn't save anyone!"

My head turns. Craig. He's sneering at me.

"Sorry?" I lean toward Craig, sizing him up. A few days ago, I fought a small army of trained samurai, but somehow this makes my stomach turn with nervousness. All of a sudden, I'm Dash again, the kid in the school hallway whose instinct is to back down.

But this time, I won't.

"What did you say?" I ask him.

Two more guys walk up behind him. I don't recognize them,

but they glare at me as Craig scoffs. "Yeah, I saw your vids. It's all tricks. If you didn't have that fancy sword that Dominus gave you, that bull samurai would have skewered you alive."

"Is that so?" I'm close enough to smell that it's not punch on his breath.

He gets in my face. His two friends close in on either side of me. "I don't think you want to do this, *Red Dragon*," Craig taunts. "Your samurai mom isn't here to save you."

Three moves. I could have all of them on the floor in three moves without breaking a sweat before they know what's happening.

"Beat him up, Dash," Braelynn urges.

I glance at her over my shoulder. Her breathing is deep, and there is a wildness in her eyes. She's ready to see blood.

The next voice I hear is Garon, whispering behind my right ear, "Dude, don't do this."

I know I should listen, but what if word gets around that I backed down? How can I be an action star if I can't hold my own at the school dance?

"Nobody's watching," Garon says as if he can read my thoughts, "but if you get arrested for beating up a bunch of idiots at a school function, you'll never go back in time again."

And I would never see Ryoko. The thought catches me off guard. I'm surprised that I'm thinking of her here at my school dance. In the present. With Braelynn Bonner at my side. I pause and take a breath.

"Maybe next time." I let Garon pull me away. Braelynn frowns and turns her attention elsewhere.

Garon throws his arm around my shoulder. "I'm hungry. Let's get out of here and go eat."

I still feel like a hot coil is wrapped around my gut, but I try to relax, to remember the breathing Kaida taught me during our kata.

"Sounds good," I agree. "Where should we go?"

"You said the gravcar will take us wherever, right?"

"Right."

"Great." He pats me on the back. "I'm bringing a few friends."

When we get outside, a handful of people are waiting for us. A couple girls I danced with and a few guys who want to hear more about my samurai training. We pile into the gravcar and ask the driver to take us to his favorite place.

The rest of the night is spent laughing and eating cheap food at a sketchy restaurant on the edge of the Dregs. The other teenagers seem like good people, but I can't shake the thought that they wouldn't have hung out with me a couple of weeks ago. Maybe it's not their fault; I wasn't always the most social person, but that doesn't mean they're my friends either.

And I can't stop thinking about Ryoko.

The gravcar drops the others off at their homes, leaving Garon and me for last. As we pull up to Garon's apartment, I realize I'm not ready to stop hanging out. "Why don't you crash with me at my apartment? I know I'm not there a lot, but when I am, it would be cool to hang out."

"Thanks, man, I appreciate that, I really do. But I need to get home."

I glance out the window at his building. I'm living the good life, but Garon is still in the Dregs. "As soon as I prove to Dominus how valuable I am, I will make sure you're on my camera crew or in the producer chair. We're in this together. It's only a matter of time."

He flashes me a smile as he opens the car door. "I know, Dash. Soon."

I watch Garon walk into his apartment building. He's always been on my team, even when it cost him. I can't let him down. I have to make sure this is not only my ticket out of here, but a ticket out for all of us. Mom, Dad, Knox, and Garon.

"I'm coming back for you." It's part promise, part prayer.

22

THE LIGHTS DIM ON THE

time platform. I'm getting used to the way it feels, the way time scientists regard me the moment after I jump from the present to a lily pad in the past. But for the first time, I see recognition on their faces. They know who I am. A few of them whisper to each other.

A man approaches me in a blue suit with a Dominus logo sewn into the left chest pocket. He extends his hand. "Dashiell Keane. Welcome to the Old West. Follow me."

He leads me away from the lily pad, down a hallway, and into a wardrobe room. The walls and ceiling are a clean, white marble, but the floors are black. A rack of Western-style clothes occupies the middle of the room, most of it black with red accents. A black vest sports my signature red *K* over the left breast, and there's a red strip of fabric to wear around my neck.

At the end of the rack hangs a black leather belt with two silver revolvers in the holsters.

Mr. Myrtrym buzzes in my ear. "The guns are real this time, Dash. We would prefer you not use them until you've been properly trained."

"How am I supposed to defend myself?"

"Your outfit is highly resistant to gunfire. You'll notice the shirt and vest are a bit heavier than you might expect. They should protect you from anything other than a shot at point-blank range. Also, we have provided a weapon in which you are already trained."

A light turns on ahead of me, shining down on a shelf built into the far wall.

My sword.

"You don't think that will look a little out of character?" I ask.

"You *are* supposed to stand out," Mr. Myrtrym reminds me.

"Good point." I walk over and take it in my hands. A week has passed since I last held it, but it feels like longer. I'm happy to have it again.

"Ramona says you should wear it over your shoulder."

I frown. "It belongs on my side."

"We did some concept art. It will look more cinematic this way. Besides, your pistols will be at your sides."

"Okay." I draw the sword from the sheath an inch to see the red blade. "Mr. Myrtrym, did Ryoko get the letter I gave you?"

"She did," he replies. "But don't worry about that now. You need to get moving."

I push the sword back into the sheath. "And who am I looking for again?"

"Duffy," he says. "Sheriff Duffy."

I get dressed, feeling strange as I strap the katana across my back, and leave the facility. When I walk outside, I'm surrounded by desert and a vast blue sky. To my right, a dark-brown horse jerks against a wooden rail to which he is tied.

"Take it easy." I rub my hand over his neck. "You and I are friends now."

The horse settles enough for me to climb into the saddle.

"Any idea where we're going?" I ask the horse.

A light flashes in the distance, an unnatural shade of green that catches my attention. As I focus on it, I realize it's a marker for my destination. It looks as if it's floating over the desert. Text appears beneath the marker: *10.8 miles.*

"That's new," I say.

"Optics tech," Mr. Myrtrym's voice says. "We just activated it. We didn't want to give you too much at once, but you might need it for what's next."

I prod the horse with my boot, expecting a trot, but it accelerates fast. We charge across the open plain, kicking up a cloud of dust. There's nothing for miles around except my horse, me, and the sky.

When we get close to the destination, a town takes shape beneath the marker. Old wooden buildings and dirt roads. My horse slows to a walk as we pass a small graveyard on my right. *I guess that's one way to welcome people.*

As we cross the threshold of the town, people sit on front porches or lean over balconies, watching me in silence.

I tie my horse to the post outside the saloon in the center of town and take a moment to collect myself. It's only then that I remember the katana strapped across my back. Probably why all the people were staring. Still, there's no way I'm taking it off.

The saloon may not be the best place to find the sheriff, but for all I know, this could be my last chance to check it out before I start training again. My boots knock on the hardwood planks as I approach the swinging doors, ready to burst through and make my presence known. But the blazing sun reflecting off the dirt makes me squint, and I can hardly see inside the saloon.

Right before I reach the doors, two men stumble out, each gripping the other's shirt. One is a wiry man with tanned leathery skin. A thick gray mustache covers his upper lip. His brow is furrowed with intensity. The other man is a round, sweaty oaf in a violet suit. His glasses fall off as the men continue to wrestle.

I jump to avoid them as they tumble into the street. The man in purple comes to his feet and dusts himself off, his skin beet red. "Please . . . *please* don't do this. I don't want a fight."

The other man stretches himself up, throwing a long shadow over the dirt. A light desert breeze catches his black duster. The brim of his hat casts darkness over his face, but a glimmer reflects in his eyes. He touches the gun at his side. My optics outline the weapon in red, showing me it's a threat. My hand goes to my side, and I remember my sword isn't there. I reach over my shoulder toward the handle.

A soft hand catches my wrist. I look to my right to see one of the saloon women, blonde with rosy cheeks, shaking her head at me. "Don't get involved, stranger."

"She's right," Mr. Myrtrym says in my ear. "Let this play out."

"Please!" repeats the man in purple. He's hunched over as if in agony. He must have taken a punch or two in the saloon before the brawl spilled onto the street. "Please, don't do this. I don't want this."

Something glints on the tall man's chest—a shimmering gold star.

The town falls quiet. My conscience screams for me to intervene, but I remember the words of Mr. Myrtrym, and I stay my hand.

The tall man draws his gun.

A loud bang shatters the air.

The tall man hits the ground, bleeding from his shoulder.

The man in the purple suit is still hunched over. Smoke lifts from the barrel of the gun now in his hand. I never saw him draw it, never saw him take aim.

He holsters his gun, rushes over to his fallen opponent, and kicks the tall man's pistol away. "Get the doc!"

An older woman in a gray dress saunters over, hauling a large bag in her left hand. "Again with this, sheriff?"

The man in purple takes the star off the tall gunman's chest. "He was drunk and teasing me, like he always does. Pulled my star, put it on himself, and started waving his gun around like he was going to kill someone. I tried to stop him. Is he going to make it?"

The doctor presses a bandage to the wound on the man's shoulder. "Yes, sheriff," she responds as if annoyed. "He'll be fine."

"You're sure?"

She nods. "I'll patch him up, then send for your deputy. He can take him to jail."

The sheriff pulls a handkerchief from his breast pocket, blows his nose, and returns it to the pocket. "Well, that's quite a relief."

The people crowd back into the saloon. A piano picks up a lively song. Men laugh over a card game. I'm still outside gaping at the sheriff.

The sheriff regards me, still breathing a bit heavily. "You appear to be new around here."

"You can't be Sheriff Duffy."

He nods.

"Sheriff Duffy . . . the famous gunfighter?"

"If you're searching for a gunfighter who shares my name, my boy, I'm afraid I've never heard of him." He heads down the dirt street.

I chase after him. "Wait! I need to talk to you!"

23

SHERIFF DUFFY'S OFFICE

shares a wall with the town jail. The outside of the building looks like a ramshackle hut held together by weathered boards, half of which appear ready to fall off.

But the inside of the sheriff's office speaks of refinement. The shelves behind his desk are filled with books arranged in neat rows. Landscape paintings hang on the wall, and I can almost see my reflection in the polish of his hardwood desk. There isn't a speck of dust anywhere.

Duffy offers me a seat next to the window at a small table with a doily on top. After I sit, he disappears into another room, then reappears holding a tea set—white with flowers— on a painted, wooden tray. He sweats through his fine clothes, which despite appearing to be the right size, look like they were cut for someone else.

"The tea is atrocious," he says as he fills the cup in front of me. "Very difficult to acquire a decent brew out here."

I take a sip. The hot tea burns my tongue. Duffy's right. It's awful, far worse than the green tea I had in Japan, but I decide not to say so. "It's fine."

"Hm." He takes a drink, making a pained expression as he

swallows. "Well, it does help calm my nerves."

I lean over the table. "What you did out there . . ."

"I'd rather not speak of it," he says. "For many reasons."

"Such as?" I take another sip of the bitter tea.

"My skills have earned me a certain . . . reputation." Duffy takes the lid off a dish between us and uses a spoon to scoop out a sugar cube, which he drops into his tea. It strikes me as odd. They never added sugar to the tea in Japan.

I scoop out a cube, drop it into my cup, and stir. "Just to be clear, you're talking about your skills as a gunfighter, right?"

He looks at me sternly. "That word is vulgar, and I'll thank you for not using it, Mr. Keane."

I take a drink. It tastes the same, so I drop in two more sugar cubes. "Gunfighter? What's vulgar about that?"

"The distinction suggests my very purpose is tied to death. My profession is that of a lawman, a peacekeeper. When I have to use my weapon, it means I have failed."

"But you're so good at it," I insist.

"My curse." Duffy shakes his head. "Perhaps penance for sins committed in a past life. It's come natural to me since the day my father raised his hand to my mother and I raised his six-shooter in response. From that moment on, I have been constantly presented with two terrible choices—take the blood of men, or allow them to do horrible things that I could prevent. On a good day, it's only a little blood that I must spill."

"And you've done this a lot?"

He gives an abrupt laugh. "You would think this godforsaken land was isolated enough to keep news from spreading, but broken men keep showing up, looking for the sheriff that people say can't be taken down in a fair match. The more it happens, the more they come, desperate to prove they're better than me. Truthfully, I hope one of them will be right."

I notice the sheriff isn't wearing a ring. This building is clearly his home as well as his office, but there is no sign of anyone else living here.

I take another drink. The tea tastes sweeter, but it's not quite enough. I reach for another sugar cube.

"Maybe I should serve you a jar of molasses," he remarks.

My hand stops as I realize that shoveling sugar into my tea might be considered rude.

"Is that why you're here?" the sheriff says, setting his teacup on a painted pink flower on the wooden tray.

I look at my cup, then at him, bewildered. "For sugar?"

He sighs. "Have you come here to challenge me? It isn't the best time. Today's altercation was as much a success as I could hope. You could say I won, I guess, and the other man still breathes. That's not a terrible day, I suppose, but it does take its toll. If you killed me now, people would undoubtedly credit the previous combatant with softening me up for you. Not to dissuade you, but you should be aware of—"

I interrupt him. "I'm not here to kill you."

"Then why are you here?"

"I want you to train me." I pat the gun on my left side. "Teach me to do what you do."

He huffs. "I might have preferred you came to kill me. Despite my stated distaste for using my weapon, crushing someone's aspirations can be more difficult than dueling. People tend to argue less with my bullets than my words."

I stare at him. "You're going to crush my . . . what?"

Duffy just continues on, "They all have the same look that you do right now. So sure of yourself, ready to take on the world and convinced you're good enough to do it."

"I can prove I'm good enough," I say defiantly. "I'll show you right now."

He yawns. "Do I have to get up?" he asks.

"No, you can stay right there." I stand and pull my sword, half expecting him to draw his gun in retaliation, but there isn't a trace of fear in Sheriff Duffy's eyes. He holds the teacup in his right hand, then raises it to take a drink.

The swipe of my sword is so fast it makes an audible *whoosh*. Before he's done taking a drink, the blade is back in its sheath. I return to my seat.

"Not bad," he observes, setting his cup down.

I point to his chest.

Sheriff Duffy looks down. The top corner of his handkerchief falls from his pocket, a perfect cut. He examines the fabric of his jacket behind the handkerchief, doubtless discovering that not a single thread is damaged.

His eyes snap up, his gaze locked onto me, and for a brief instant, the mask he wears slips away. "Impressive, though now I must consider whether it would be unwise to teach you the way of the gun. You appear to be a very dangerous individual."

I lean forward. "Don't do it for me. Do it for yourself. By training me, you set yourself free."

"How so?"

"Give me a few weeks," I say. "I'll work for you in exchange for training. If by the end of that time, I'm not as good as you, I'll leave."

"And if you are able to achieve my level of skill?"

"Then I'll become more famous than you. I'm younger. I stand out. It will be my name that broken men whisper over campfires. They won't come gunning for you anymore. They'll come gunning for me. You can escape the life of gunfi—err—dueling, and you won't even have to die."

The sheriff goes silent, taking time to finish his tea. Several times I consider speaking up to further my case. After all, I'm not certain what would happen if he refused. Would I ask for Mr. Myrtrym's help? Is this a test? And if I fail again, how many times will Dominus cover for me before they cut my contract?

"Have you ever been in love?" Sheriff Duffy asks.

The unexpected question makes me think of Ryoko. I wonder what she's doing and if she's thinking of me. I want to see her again, but if I do, what will I tell her about where I've been?

"No," Sheriff Duffy is answering for me. "You're too young, so I caution you, young man, this is a lonely road. You seem to have a kind soul, if you believe in that sort of thing. I do. I've looked into the faces of people in their darkest moments. Usually, I see at least some conflict there, even if they aren't aware of it. I see someone who, if they did manage to kill me, would be tormented by my face in their dreams for the rest of their lives.

"But sometimes, I see . . . emptiness. There are soulless creatures roaming this universe who can kill a person and feel nothing about it at all. I don't know if they're born that way or if something happened to make them such. I wish I knew; it would make decisions like mine far simpler."

I want to respond, to tell him that I'm not one of those people. I want to tell him about Knox, about my friends, and about Ryoko. If he needs to know that I have a heart, then I have enough in my life to show him it's true.

But for some reason, I keep quiet.

"I'm not going to ask which type of man you are. If you were the latter, it's quite possible that I wouldn't know you were lying to me anyway. So, you see the dilemma. But for what it's worth, if you are the first kind of man . . ."

Sheriff Duffy slams his gun down on the table, rattling the spoon against the cold cup of tea. "Don't let *this* turn you into the second."

MY NEXT FEW DAYS ARE
spent following the sheriff around town, mostly checking in with shopkeepers. Duffy alternates between complaining about the heat and complaining about his severe desert allergies. He seems to hate everything here except the people. As we make our way through town, he calls out children by name, asks people about their health conditions, and inquires about previous disputes between neighbors. Everybody seems happy to stop and speak with him.

But as much as they admire the sheriff, they seem uncertain about me. More than a few ask about the sword on my back. Duffy tells them I'm a traveler who feels more comfortable with a sword, then changes the conversation. Despite his reassurances, they keep a wary eye on me.

His deputy, a man named John Carlson, manages the prison during the day, though we check in from time to time. John is slightly overweight and looks halfway between Duffy's age and mine. He comes off as kind enough, but I doubt he has the intimidating quality I would expect from a lawman. Sheriff Duffy confirms that impression one day as we leave the jail.

"It's good to have him in the jail," Duffy says. "John's

greatest gift is a comforting presence. He has a way of calming people down."

A man of his word, Duffy and I spend any extra time training with six-shooters. The lessons start by shooting empty bottles off a fence post near the edge of town. The target practice is easy for me, though I don't tell Duffy about my optics technology homing in on the bottles, providing me with crosshair targets that account for wind speed and distance. The optics even adjust after every shot by observing the arc of the bullets.

More than once, Duffy pulls his glasses out of his inner pocket and asks to inspect my revolvers. I'm not sure what he's searching for, and he never tells me if he notices anything different. Usually, he makes sounds like "hmmm," then hands them back to me.

Regardless, Duffy is a great teacher. He explains the proper angle for my holsters and how to position my hand when drawing to shave microseconds off the time needed to pull and fire. I spend hours pulling from both sides with my eyes closed, which Duffy says will help me focus more on the action.

"Shorter" becomes a word I hear over and over again as he emphasizes the importance of completing the draw-and-fire action as fast as possible, rather than taking time to extend my arm. "Aiming is something you should have already completed before you pull."

Like Shimizu Kaida, the sheriff emphasizes a focus on breath as well as finding my natural motion. "It should be as unique as poetry," he says. "A perfect draw is unlike that of any other human being throughout history. It is also an unobtainable goal, a true name never to be discovered in this lifetime, but for which you must constantly strive. The closer you get, the more unique your technique shall become, and the less I can teach you."

A few days into our training, we shift from stationary targets to moving ones. Duffy makes John fling bottles in the air. My optics recognize the targets and soon work in harmony with the forms I have learned. Within an hour, I'm shattering every bottle John tosses. He tries throwing them farther, but my aim remains perfect. He grows frustrated with his inability to get a bottle past my bullets. I can't help but chuckle, which infuriates him more. Finally, John grabs the hat off his head and hurls it down at the ground.

My bullet rips through the hat before it hits the dirt. Duffy and John look at me as if I've sprouted a third arm.

"That will do for today," Duffy says between coughs. "This dry desert air is getting the best of me."

I spend the nights writing letters to Knox and Ryoko, though most of Ryoko's wind up crumpled on the floor. The problem is the pen. As soon as I fall into a rhythm, it betrays me by telling her things I'm not ready for her to know. Things like *I'm from the future* and *there are millions of people watching my every move.*

But a few times, I manage to craft letters that focus instead on her. I write about our night together and how often I think about it. I drop the letters at the town post office at the instructions of Mr. Myrtrym, who says I should tell the postman that they are for Dominus Corporation. He assures me the postmaster will handle the rest.

25

I STROLL INTO THE JAIL

one morning, well-rested and ready to train. But when I see the look on John's face, I know something's wrong.

"The doctor thinks it's consumption," John tells me from behind his wooden desk in the jail. "At least, it seems to have those symptoms."

The news hits me like a wave. "So, he's at home?"

John nods. "Doc said he needs to rest, and it's advised that nobody goes to see him. She's unsure exactly what we're dealing with, and we don't know how contagious it might be."

But Dominus could figure it out. Mr. Myrtrym brags about his medical division all the time. Surely they could help the sheriff, but maybe they don't want to intervene. I decide to ask him about it when I can.

"In the meantime, I've been told to give you this." John slides a gold star across the desk.

My eyes widen slightly, and I pick it up. "Duffy gave this to . . . me?"

John winces. "He's been feverish, but that's what the doctor said." No doubt John is disappointed, though Duffy made the right call. John's a great jailor, but he doesn't have the mindset to be a lawman. He's not fearsome enough.

"You'll be around to help, right?" I ask him. The last thing I want right now is to deal with drunks who need to sleep it off behind bars. "For Duffy?" I add quickly.

"For the sheriff," John says. "He's been good to me."

I shake John's hand before walking outside. I don't want him to see me pin the badge on my chest, but I make sure to step out from beneath the awning of the jail so I'm in the light. The cameras should have a clear shot of me from here as I place the star over my heart.

I'm a lawman.

What do I do now?

I start by mirroring what I saw Duffy do, which means visiting the shopkeepers around town. Each time I cross somebody's threshold, I make sure that the star on my chest is showing. The message needs to be clear.

Most of the town has already heard about Duffy's condition. When I walk through the door, I'm greeted with a combination of condolences over his sickness and expressions of gratitude that I'm around. A few mutter their relief that John hasn't assumed the role.

"I'm not sure he'd pull the gun when needed," the town grocer says.

"Hopefully I won't have to pull it either," I respond. For some reason, I feel loyal to John. I prefer to steer the conversation away from his shortcomings.

"I don't know," the grocer eyes me doubtfully. "New kid walking around wearing the star, especially one as young faced as you. Someone's bound to test you, son. Hope you're ready. Ever had to kill anybody?"

I shake my head, remembering the bull samurai and my disobedience of Dominus' orders. I thank the grocer and leave.

The next few days pass without major incident, but on the fourth night, a commotion at the saloon sends me rushing through the swinging doors to find four young men shouting and hurling glasses. The instant I appear, they charge me. I catch the first with a punch that drops him to the floor before I grab the next guy and use his momentum to throw him out of the saloon.

The other two approach. My heart races. They throw punches that I dodge, but my optics pick up on the loaded guns at their sides. I have to get this outside as soon as possible. Someone's going to get killed.

I backpedal through the doors. They follow me outside where their friend stands waiting. They're scared. It's evident in the way they take their time circling me, each of them afraid to make a move, but their hands are near their guns. People are watching from the porch of the saloon, but everyone is quiet.

I pull my sword as I turn a slow circle. A few of them snicker. They're expecting a gunfight, but I would prefer to end this without taking lives. Mr. Myrtrym is watching, no doubt, but I hear nothing from him.

The moonlight glints off the red blade. My muscles tense. "Are you guys going to make a move or what?" Not the best challenge, but it will do.

The first one draws his gun. He's slow. I lunge forward, slice through the barrel, then spin and deliver a hard kick to his gut. The man to his left draws as well, and I swing the blade and catch his arm, sending a spray of blood into the air.

My optics flash red as the other two across from me pull their guns. Two red lines appear in my vision. I swing toward the lines a heartbeat before they fire. My blade rings twice. I draw one of my guns with my free hand and target the flesh between their necks and shoulders, the spot Duffy showed me.

Two shots later, they're down.

The gunfighter behind me reaches for his revolver, which is a few feet away. I jump and bring my blade down through his palm, pinning it to the ground. He cries out and drops onto the sand. I leave the sword where it is, holding him in place as I draw my other gun.

"The next time I use a weapon," I warn, "somebody dies." I hope they don't test me. They're echoes, but I'm not sure I'm ready to cross that line, not for low-level thugs like these guys. They stink of whiskey; it's seeping out of their pores. I would rather not kill anyone, even an echo, simply because they got drunk and stupid.

The men raise their hands in surrender. At least, the ones who *can* raise their hands.

I holster my weapons.

After the wounded are bandaged up and all of them are delivered to the jail, I'm sitting in the saloon as people raise drinks in my honor.

"To Sheriff Keane!" one of them calls out.

The rest of them cheer in response. "Sheriff Keane!"

I sniff the whiskey in my glass, then toss it back, feeling it burn all the way down my throat. I take a quick look around the room. When I check my glass again, somebody has refilled it. I only take a sip this time, very aware that many people are examining my every move. Several come to congratulate me. They tell me they're glad I'm here, and a few confide their fears that Duffy might be too old to keep the peace, that maybe his illness is a type of mercy.

"I hope he survives," is a common refrain, "but better to pass on in your bed than die bleeding in the street."

I'm unsure how to respond, so I give a polite raise of my glass and say I'm grateful for what he's taught me and hope he has a long life ahead of him. That seems to satisfy people enough to move them along, but more always walk up.

More than once, they remark that I'm not paying enough attention to my drink and make me promise to let them buy my next round.

Pretty soon, I feel more like a carnival attraction than a hero.

26

I SPEND THE NEXT FEW

days making my rounds in the mornings and exploring the countryside in the afternoons. With Duffy in sickbed, I'm left to train on my own. I ride out to remote areas that give me a chance to push my enhancements to their limits. My speed and aim improve fast. Within a couple of days, I can quick draw and hit a bottle a hundred yards away with almost one hundred percent accuracy.

The training is nothing if not relaxing. I ride and shoot until the sun dips toward the horizon, the movements becoming automatic. While I practice, my mind always finds its way to Ryoko.

But as I ride back one day, the instant my optics recognize the town in the distance, a gunshot echoes across the desert, shattering my solace. Something's very wrong. I feel it in my bones.

"Go!" I command. My horse bursts into a full run, but it doesn't seem fast enough. My muscles tense. I want to jump off and sprint on my own legs, pushing my abilities to their limits, but I know it wouldn't be any faster.

When I reach the town, the streets are empty and quiet except for the bartender standing outside the jail, waving frantically to get my attention.

"Where were you?" he asks impatiently.

"What happened?" I don't bother tying up my horse after I dismount.

John appears in the doorway of Duffy's office, his white shirt covered with blood. "Dash . . ."

It isn't real, I tell myself as I follow John inside. The office is crowded but quiet as we head back toward Duffy's room. Everyone is glaring at us. *It isn't real.*

Duffy's lying still on the bed, the life stolen from his eyes, a blood-soaked bandage on his chest. The doctor stands at the sheriff's side, her eyes down as she carefully places medical supplies back into her bag.

I go to the side of the bed, placing my hand on Duffy's. The skin is still warm. I close my eyes.

"Who?" I ask.

"Dash," John starts. "Maybe you should—"

"Tell me!"

John sighs. "I was across town when it happened, but the bartender saw the guy walk in. Said he wasn't here five seconds before the gunshot. The man came back out slow and with pistols drawn. He wanted people to see."

"Did anybody recognize him?" I ask.

"Maybe you would have." The bartender appears in the doorway, frowning at me. "He said this would get your attention."

My blood runs cold. "My attention?"

"Said he'll be waiting for you."

"The guy was insane." John steps between the bartender and me. "He was talking nonsense."

But I look past John to the bartender. "Waiting for me where?"

"He said he'll be waiting for you at the mouth of the abyss. The place where you entered this world."

The facility. Could this man know where that is? Does he know what I am? My heart jumps into my throat. "Did he say when?"

"Sundown." The bartender studies me like he realizes I'm hiding a secret, that the words of this madman make more sense to me than they should.

I take a last look at Duffy and wonder if somehow I might see him again. If I had enough money and power, I could open another lily pad earlier in the timestream and save his life.

He warned me this would happen. Now, there's only one thing I can do.

No one says a word as I leave Duffy's office and walk next door to the jail, all the time thinking about what the bartender said. Is this some gunslinger trying to make a name for himself?

No. He knows something more about me. I need to find out what.

Sundown is hours away, but I want to get to the facility sooner. I reload my revolvers and run a whetstone along the edge of my sword. The blade never needs sharpening, but I like the ritual of it. Perhaps I'll use the sword against my enemy rather than giving him a quick death. Maybe it will be more entertaining that way. A good show would make Dominus happy.

My horse waits for me when I leave the jail, not tied up but standing as if expecting me. On my way out of town, I stop at the post office to drop off another letter to Ryoko, knowing it might be the last.

I ride to the cliff that hides the Dominus facility. I don't bother to tie up my horse, but he stays with me as I walk to the cliff edge. I know it might be foolish to lower my guard, but I sit and close my eyes, trying to center my mind, to push away the distractions. Lessons from Shimizu drift back into my thoughts, telling me never to underestimate my enemy, never to allow the reason I fight to cloud the fight itself. She once compared passion to a whetstone; it can sharpen the blade but must be put away when the battle comes.

A warm breeze lifts me from my meditation. I open my eyes

to see the sun hanging halfway below the horizon, the moon already visible in the sky.

When I stand and turn around, the gunslinger is waiting.

He wears black and has his head down. A dark hat hides his face. "I should have killed you already."

"That wouldn't have been honorable," I say. My nerves are strangely calm. "And besides, when you drag my body back into town, you want the bullet to be in my chest. No one will tell tales of the coward who shot Dashiell Keane in the back."

"You think this is about fame?" the gunslinger asks.

"Can't think of another reason," I remark. "Though I also can't think of an act more cowardly than gunning down a man while he's sick in bed."

He raises his head, revealing eyes that glint in the light of the setting sun. He looks like a hawk that has spotted its prey. I try to ignore the shiver that runs over my skin.

"This is not about people knowing my name," he says deliberately. "The sheriff was a casualty of war."

"War?" The mention of Duffy has me ready to gun him down right now. My optics identify the kill shot, targeting his heart. My finger twitches.

His face hardens. "You're a demon, an unnatural element in this world, and your presence reaps destruction."

He knows.

"Your people," his voice is as stern as his face, "are a tyranny. You come to rob and pillage and kill, but I am a defender of this land. The sheriff was corrupted by you, took you in, even trained you. That cannot stand. No quarter can be given to the enemy."

I grit my teeth. "I don't want to kill you."

He spits. "I don't think that's true. Your kind is all lies."

"Fine," I say, exasperated. "I absolutely want to kill you, but I won't, if you come peacefully."

"And what will happen to me?"

"You'll stand trial for your crimes."

"And will you stand trial for yours?" he counters. "Will you stand in representation for all the crimes committed against the people of this world, of this *time*?"

Mr. Myrtrym buzzes in my ear. "You have to, Dash."

The gunslinger pushes back his long jacket to reveal the gun on his side. "I know they're watching. I want them to see you die."

"Don't." I hold my hand over my gun. "I swear, I will kill you."

"Pull," Mr. Myrtrym says. "Do it now. Finish this, or you're done."

I wish he would shut up. My breath stops. The wind pauses. It's as if the timestream itself goes still.

The gunslinger draws.

I draw faster.

Seconds later, time flows again, spurring the wind as it pushes a thin layer of dust over his body.

And I know I'll never be the same.

27

I WALK BACK INTO TOWN
with the gunslinger's body draped over the saddle. There are
cheers from some, silence from others.

But everyone is looking at me.

Good. I want them to know what happens to those who hurt
the people closest to me. I'm glad Ryoko will never see this, but
I can't help but wonder what Knox will think. In many ways, I
did this for him. I'm making a better life for us.

I leave the body on the steps of the morgue–which also
doubles as the pharmacy–and ride away. The undertaker will
have to decide what to do with it.

When I return to the jail, John waits for me outside.

I wave him away. "Not now, John. I'd prefer to be left alone."

"I understand," he says. "But there's someone who insisted
on seeing you."

On instinct, my hand goes to my sword. "Who is it?"

"Myrtrym. He said his name was Mr. Myrtrym."

The tension releases from my shoulders. "Thanks, John. I'll
handle it. Do me a favor and keep an eye on the town tonight,
okay? I may be a little distracted."

He agrees. I shake his hand before going inside the jail.

Mr. Myrtrym sits with his shiny brown boots propped on the desk. He wears a brown vest with a white shirt underneath, the sleeves rolled up to his elbows. The casual look doesn't suit him. Even in such common clothes, his polish stands out. "How are you holding up?"

"I did what you told me." I walk across the room and hang up my duster.

"You did well." He produces a bottle of whiskey and two glasses from behind the desk. "You did very well, Dash."

"So why are you here? I did what you asked."

"I'm here *because* you did what I asked." Mr. Myrtrym hands me a drink. "I know this was difficult, but it was important. It will get easier, I promise. The more you do it, the more you'll be reminded it isn't real."

"It felt real." I swirl the whiskey in my glass. "It was like I could see his soul leaving his body."

"We're hardwired to think that way. Thousands of years of programming," he taps his head with one finger, "to teach our species that killing each other is bad. But it's in the past. All of it. In many ways, that man is still alive right now and he's also been dead for over a hundred years. It's all just energy."

I know that he's right, but I don't feel like it's true. The tension is difficult, the inability to convince my heart of what my brain knows to be a fact.

"Plus, the ratings . . ."

That brings my head up. "What about the ratings?"

Mr. Myrtrym smiles. "They keep going up. People love you. The fact that you didn't kill the samurai played well too. The audience viewed it as you rebelling against Dominus. We're going to use that. We're going to make it look like we wanted you to kill those outlaws at the saloon, but you turned us down."

"You want people to think I disobeyed Dominus?"

"It's a great narrative." He leans back again, flitting his hands like he's composing a story. "The young hero defying the corporate overlords, a lone samurai forging his own path. Then when you are forced to drop the gunslinger because he killed that poor, sick echo sheriff with a heart of gold, the audience knows it was a decision you made on your own, not because we told you to do it. You were protecting people. Seriously, we couldn't have hoped for better."

The word *echo* stings. Duffy was so much more than that. I decide to keep my mouth shut. He was an echo. Arguing about it doesn't change what happened. "So, am I getting that contract?"

"You are," Mr. Myrtrym says. "I can bring you back to the present right now and sign you up, if you like. But my conscience is forcing me to tell you I'm not sure it's the best thing."

I take a drink of whiskey. "What do you mean? That's what this has all been about, right?"

"Absolutely. I can offer you a very lucrative deal right now." He leans forward. "But I don't think you've peaked. Look, I'm rooting for you. You're *my* project. I convinced Dominus to make a big bet on you. It's in my best interest that you succeed. But I also see something special in you. I've only told one other person that, and he became one of the biggest timestars we've ever had.

"If you sign now, you and your family are set for a while, but not for life. You're high in our ratings, but you're not number one. The first real contract you sign is going to set a benchmark. Dominus will have you locked up for years at that rate. If you hold out and bet on yourself, I think you can get an even better deal."

My brow furrows. "I don't understand. Aren't you supposed to be getting me at the best rate you can?"

"My job is to make you the best you can be," Mr. Myrtrym responds. "I want you to be hungry. I believe you can do better. The question is, do you believe it?"

I pause to consider it. A few months have passed since I

became a timestar; I'm still getting used to my implants and the speed at which I learn new skills.

Plus the things that the gunslinger said keep eating away at me. "The man I killed, did he know that I'm from the future?"

"You're not from the future. The future doesn't exist. You're from the present. This is the past."

"Right, sorry." I try again. "Did he know that I'm from . . . another time?"

Mr. Myrtrym pauses. "It's possible. We go to great lengths to preserve certain time periods, including this one. We try not to let the echoes understand what's going on. It makes the experience more authentic, but there are slipups from time to time."

"So the audience will know that he knew I didn't belong here?"

Mr. Myrtrym shakes his head. "We'll edit that out. Any details he might have known about you are irrelevant to the narrative. He killed someone in cold blood, and he would have killed many more to get to you. You stopped him by doing what you had to do. That's all the audience needs to know."

Something bites at my gut. "Yeah, I know you're right. It feels so weird, though."

"It's a lot to think about," he acknowledges. "I know you're still experiencing compassion for the echoes. Hold on to that. The audience connects with it. You're a hero in your heart. That's probably why your brother looks up to you."

Mr. Myrtrym picks up his glass. "Listen, don't make any decisions right now. We've got plenty of content for several episodes. You deserve some time off to sort through what you want to do. It's on our dime, of course. Where do you want to go?"

My first instinct is to visit Ryoko, but I'm not ready to see her yet. I have to wash this blood off my soul first. "Actually, I do like it here. Can I stay in this time period for a while, but away from this town?"

Mr. Myrtrym raises his glass like a toast. "I know the perfect place."

28

THE CABIN SITS ON A SMALL

hill, a few hours' ride from where the desert sands drown in the grass of the prairie. As I tie my horse to the post outside the cabin, I see a town in the distance. It's far enough away that I doubt I'll hear any noise, and I assume they can't see me. My horse munches on grass as I walk inside.

Dominus must have sent somebody to clean the place before my arrival; a faint scent of pine lingers in every room, and the furniture all shines like new. There's a living room area with a lamp, a wood-burning stove, a couple of chairs, and a sofa. In the adjacent room is a bed, a wooden dresser, and a nightstand. Books lie scattered throughout the cabin, but there seems to be little else.

My optics detect a trapdoor in the main hallway beneath a rug. When I pull up the door, a light comes on to reveal steel steps leading into some type of underground bunker. At the bottom of the steps, I discover another floor that appears as big as the cabin itself.

The first thing I notice is the air conditioning—much cooler than upstairs, but a little stuffy and artificial. Steel walls surround me. An array of monitors occupies one wall of the main room, which also includes a leather couch and two matching chairs.

The monitors blink on as I step in front of them. The sound is off, but some are tuned to different vidstreams on the timenet. Others show feeds from cameras that must be placed all around the outside of the cabin. That idea is comforting. If anyone comes looking for me, I'll know long before they get here.

In other rooms, I find machines for washing clothes, a bathroom with a modern shower, and a kitchen stocked with frozen foods. Another room contains training equipment and a VR station.

None of the rooms have doors except for one. It appears locked, but as I approach, a confirmation blinks green on the keypad, and the steel door slides open. Inside, I discover racks filled with energy rifles and other combat gear. In the corner of the armory is a small lily pad encased in a glass booth. I'm still not sure how they work, but I've heard companies can create multiple lily pads at different geolocations without exerting a lot of extra power, so long as they exist at the same precise moment in the timestream.

Mr. Myrtrym's face appears on the glass of the booth. "Dash, you can use this lily pad whenever you like. The controls are intuitive. You'll be presented with a variety of options of places and times to which you can travel."

"Thank you." I'm unsure whether the video is live. I assume Dominus is monitoring me, so I err on the side of gratitude.

The next couple of days pass in silence, for which I am grateful. I go to the bunker to prepare food and shower, but not much else. Most of my time is spent in a chair on the front porch, reading or watching storms roll across the prairie. I find time for my kata and quick-draw drills. Despite the fitness equipment, I exercise in more natural ways like splitting firewood and practicing my swimming in a nearby lake.

Every day, I go for long horseback rides, exploring the surrounding areas but not finding much. At night, I write more letters to Knox and Ryoko, then read by candlelight in my bed for as long as I can stand it, occupying my mind until my vision blurs beyond my control. More than once, I wake up in the middle of the night with the lamp still on and an open book on my chest.

After a few days, I decide to check out more of the technology downstairs. It doesn't take long to figure out how to contact the present using one of the monitors. My first call is to my home, and as much as I miss them, I hope my parents don't answer.

I breathe a huge sigh of relief when Knox's face appears on the screen.

"Are Mom and Dad home?" I ask, my stomach in a knot.

"Nice to see you too," Knox grins.

"Ha, ha. Seriously, it's great to see you. How's everything there?"

"It's okay, I guess," he replies slowly. "I'm pretty popular at school now. Dash Keane's little brother."

"You should tell them you're Dash Keane's original costume designer." I sit on the couch. "And future costume designer too. Have you been watching?"

"As much as I can. Dad's keeping a closer eye on me lately."

"They won't let you watch my shows?"

Knox hesitates. "They haven't exactly said I can't. It just seems like a better idea not to deal with it."

The air-conditioned room suddenly feels too hot. Why can't my parents be happy for me? I've made my decision; there's no turning back. They could at least accept reality and make the best of it. This is supposed to be a fun time for me, but their disappointment casts a dark cloud over all of it.

I run my fingers through my sweaty hair and force a smile. "You know I'm doing this for all of you, right? So I can make enough money to give us a better life, and so that you can get treatment to—"

Knox pulls back a little. "I don't need you to do anything for me, Dash. I'm doing fine."

"I know, I know." I look at the floor, shaking my head. I decide to change the subject. "Hey, speaking of my costumes, what do you think?"

"About what?"

"About how Dominus has been dressing me. They've been using your shade of red and keeping the *K* logo."

He nods. "The black and red is cool, and they've done a good job with the fitting. The red sword is kind of over the top, though."

"Maybe. I think they do that so it will stand out."

"I'll tell you what I liked," Knox says. "That girl, Ryoko? The blue dress she wore when she was dancing."

I feel myself light up at the mention of her name. "Yeah? What'd you think of her?"

"I can tell that you like her."

My cheeks get warm. "How can you tell?"

He just grins. "I know how you normally are with girls, I guess."

"Most girls didn't pay me much attention until recently."

"Well, you're different around her. You couldn't stop looking at her, and you had this goofy look the whole time." He gives me a weird, crooked smile and makes his eyes bounce in different directions.

I laugh as I hurl a pillow at the screen.

"Are you going to see her again?"

"Uh . . ." I wonder how much I should tell him. Writing letters to an echo still strikes me as kind of silly, but I want to tell Knox everything. "I've been writing to her. I hope I get to go see her soon."

He seems satisfied with that. "What do they have you doing right now?"

"I'm on break while they put together my next few episodes."

"Why didn't you go see her?" Knox asks.

I bite my lip. "I'm not sure if I can talk about it before it airs, but some things happened, and I need a little time to recover."

Knox looks at me closely. "Are you okay?"

It's a question I've asked myself a lot over the past few days. Killing the gunslinger has stuck with me, but at the cabin, I've found some peace. I realized that even if he had been a real person, I still would have had to kill him to protect myself and to stop him from hurting anybody else. It was justice. Retribution. Thinking about it made me realize that my biggest problem has been doubting myself, expecting good things to fall apart at the last moment, expecting to fail.

But this time, I didn't.

I've reminded myself of that fact many times as I rode across the stormy plains, alone with my thoughts and the sound of my horse's hooves pounding as the thunder rolled in the distance. When I drew that gun and fired, I trusted myself for the first time, letting loose the fire that has burned inside me my entire life.

"Yeah, Knox. I'm great."

"DID YOU EVER IMAGINE ALL

this would happen?" The reporter leans back in his chair with a fake grin on his face. He wears a tight black suit with a vivid blue shirt, collar unbuttoned.

My gaze bounces around the lobby of the hotel. Everything is glass and daylight and wooden tables and fancy people drinking absurdly overpriced beverages. If I had walked into this place a few months ago, security would have descended on me immediately, whisking me away quickly and quietly so as not to disturb the elites of society.

As it is today, the man who greeted me in the lobby called me Mr. Keane and escorted me to the table for this interview, my first appointment of Press Day.

The reporter leans forward and narrows his gaze at me. "Dash? You okay?"

Dash? He says my name like we're old friends. Maybe I'm in the club now. I've moved beyond that invisible threshold into the realm of famous people and those who surround them, where everybody knows everybody, even if they've never met.

This is the part where I'm supposed to say I never believed this could happen, but it isn't true. I used to envision this and much more on nights when Knox and I sat staring at the timenet together in our bedroom. I pictured my face on all the timestars and thought about how I would do things differently. Does that make me arrogant?

I decide to play it safe, throwing out the humble smile and laugh that Ramona worked with me to develop. "Sorry, Jack. I'm trying to take everything in. I never expected success like this. I'm just a kid from the Dregs."

"And now you're a timestar." He eases back again, apparently pleased that I'm following the prescribed narrative. "There are even rumbles you might be up for the Suvea."

I shake my head. "I don't know about that. There are so many great timestars. I'm just humbled that I get to go on all these adventures." It's all rehearsed lines, and I'm sure the reporter will see right through it.

Instead, he smiles. "That's incredible."

Incredible? It's not, but I won't call him on it. I wonder if he'll applaud whatever I say because I'm famous. "But don't think I'm not going for that award either."

"So you're competitive?"

"It's like this, Jack," I say, leaning forward. "I'm taking people on a journey. I remember how I used to live vicariously through timestars. It's my responsibility now, and it's an important one. My job is making people believe that their dreams can become their reality." I can hardly believe the garbage coming out of my mouth, but the reporter keeps nodding, eating it up.

It goes on like that for an hour—me saying whatever comes to mind without thinking about it beyond trying to sound as confident as possible. When Jack is done with me, another reporter sits and asks all the same questions. Ramona oversees it all from the bar ten feet away, sipping a sparkling water with some exotic fruit on the rim of the glass. When my answers start to get too outlandish, she tells me so with a slight cock of her head and narrowing of her eyes. The endless line of reporters is loving it, but her message for me is clear. She wants me to rein it in.

After several interviews, I'm taken upstairs to an exquisite hotel room. Dinner waits on a small table—chicken, vegetables, and rice, which Ramona tells me won't upset my stomach. I eat, shower, and get dressed. The moment I'm ready, there's a knock at my door. It makes me wonder if they've been monitoring me the entire time.

Ramona and a driver take me to the set of a talk show that's well-known for interviews with timestars. Before I know what's happening, I'm sitting on a couch getting peppered with silly questions about the food in feudal Japan and whether I've had any off-camera romances with echoes. The host is an older guy, though his skin is pulled tight to fight off the wrinkles, making it difficult to nail down his age. He calls himself J3ST3R and wears an old-fashioned black suit and tie, but his hair changes color and shape every thirty seconds or so.

The audience is composed entirely of holograms—people viewing from interfaces in their homes that project their chosen avatars into the chairs. Some look like normal people, but I also see orcs, robots, and even a panda bear in a top hat. They laugh as I volley quips back and forth with the host, always feeling as if I'm teetering on the edge of destruction.

"We've got a challenge for you, Dash," he says.

I raise my eyebrows. "Alright. I'm up for a challenge."

"You're a pretty good samurai now, right?" he asks.

I smile. "I can hold my own."

The holographic audience applauds.

"I thought maybe you could teach me a few things." J3ST3R pulls two plastic swords out from behind his desk and tosses one to me. He has me stand up and show him a few moves. He's purposefully clumsy, but I play my role, telling him that he's doing great. The audience laughs and claps in all the right places.

After a few rounds, a group of children rushes out from behind the curtain, all wearing samurai costumes and carrying plastic swords of their own.

When I see them, my breath catches. I freeze.

One of the kids is wearing bull horns on his helmet.

"Oh no!" J3ST3R says. "It's the samurai horde! They're back!"

Ramona catches my gaze from side stage, snapping me back to what I'm supposed to be doing. The kids run toward us, swinging their swords as the virtual audience rolls with laughter. My hands shake as I try to steel my nerves, playing along with their game, but my insides are trembling the whole time.

It's just a game. It isn't real. I say it in my mind again and again as we joke with the kids. The one with the bull helmet charges at me, as I'm sure he was instructed to do.

J3ST3R clutches his stomach and falls forward, pretending to have been stabbed by one of the kids. "Finish him, Dash! Avenge me!"

It isn't real. But my heart pounds as memories of the real battle flash in my head. The smell of blood returns. I see Akinari before me, staring into my soul as blood pours from his stomach. I hear his words.

My blood is real.

I let the child hit me with his sword, and I fall over as the audience cheers and laughs.

Then thankfully, mercifully, the show ends.

30

Dear Ryoko,

I hope you're doing well. I think of you often, though I apologize for not writing in quite some time. The truth is I have a stack of letters I haven't sent you, mostly because I never know exactly what to say.

There are a lot of things I want to tell you. I should have said them sooner, but I didn't trust myself.

I'm done with that now.

This needs to be a conversation we have in person. I have started another mission, but it shouldn't keep me away for long. I will return soon. I hope you will allow me to sit and speak with you.

Until then . . .

I tap my pen on the captain's desk, trying to think of a good ending. In my previous letters, I've simply written my name, but it never feels like enough. I always try to think of something poetic. *Until the river of time brings us back together?* I almost laugh at how ridiculous that sounds, plus I have no idea how it would read after some Dominus intern runs it through a translator and delivers it to Ryoko. So instead, I scribble my name and fold up the letter.

Maybe next time.

The deck of the ship rocks back and forth. The sound of waves slapping against the hull faded away as I wrote, but now returns. I had almost forgotten where and when I am. Occupational hazard, I guess.

The salt of the sea air hits my face when I emerge from the captain's quarters. The first mate shouts orders at a crew of men rougher than any I've seen in any other time. "Adjust the sails! Catch the wind, you fools!"

The order is not for me, but I move to the pulley on my left and tug on the rope until the white sail turns to port. The sail bows out when I've found the wind. Other crew members adjust the sails in front and behind mine, giving the ship maximum speed.

"Much obliged, Mr. Keane," the first mate says. His name is Leone. He's bald with a thick black mustache and more muscles than I would have if I worked out every day for ten years. When I first met him, I pegged him as a muscle-bound moron, but judging from the way he interacts with the crew and charts courses for the captain, Leone is as bright as they come.

I can't say the same for the captain, not because he's dumb, but because I can't figure him out. The crew calls him Captain Shadows. I have no idea why. The first time I met him, at the direction of Mr. Myrtrym, I called him *Captain* and that seemed fine enough with him. He's not a bad-looking man, and has hair the color of milk chocolate that always seems to catch the wind the right way.

The one thing I'm unclear about is whether he's a genius or a madman. No one ever sees him sleep. He gave me his quarters when I caught on with him and his crew. On the first night, he sailed us straight into a storm and stood on the ship's mast the whole time. Amazingly, the wind and waves settled right before we reached the worst of it. He neither celebrated his apparent triumph over nature nor seemed surprised. The rest of the crew refers to him as a cursed man, but then again, they act as if they are all cursed. I hear them muttering under their breath about demons and witchcraft, about dark souls that drift across the water in the night. They never seem afraid, but more like this life is what they deserve, where they belong.

I'm not sure what that says about their acceptance of me.

I climb the steps to stand beside the captain as he holds the wheel. "Any sign of them?" I ask. We've been chasing another ship for days after learning that they beat us to the treasure we seek. This might have been Mr. Myrtrym's plan all along, pitting me in combat against more echoes. I'm ready for it. Dominus let me keep my katana, though the flintlock pistols at my sides have me missing my revolvers. At least my tech has been upgraded. My outfit has lots of hidden new toys I'm dying to test out.

"Our man in the crow's nest hasn't seen their ship," the captain replies. "But we should be close."

I look to the top of the mast. I had half expected a Jolly Roger flag, but Captain Shadows has chosen a rose of fire against a field of black.

"Let me have a look." I wait for the captain's nod before I start down the steps. It's not that I need his permission, but he seems to appreciate the gesture. I'm not sure which of us is in charge, but until that becomes a problem, I'm happy to keep up the pleasantries. After all, it's *his* ship.

The wind whips my face as I climb the mast to the crow's nest. I don't know the young boy's name looking through the spyglass, but he offers it to me as soon as I'm up there. "Do you want to look, Mr. Keane?" The wind forces his long, knotted hair away from his face, revealing a scar stretching from jawbone to scalp.

I pretend to use the glass, but my optics have already spotted what I was looking for and outlined it in red against the horizon.

"I see them!" I shout as loud as I can.

The captain's head tilts up toward me. "Where, Mr. Keane?"

"North by northwest." I could give an exact heading, range, wind speed, and an estimated amount of time it will take us to reach the other ship. All that information appears in front of me, but it doesn't matter. We're sailing faster than they are—I know it, and the rest of the crew will know it soon enough. All I need to do is point us in the right direction.

I have so much adrenaline that I almost jump down from the crow's nest and let my gravboots catch me, but instead I climb down the rungs of the mast. The crew stirs into a flurry beneath me, anticipating a fight. The captain orders some of them to adjust the sails while others load the cannons.

When I reach the deck, I find Leone berating a small group of men for being unable to locate the direction of the wind to his liking. He stops talking the moment he sees me.

"Don't fire the cannons until we've taken what they have on board," I instruct.

"Aye," he says. "But after you have what you want, you'll let us have our fun?"

"Of course," I say. Mr. Myrtrym was right; this is the change of pace I needed. There are no innocent men out here, not on my ship nor the other. I won't feel bad about killing them. They're all thieves, scoundrels, and worse. I'll be doing their fellow echoes in this time period a favor by removing them from existence. The hardest part will be making a good show of it.

Our quarry tries to run, but Mr. Myrtrym was right when he told me this was the fastest ship and the best crew, even if they do stink like dead fish. The ship is in sight. The men snarl like hyenas that have caught the sight of their prey. Those not manning the sails scream challenges across the water. They're beasts, but no matter. I can be a warrior among beasts if need be. A light in the darkness.

I climb halfway up the mast and take hold of the rope. A quick press of the center button on my shirt sends an electric signal throughout my clothes, hardening the fabric to protect against bullets. It won't stop a point-blank shot, but it's an advantage.

As we pull alongside the ship, both crews open fire—ours with rifles, theirs with cannons. Smoke and shouting fill the air. Men fall on both sides. Some in our crew hurl grappling hooks attached to ropes and nets at the other ship.

I wait for the right moment. Every man on the opposing deck is busy trying to fight off our crew and cut the ropes. *They won't see me coming.*

"Go," Mr. Myrtrym says into my left ear, but I'm already using my rope to swing across. I picture how this must look on camera, the hero glides from one ship to another amidst the chaos of battle. My gravboots and repulsor gloves give me a boost, lifting me a little higher into the air. I let go of the rope and pull my sword as I descend toward the enemy.

I land on the deck, pull my flintlock pistol, and shoot the man in front of me. My crew is seconds behind me, scrambling across nets connecting the two ships. I thrust my katana into one man's gut, then grab his pistol and shoot his crew member.

The smoke clears. Gunshots are replaced by the clang of swords. I sweep through the fight like a phantom, dancing between their blades and cutting them down one at a time.

A giant beast of a man tosses one of my crew members overboard and lumbers toward me. He wields a large wooden plank like a club. A roar escapes his mouth as he brings the plank crashing down at me.

I jump back, swinging my sword at him. He's too far away, his weapon far longer than mine. He strikes again, missing me by inches but hammering one of his own in the back. The man stumbles forward and catches a dagger in the gut from one of my allies.

"Oops." I taunt the large man with a grin.

"Die!" He lifts the plank over his head and brings it down with his full strength. I leap back again to dodge the attack, then rebound forward, stepping on the wood as he raises it back up. My gravboots pulse, and I go flying into the air toward their mast.

My boots hit the wooden pillar and I ricochet off, sailing back over his head. He tries to track me, but he's too slow.

I land and thrust my blade backward without looking.

His body thuds against the deck.

My crew watches in silence. The fight is over, my enemy's blood washes over the deck. My stomach turns.

It's all a game, I remind myself, *and I'm the hero.* I raise my sword, blood dripping from the blade. The crew cheers.

"Well, what are we waiting for?" I yell. "Let's find what we came for!"

The crew picks their way through the scattered bodies of the echoes as they search the ship. I could use my optics to scan the vessel from bow to stern, but I would rather test their loyalty. Will any of them try to hide the treasure from me? Will they betray me? After all, I'm not one of them.

I pace the deck, enjoying the warmth of the sun on my skin, the waves breaking against the side of our new ship. Aside from the gore, the deck is in good condition, and there are decorative flourishes everywhere. An image of a man slinging lightning bolts is carved into the wood in front of the steering wheel. In other places, I see Minotaurs, swords, goddesses. A curious thought catches my mind, and I look at their flag again. *A Pegasus.*

Studying the ship becomes like a scavenger hunt as I search for more of the symbols. Some are carved into the wood; others are simply painted on the deck. Did they believe these would bring the favor of the gods? And why don't I see any aquatic figures? On a ship, I would have expected to find an image of

Poseidon, but I don't see tridents anywhere.

A small group of the crew emerges from the lower decks, carrying a chest between them. It's exquisite–black wood with golden flourishes. There isn't a scratch on it.

"How do you open this thing?" one of the men asks.

I kneel in front of it. There are no hinges or locks. It looks like a single, solid piece of wood.

"Is it heavy?" I ask.

"Light as a feather," one of them replies. "Two of us lugged it together to be careful, but I could have tossed it up the stairs with one hand."

No doubt this is the work of Dominus, amusing themselves and their audience by leaving little mysteries in the world. I've seen similar things on the timenet before, as if the corporations thought the actual past wasn't interesting enough, so they planted elements that would create mystery and wonder. To echoes of this time period, who have no experience with advanced technology, it would be logical to assume these artifacts are magical, bearing the fingerprints of the gods.

When I reach toward the chest, the top opens on its own. A gasp escapes the crew. My heart seizes as smoke drifts from the opening. Several men scramble away. I hear the word *cursed* whispered a few times, but my optics identify the smoke as harmless. It's vapor, created by dry ice, probably placed inside for dramatic effect.

As the fog clears, I peek inside the chest and see a device. It's black, sleek, and in the shape of a large pill. I reach for it.

"No, Mr. Keane!" one of the crew members bursts out.

I almost tell them it's safe, but Dominus needs me to make this entertaining. "Gentlemen, where's your sense of adventure?"

None respond. A few sheepish looks pass between them as I reach into the chest and take hold of the device.

The instant my skin makes contact, it glows red, though there is no sound. A light from it shines in front of me as if illuminating a path, then begins to send streams of energy pulsing through the beam. I rotate the device in my hands, but the pulsing light continues to point in the same direction.

"Some kind of compass?" one of the men ventures.

"But it isn't pointing north." Leone crouches next to me, marveling at what he's seeing. "So where does it lead?"

Mr. Myrtrym buzzes in my ear. "This will take you to Ryoko."

Her name causes a spark inside of me. I doubt that Dominus would bring her to this time period. *This device must lead to a lily pad.*

I place the device into my jacket pocket without answering. The fabric is thick enough to muffle the glow.

The crew finishes looting the other ship, then boards our vessel. I stand at a cannon as we pull away. When we reach a short distance, we circle the dead ship. It seems wrong to sink something so beautiful, but there's an honor amongst these thieves. Respect demands that we lower the ship to the watery depths with its crew on board so they may sail into the afterlife. Our captain angles our ship back around so I have a clear shot. My optics zero in on the target and help me adjust the cannon to achieve the proper trajectory.

My shot is perfect, blowing a large hole into the side of the vessel.

As the ship is swallowed by the sea, I take the device out of my pocket and hold it above my head, lighting the way. Our heading is south by southeast. I'm unsure if anything of value awaits the crew at the end of this light.

But for me, Ryoko is well worth the voyage.

31

AN HOUR LATER, I SIT

before the bowsprit and stare across the water, listening to the ocean and the chatter of the crew as they tinker with the sails and stow the loot from the other ship on the lower decks. Dark clouds collect on the horizon. Thunder drifts across the sea. Somewhere out there is a portal that will take me to Ryoko. It's funny. Not long ago, all I wanted was to be a timestar, setting out on adventures and becoming world-famous.

But right now, all I care about is seeing her.

The boy in the crow's nest shouts something, jarring me from my thoughts. Between the rush of the wind and the water, I can't make out his words.

"What?" Leone calls back.

Everything falls silent, as if Poseidon has calmed the waves so that the single word may fill us all with terror.

"Monster!"

I rush to the port side of the ship, scanning the horizon with my optics. A red outline blinks on a row of spikes breaching the water in the distance. I'm unsure what I saw, but it was big and heading right for us.

Cameron Cooper's words flash into my mind. "They use my

work to make their timenet programming more . . . exciting."

The dinosaur embryos.

Some of the crew shout orders at each other. Others load the cannons, as if we stand any chance of hitting the thing.

"Full speed!" I shout. "Maybe we can outrun it." But I know there's no chance. Storm clouds push in overhead, and the deck rocks back and forth as the ocean grows choppy.

Captain Shadows draws his sword and points at me. "It's *that.*"

Realizing what he means, I pull the power cell from my pocket. The light continues to pulse and shine in the same direction. Maybe he's right. Maybe it's emitting some kind of signal that the creature is following.

But it's also my way back to Ryoko.

"Throw it overboard." Leone steps toward me.

"No." I draw my katana as the crew surrounds me, many of them pulling rusty swords. "You can probably take me," I challenge, "but how many of you are ready to die trying?"

They hesitate, all looking at each other. These men have seen me in action. At night, the pirates tell stories about me in hushed tones after the day's work is done, when calm seas allow them to indulge in their mugs. Some believe me to be some type of god or the illegitimate son of a deity who amused himself among mortals.

Maybe I should have done more to stoke the fires of their imaginations. Mr. Myrtrym hasn't told me that I couldn't use my tech in this time period. They might fear me more if they had seen more of my abilities.

The deck lurches as something brushes against the ship. *The beast is testing us.* I cast another glance over the side. Beneath the surface of the water, the behemoth swims away from us. Its back breaches the water again, reaching higher this time. It's easily as big as our ship. Maybe bigger.

Lighting crackles as black clouds cover the sky. It's almost as dark as night. The rain begins to pour. The crew saw the monster as well, and any lingering doubt melts from their faces. They're not taking any chances.

"Grab him!" Leone commands.

Different scenarios race through my mind. I'm going overboard; there's no way around that. The beast could destroy the ship with its next strike. Even if it doesn't, the crew will likely overtake me. I would kill a few of them at best before they toss me into the water.

If I'm going over, I'm going over my way.

I sprint toward the front of the ship, slashing my katana at the men in front of me to clear a path.

Suddenly it's as if I'm back in the Dregs, racing along the rooftops, feeling the familiar rush of adrenaline and danger. I'm not thinking about the crew anymore as I run up the bowsprit, sheathing my katana. The deck pitches back and forth with the rolling sea.

More lightning flashes across the sky. I catch sight of the beast out of the corner of my eye. Huge black eyes look up at me from below the water's surface.

I grab the power cell from my pocket and hold it tight as I jump from the ship.

The beast explodes out of the water, jaws opening. My gravboots activate and lift me higher. The monster snaps its jaws together, missing me by a few feet.

"Got a surprise for you," Mr. Myrtrym says as I arc through the air. "Knock your heels against each other."

I hit my boots together as I start to descend toward the water. My boots lock as if an invisible field holds them in line with each other. A holographic board appears beneath them, black with my red K logo.

The thrusters on my boots catch me before I hit the water, keeping me above the surface and propelling me forward. I'm surfing on air, but I'm leaving a churning wake in the water behind me. The wind whips at my face, the waves crashing on all sides. The light from the power cell shows the way forward. I lean left and right. The holographic board responds with me, carving lines in the water.

A huge wave appears before me, and I head right for it. My board climbs the wave. When I reach the crest, I'm airborne again. I let out a shout of exhilaration.

My head twists as I hear a roar at my back. Teeth and eyes emerge out of the wave behind me. The sea monster screams for my blood. It has a long gray body, four massive fins on its underside, and a mouth filled with fangs as big as me.

For an instant, we're both flying, predator and prey moving through the sky.

I hit the water a second later, my boots skimming the surface before the boosters lift me back into the air and surge me forward. I dodge back and forth between the waves, hoping I might lose the beast before my boots run out of power.

Through the storm, an island appears ahead of me, a green mountain towering above the sea. My optics identify my destination with a green outline. My blood surges as I try to will the gravboots to push me faster. Every snap of the beast's jaws is a little closer than the last.

The island rushes toward me. *I'm going to make it. I'm going to see Ryoko.* I picture her on the shore, dancing along the beach, blue robes billowing in the storm winds.

Pay attention, Dash. A few seconds have passed since I heard the beast behind me. Did I actually lose it? I look down at the dark-blue water, trimmed in the white wake of my holoboard.

Then I see the creature coming up out of the abyss.

"No!" I shout as gaping jaws come out of the water beneath me. My gravboots surge, pushing me forward enough that the jaws don't swallow me whole. I balance on the edge of the beast's mouth. The holoboard disappears.

We rise out of the water together, me on the lips of the

monster, climbing higher and higher into the storm. Its entire body breaches the ocean, and when I look, the waves appear to be miles beneath me.

With every ounce of strength, I push my legs against the creature's lower jaw and launch myself forward as far as I can.

My gravboots ignite again for a moment, one last burst of energy that lifts me away from the monster. My focus quickly turns toward the beach, the beast forgotten as I careen toward land, totally out of control. The gravboots are dead, and the repulsor gloves aren't powerful enough to hold me on their own. My legs and arms flail as if I could grab onto the clouds to slow down.

I'm not going to make it. I fall toward the edge of the water, fighting for every inch. At the last moment, I hurl the power cell forward with all my strength.

When I hit the water, everything goes dark.

My thoughts drift in a flurry of hallucinations. I'm walking through the school with Garon. Knox and I lie in bed, bathed in the glow of the holoscreen. Ryoko's body crumbles in the flames of a burning village.

No. That didn't happen. No!

I open my eyes. Water spews out of my lungs. I cough uncontrollably as my body fights to purge itself. I lie on the sand, gasping for breath.

The air comes. My muscles relax. I'm soaking wet and covered with sand.

But I made it.

The rush of the ocean reminds me I may not be alone. I sit up and scan its surface. The storm has moved on, surrendering to blue afternoon sky. I see only clear water, but there are dangers in those depths. *Can that thing come on land?*

I scramble up the beach. Every few steps, I dare to look back, expecting to see the beast emerging from the water.

When I see only ocean, sand, and sky, a worse thought comes over me.

The power cell . . . is it broken?

I jog up the beach, trying to remember the direction in which I threw the device. The sand gives way to a thick forest that leads up to the mountain. Did I manage to throw it this far?

I move along the beach, combing through the sand, desperately searching for the power cell, for my pass to see Ryoko again. Who knows how far the waves carried me off my original trajectory? For all I know, I may be on the wrong side of the beach.

My heart seizes with the idea that I may never see her again. The island appears to be deserted, which is fortunate. In this state, I would be worthless in a fight. Shimizu Kaida warned me about letting emotions damage my focus.

The thought of my sensei centers my mind. I stop and take a deep breath. The smell of the saltwater wafts over me with a warm breeze. Leaves rustle overhead. My eyes close, and I think about how I got here, flying across the water, dancing with a creature unlike any I've ever seen.

When I open my eyes, I survey the area again, taking my time. The island is beautiful, and there is no apparent danger here. If there is, I have my katana. I have the protective layers of my clothes. I press the buttons on my sleeve to deactivate the armor, and the fabric softens against my skin.

I finally find the device in a cluster of trees, the red light pointing in the same direction. Doubtless, I walked right by it before. In my panic, I couldn't see the truth right in front of me.

The red light leads me into the jungle. I use my sword to cut a path through the vines and brush. The mountain looms before me.

After a short distance, the trees clear away to reveal a sparkling pool being fed by a waterfall. The light from the power cell shines up into the source of the waterfall, a dark cavern that goes into the belly of the mountain.

When I reach the pool, I slip into the cool water, letting it rinse off the sand and sweat. I walk until my feet no longer touch the bottom. My head dips below the surface, the light of the power cell shining like a laser in the water.

Thousands of tiny fish of various colors and sizes, though none bigger than my hand, swim toward the power cell, toward me. My muscles tense, but none of them attack. Instead, they move back and forth through the beam.

Soon fish are all around me. It's like drifting through crystal blue space surrounded by swimming stars of a million colors, nebulas of coral beneath. Knox would love this. When he's old enough, I'll bring him here, and Ryoko as well.

Of course, to do that, I have to tell her the truth about me.

That sobering thought lifts me back to the surface of the water. I swim toward the rocks near the base of the waterfall, its cool spray misting my face.

My physical enhancements make it easy to climb up the rocks and into the cavern. I look back at the ocean, the blue darkening with the fading light of the day. A chill runs up my spine as I remember the creature. My tech was extraordinary, but I barely survived. Did Mr. Myrtrym expect me to live through that?

The thoughts rattle my mind as the power cell leads me into the damp tunnel. Was he *trying* to kill me? And if so, what could that mean?

But I push those ideas aside when I see a tube just large enough for a single human appear in front of me, the modern technology a stark contrast to the rock walls of the cave.

A time platform.

I place the power cell into the lily pad, and it lights up. As I step inside, the lights activate.

When they fade moments later, I'm back in my cabin.

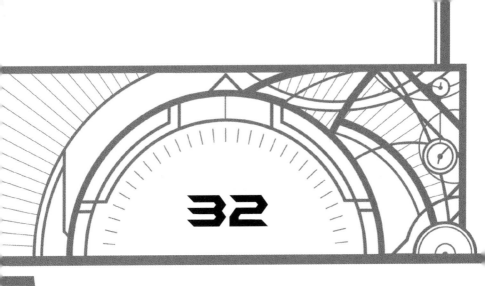

32

"REALLY?" I'M TALKING TO

Mr. Myrtrym via the monitor in my cabin. "Because it almost seemed like you were *trying* to kill me."

Mr. Myrtrym glances from side to side like he's checking to see if anybody's around. I can't see anything but his face and the wall behind him, which is covered by a painting filled with dark, swirling colors. "You want to know the truth?"

"Yes!" I answer. "I could use a lot more truth right now."

"We are absolutely trying to kill you."

The statement catches me off guard. I would have never expected him to admit it. My first instinct is to grab my weapons and run. Can I jump to another time segment without them knowing? The dinosaur period would be the easiest place to disappear. The fewer people, the better. Plus, I loved being in that valley.

But Ryoko isn't there.

Mr. Myrtrym cracks a smile. "Take it easy. You need to understand the nuance of what I'm telling you. If you're to become our most popular timestar, you need to see the bigger picture. We don't want you dead, Dash, but we must *try* to kill you."

A wave of relief washes over me. "The ratings."

"They're astronomical," Mr. Myrtrym says. "But we have to keep your show interesting. Some people already think everything we're doing with you is rigged. If they know you'll dominate every single time, they'll stop watching." He pauses to let his words sink in. "They care about you, Dash. That's good, but they also have to believe they might lose you. That's how we keep their attention. You need to succeed, but not by much. And it has to be real danger."

The conversation is surprisingly exciting. "Am I number one yet?"

"Really close," is his response. "We're going to keep making it harder for you; I won't lie about that. If you want to quit—"

"I'm not quitting, but you promised I could see Ryoko. I want to tell her the truth."

Mr. Myrtrym sighs and shakes his head. "We need to talk about that. You know how important authenticity is to your vidstream. If the echoes from that time period learn that you're from the present—"

"We can trust her. Listen," I say, pressing him, "I know she's not real, but I have to keep my head straight. To do that, I need to be honest with her."

"Well, your relationship with her *is* popular," Mr. Myrtrym admits. "It adds a nice dimension to your story, but it's a risk. If she doesn't believe you, if she thinks that you're insane . . ." He gazes upward as if pondering the consequences. "Or even worse, if she does believe you, she might hate you for lying to her."

I already hate myself for not being honest with her. "To be clear, are you telling me it's not a good idea, or are you ordering me not to tell her?" The question is a gamble. It's the first time I've measured how much sway I have with Dominus. This is something he doesn't want. His response will tell a lot about how well I'm doing.

Mr. Myrtrym purses his lips. "I'm advising against it, but it's your decision."

I want to pump my fist in victory. My first inclination is to thank him, but that doesn't feel right. I survived an attack from a sea dinosaur by riding a jet-powered holographic surfboard across the ocean after being forced overboard by a crew of pirates. At one point, I stood on the jaws of the monster, and somehow I'm still breathing. I'm giving people content they've never seen on the timenet before. This is my moment. Dominus needs to respect what I've done.

"I'm going to tell her the truth," I say. "Keep the cameras rolling if you want, but don't speak into my ear while I do it. If you want the audience to see a real moment, let me do it my way."

I could almost swear that a look of pride flashes across Mr. Myrtrym's face. "Okay, Dash. Do it your way."

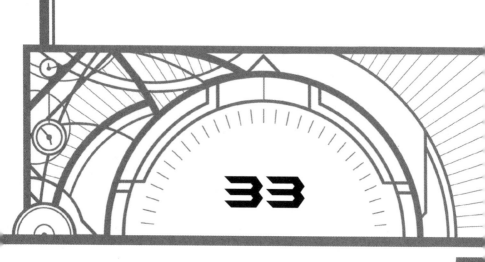

I'VE JUMPED FROM ROOFTOPS

in the rain without seeing where I would land. I've faced rogue samurai, demented gunslingers, and bloodthirsty sea monsters.

But as Ryoko and I walk side by side to the hill behind the pagoda, I'm not sure I've ever been so afraid. Questions stumble out of my lips. I try to keep her talking about herself and what she's done over the past few weeks so I can avoid answering the same questions about where I've been and what I've been doing. Maybe if I can reach the hill where Shimizu Kaida taught me to find peace in meditation, I might also find the courage to be honest.

As we walk in the fading daylight, the sky shifting to shades of radiant pink and gold, Ryoko tells me about the efforts to rebuild the village. Shimizu Kaida requested assistance from the emperor, which was granted in the form of labor and materials. Ryoko doesn't say it, but it sounds as if Kaida has put her in charge of much of the restoration. She's a great candidate for the job, but a sadness comes over me when I picture it. Ryoko should be dancing, not rebuilding villages that were burned down in defiance of a distant ruler.

As she talks, the gunslinger fills my thoughts. If he knew the truth about me, could the bull samurai have known as well? Did the destruction of Ryoko's village have something to do with me?

When we reach the top of the hill, we sit on the grass, allowing the day's last light to warm our bodies.

"I know you're trying to keep me talking." Ryoko runs her fingers along the ground. Even that seems beautiful, the way in which her hands move across the blades of grass. She can't help but dance in whatever she does.

I allow her statement to swirl on the breeze as I build the courage to respond. The hill does calm my spirit a little. Ancient religions believed certain places were more closely connected to the spiritual realms. I suppose it isn't so different from the portals we create in the timestream—gateways leading from one moment to another. Maybe this hill is one of those places. Maybe there's much more to this world than moving between time periods.

Either way, it feels as if this place is lending me strength. If there is another side, I offer a silent prayer to whatever may be listening. I can't tell Ryoko everything right now, maybe not ever. But perhaps fewer secrets, at least, will make this all simpler.

"I'm not from here," I say, then laugh a little at the absurdity of the comment.

Her eyes widen. "If you have to begin there, this conversation is going to take a long time."

"I'm not sure how to explain this," I say, "but I'll try. My one request is that you listen. I promise to keep it short, and I will do my best to answer every question you have once I'm done. Is that okay?"

She nods.

I take a deep breath and release it. "Imagine you tip over a bucket of water and allow that water to go trickling down the side of a large rock. The stream of water grows longer each moment as it makes its way further down the rock.

"Where I come from, we have discovered that time is somewhat like that stream. In the present, we are at the very tip of the stream. No water . . . no time . . . exists in front of us, but it does exist behind us, the stream of time constantly getting longer. But also, the water moving down that stream is all progressing at the same speed." I can't tell what she's thinking. "Do you understand?"

She gives me a long look. "You told me not to interrupt."

I smile. "You're right. Anyways, time is like that stream, if the bucket never runs out of water and the rock itself is endless. But imagine that stream is not a trickle, but a river. There are lily pads floating along the river."

"Lily pads don't float along the river," she says. "They stay in one place."

I snicker. My father would like her. "I know, but just go with it. Where I'm from, we have learned how to move, or jump, from the present to those lily pads in the past. Remember, the lily pads are constantly moving. If the lily pad is at this precise moment in the timestream, tomorrow it will be one day ahead. You can't jump back to this exact time until another lily pad reaches this moment in the timestream."

I try to read Ryoko's face, but all I can tell from her expression is that she's listening. I assume she believes that we are in the present, but I've told her that I'm not from here, so she may have pieced together the truth. How do you tell somebody they're not real?

I consider saying more, but I'm not sure which direction to go. There's so much to explain, but I don't really know how any of it works. She could ask a million questions that I can't answer.

And a handful that I'm afraid to.

"So, does that make sense?" I finally ask.

Ryoko looks to the sunset. "You're telling me you can travel through time?"

"Anybody can," I say quickly. "Anybody who steps onto a lily pad. It's not magic. It can be programmed . . ." I pause for a second, realizing that word might not make sense to her. "There's a way to tell the lily pad that you want to be sent to another lily pad in the timestream and then, suddenly, you're there."

Her attention goes back to the grass, picking blades and letting them fall through her fingers.

"Please, Ryoko, talk to me."

"I'm trying to decide if you're a liar or a lunatic."

I may be both. "If you'll come with me, I can prove it to you." Her breath stops. I see the hesitation on her face. Why should she trust me? I haven't been really honest with her since the day we met.

And yet, in many ways, I've been more honest with her than anyone. "Ryoko, please, you have to trust me." I take her hand. She looks at me, and I see fear in her eyes, but also a trace of hope. Maybe she can dare to believe me, to trust me. Not that I deserve it.

"Does Shimizu Kaida know?" Ryoko asks.

"I think so. We've never spoken about it, but she must know something to take me in and train me the way she did. The people who sent me are very powerful."

Her eyes flicker. "Why did they send you? What do they want?"

Possible answers flood my mind. How do I explain this? "They want me to train to become a great hero." It's true enough, but it sounds beyond arrogant, and a nauseous feeling rises in my stomach. It must be the nerves. "Please, Ryoko, let me show you."

"Will I be able to come back?" she asks, withdrawing her hand from mine.

"Yes, absolutely," I promise. "Although it will be a few hours from now when you do, near morning. However long we spend in another time period, that same amount of time passes here."

She nods, and my heart lifts. But I can see the reservation hiding in her eyes.

We return to the pagoda, where we mount horses and ride to the time platform. Darkness has long since fallen, but my optics' night vision allows me to navigate. Ryoko follows in silence.

She grips my hand as we enter the facility, her gaze bouncing between the Dominus employees, the modern technology, and the time platform.

I hold both of her hands as we step onto the platform. "This is the scariest part. But I promise—you won't feel a thing."

Ryoko swallows and tightens her grip, our fingers weaving together. I can't imagine the courage she must have to step onto the platform. I grew up with time travel being an ever-present part of reality. She had no concept of it until an hour ago. That makes her the bravest person I've ever met.

The light envelopes us.

Moments later, we're in the basement of the cabin. I half expect her stomach to revolt after what we've experienced, but she holds it together, her eyes taking in everything around us.

Rather than explaining the modern technology, I get Ryoko upstairs as quickly as I can. She seems to calm down. Some of what she sees is more advanced than her own time period, but not by as much. When we go outside, I show her the horses, the countryside. It's daytime here—a clear blue sky and green grass as far as we can see.

"It smells different," she says when we're outside.

"Is it bad?"

"No." Ryoko smiles. "Only different." The lurking fear in her eyes is replaced by a wild wonder as she surveys the land, fixing on a small valley in the distance. "Are those wildflowers?"

I follow her gaze to a field of bright yellow flowers covering the ground like a blanket that sways in the breeze. "Yes. Do you want to go?"

Her smile is her answer.

We mount our horses and ride down to the meadow. When we arrive, the animals nibble at the flowers as Ryoko walks among them. The wind picks up, playing with her dress as she runs her fingers over the petals, bathing in the sunlight. She twirls. "This is your home?"

I glance back at the cabin. My first instinct is to say no, but my parents' place doesn't seem like home anymore, and I haven't stayed many nights in the apartment Dominus gave me. This place doesn't belong to me, but it may be the closest thing to a home that I have. "Yes, it is."

"It's wonderful," she breathes.

"Come visit whenever you want," I say lightly. "Right now, I have people from the town who check on it for me, feed the horses, that sort of thing. But I would much rather you be here."

She picks a flower and holds it to her nose. I know what I've asked isn't fair. Ryoko would be lonely here. I also haven't asked Dominus if this is alright or even possible. Most corporations offer people the option of buying the rights to certain echoes from their time segments. When that happens, they're still not allowed to bring those echoes to the present, but they can live with them in the past, marrying them and such, never having to worry about the corporation treating the echoes like property. Corporations aren't required to offer that option, but if they do enter into such an agreement with a person—a *real* person, that is—they have to honor it. *Maybe I could purchase Ryoko's rights from Dominus.*

"Yes." The joy on her face interrupts my thoughts. "I would love to come here more often."

And with that, my fears melt away.

34

MR. MYRTRYM'S OFFICE IS

easily as large as the Dominus conference room two floors below us. But as soon as I step off the elevator and onto the polished dark wood, it feels as if I'm stepping back in time again, though to what period, I don't know. There are windows throughout the room, but the light from each of them shines with different hues. I realize they're time windows, each showing a different segment. Through one of them, I see the Colosseum. Through another, Saint Basil's Cathedral.

The walls and ceilings are carved with simple but elegant flourishes. A large rectangular painting covers most of the far wall. The painting appears as if a cathedral has been turned on its side and the roof ripped off. There are winged beings among clouds and rays of light, with the golden and white walls of an ornate church framing the sides. It's probably a famous piece of art, but I don't watch The Fine Arts Collective timenet channel enough to know for sure.

Ramona leans on a massive desk in front of the painting, her arms crossed and a knowing smile on her face. To her right is a small sitting area with leather chairs, an end table, a lamp, and a fireplace with crackling logs that fill the room with the smell of smoke.

On her left, Mr. Myrtrym sits at a grand piano, his eyes down, his fingers dancing over the keys. I pause and listen to the music filling the room. The melody, I realize, is composed of the same few notes over and over again, first climbing the scale in one order, then falling back down in reverse.

"That's a nice song," I comment as I approach him.

Mr. Myrtrym looks up at me, continuing to play. "Thank you. I've been working on it for quite some time, trying to find just the right notes. Time well spent, I think. A great piece of art lives forever."

A piece of sheet music sits on the piano's music rest, hand-drawn notes dotting the clefs. Many are faded almost to the point of being invisible, clearly notes that were once tried, found unsatisfactory, and erased. The piece's title, however, is written in clear, beautiful script.

Echo Nova.

My attention returns to his hands playing swiftly but deftly, and I notice his watch again.

I gesture to his wrist. "You know, I've always really liked that."

"It's a 1904 Cartier," he says, returning his gaze to the piano. "The first wristwatch ever made."

I let out a whistle to show I'm impressed. "Must've been very expensive."

"Actually," he says, "it was given to me."

I narrow my eyes in disbelief. "You're kidding."

"Peculiar thing, wealth," he remarks. "The more you accumulate"—he moves his right hand farther down the keyboard, shifting the melody up an octave—"the less important it becomes. You stop wanting things you can buy, and nobody who owns anything you would want will sell it to you anyway. When something is sold, the transaction is over. A gift that carries an implied debt is much more valuable."

Somehow, I doubt that Mr. Myrtrym has many debts. "Do you collect watches?"

"I'm not a collector," he answers. "More like a steward of important artifacts. There are some things I don't trust anybody else to maintain, so I acquire them. I see it as a responsibility for a man of my resources."

That piques my curiosity. "What else do you have?"

"The body of Dr. Suvea." Mr. Myrtrym says it with the casual air of a man talking about a pair of shoes.

I stare at him. "You're kidding."

"Well, I purchased the land upon which he rests. I pay for the upkeep of the grounds and his mausoleum."

"I've seen it." I remember the images shown to me in school. "Wildflowers, Spanish moss hanging off the trees. It's beautiful."

Mr. Myrtrym shrugs. "I haven't been there. Truthfully, I never cared much for what I learned about the man himself. For such a brilliant mind, he appears to have been very shortsighted. But sometimes talent strikes the unworthy. Regardless, the discovery should be properly memorialized."

His words give me pause. Why would he pay so much to maintain the gravesite of someone he didn't like?

I decide to change the subject. "You wanted to see me?"

Mr. Myrtrym tilts his head to Ramona. She's still in front of the desk, her face beaming. "Your ratings are higher than ever, Dash," she says.

A holographic chart appears in the air in front of her. I don't know how to read it, but the green line makes a steep climb as it runs from left to right, and I know that's good.

I try to play it cool. "People liked the pirate stuff, huh?"

"We haven't aired that episode yet."

I raise my eyebrows. "Seriously? The Old West stuff is getting the ratings?"

"Better than that," she says. "We aired you telling Ryoko that you're a time traveler."

"That was quick," I say, feeling equally surprised and embarrassed.

"We didn't have to edit much." She smiles brightly. "And now the audience is invested in your relationship, so when that beast chases you across the ocean, the emotional impact will be much more significant. We have metrics suggesting that some people expect you to die soon. They think we wouldn't let you do what you did unless we were about to kill you off." She laughs.

"What I did?" I'm not laughing. I'm too confused.

"Breaking the time wall." Mr. Myrtrym stops playing and speaks loudly as if he's been waiting for the right moment to say the words. He stands and walks to one of the time windows, his back to me. "We've done love stories between echoes and real people before. He can't tell her the truth about being a timestar because she would never understand, and so he must leave for her own good, blah, blah, blah." He waves his hand like he's disgusted with the frivolity of it. "Honestly, we thought it was passé at this point. Otherwise, we would have planted a love interest for you. Call it a happy accident that your relationship happened the way it did."

"And that's good?" I ask.

"It is." Mr. Myrtrym turns and looks at me. "You're a great action hero, Dashiell Keane, but I'm not sure you're much of an actor. The fact that this happened naturally was fortuitous; the audience wouldn't have bought it otherwise. When you told her you were a time traveler, our sensors detected an unprecedented number of audible gasps from viewers. It's never happened, and thanks to you, anybody who does it now will look like they're copying us. The moment after you said it, our vidstream shares skyrocketed. That type of enthusiasm is gold."

Maybe it wasn't so embarrassing after all. A huge smile spreads across my face. "So what now?"

"That's the best part." Mr. Myrtrym nods at Ramona.

She looks at me with her own huge smile. "You should take Ryoko on a date."

"Great!" I exclaim. "I want to see more of Japan."

Ramona and Mr. Myrtrym share a short laugh that makes

me feel left out of some joke.

"That's not what we had in mind," Ramona says. "We're breaking new ground here. Ryoko dealt with the concept of time travel much better than we would have anticipated, which opens new possibilities."

Mr. Myrtrym puts his hand on my shoulder. "You like her, right?"

I nod. "In fact, there's something I'd like to talk to you about."

He lifts his hand. "I already know what you're going to say. But before we go there, you should solidify the relationship, don't you think?"

"I guess so."

"We want to help you win her heart," Mr. Myrtrym says. "And our audience wants to be dazzled by this whirlwind romance. When this is over, Ryoko will realize you're a man who can show her things and take her places she never thought possible."

35

"HOW MUCH DO YOU TRUST

me?" I ask Ryoko as we stand on the hill behind Shimizu Kaida's pagoda. The morning sun pours over us, drying the dew on the grass. I sent a note to her home yesterday, asking her to meet me here. Thankfully, she did.

Ryoko looks at me sideways. "Why do you ask, Dash?"

"I want to take you somewhere, but I need you to trust me." I flash her a grin. "Again."

"I still have a lot of work to do in my village."

"I know, but you've been working so hard. You deserve a break." I give her a mischievous look. "Besides, a lot of planning has gone into this, and not just from me. I had help."

She lifts an eyebrow. "Help? From who?"

"It would take a long time to explain, but it's easier if you trust me."

The doubt is evident on her face, but I'm not sure I've ever been so determined. Dominus bent over backward to set everything up for us. I've spent the past couple of nights thinking about how incredible it will be to take her on this date.

"I told you a dangerous secret," I reach out my hand, "because I want you to know who I am. I promise this will be a day you'll never forget."

She pauses, and for a second, I think she's going to turn me down. The rejection will be caught on camera, and if Dominus airs it, I'll be the laughingstock of the present. I've had girls pass on me before, but never in front of millions of viewers.

Ryoko accepts my hand. "Let's go."

She laughs as we run down the hill, sharing in my happiness. We take horses to the time facility and go inside. The Dominus employees nod as we take our places on the lily pad. I'm sure we're being monitored from every angle.

When our time jump is complete, we're in a room made of clay bricks. The first thing I notice is the warmth and the humidity, which must wreak havoc on the modern technology.

A Dominus time scientist addresses us from the other side of the platform. "Mr. Keane, welcome to—"

I raise my hand to stop him. "No, please. It's a surprise."

"Of course." He bows his head slightly. "My apologies. Right this way. The celebration has begun."

Ryoko squeezes my hand as we step off the platform. Her fingers shake, though I can't tell if it's anxiety or excitement. I wink at her, and she responds with a smile.

The man shows us into a room filled with dresses, shoes, and masks. Ramona waits for us there.

"Ryoko"—Ramona steps forward—"it's so wonderful to meet you. My name is Ramona. I'm here to help you."

Ryoko appears to understand, which must mean Ramona is actually speaking Japanese. Impressive.

Ramona glances at me and gestures toward a large divider in the center of the room. "We'll let you know when we're ready, Dash."

"Are you okay?" I ask Ryoko.

She gives a shy nod.

"Great." I grin. "I'll be getting dressed." I walk around the divider to find clothes waiting for me. I choose a robe of my signature red, trimmed in gold, and a pair of sandals. A small table presents several options of masks—some cover the entire face, some with designs similar to horns or wings extending from them.

I pick the simplest one I can find. It's black with swirling flourishes and will cover only the areas around my eyes. Wearing a mask is a requirement for this party, but I assume that the more of my face Ryoko can see, the better.

Ramona's head appears. "She's ready for you."

Butterflies fill my stomach as I come around the divider. When I see Ryoko, it feels as if the world has stopped turning.

She wears a dress that begins with flowing blue at her feet and drifts into a creamy white as it makes its way up her body. Golden clasps that look like dragon's heads adorn the straps at her shoulders. Her mask covers almost her entire face— everything but her lips and her eyes. The mask is white with gold fringes. Blue feathers adorn the top of it.

"You look beautiful," I say.

She smiles.

"Have fun," Ramona calls after us as we leave the room.

"One thing," I say to Ryoko as we head toward the stairs at the end of the hallway. "You won't understand what people are saying. This is a different time and place."

"I'll be alright." Ryoko brushes her hair back, revealing a small black device nestled inside her ear. "Ramona said I'll understand everything, but I won't be able to speak the language."

When we reach the top of the stairs, the first thing I see is the evening sky. A Venetian estate surrounds us—an enormous palace of white brick nestled into the side of the mountain, a small pond in front with a fountain in the middle. All around us are sprawling gardens and people in decorative costumes and masks. Minstrel music fills the air along with the smell of food.

Ryoko and I spend an hour strolling through the gardens,

sampling food and wine offered by servants wearing masks. I ask about her family. She tells me her parents met during a civil war, where her mother was disguised as a soldier.

"She told me she did it for the adventure," Ryoko says. "She was the bravest person I've ever met, but it wasn't just about courage. She had a wild spirit."

"They fought side by side?"

She shakes her head. "They fought on opposite sides but never told me who fought for which. They just said that they left many horrible things behind them and moved away to start a new life."

I consider it for a few seconds. "Did you ever figure out who fought on which side?"

"Of course I did." Ryoko's eyes twinkle. "They were my parents."

Her expression turns quizzical. She points to an elaborately trimmed array of bushes ahead of us. There's a large opening in the center of the greenery. "What is that?"

I laugh when I realize what we're looking at. "That's a hedge maze."

She scrunches her eyes in confusion, but she's smiling. "A what?"

"Some people . . . rich people . . . have so much money that they create large, complex mazes out of plants so that their rich drunk friends can get lost inside them."

I expect her to comment on how wasteful it seems. As a kid from the Dregs, my friends and I have spent a lot of time making fun of the stupid ways wealthy people choose to burn through their money.

But to my surprise, her eyes light up. "How wonderful."

To my further surprise, Ryoko takes off into the maze, not turning her head as she calls out to me. "Come find me!"

I give her a three-second head start before I run in after her. I twist and turn through the hedged pathways. Ryoko's laughter blends with the music. She sounds close. Many times I turn a corner, certain I have found her, only to be disappointed by more hedges. I could swear we've gone in a complete circle. Judging by her laughter, she doesn't care. The sound of her delight and the knowledge that I could give her a moment like this make me feel like somebody turned on a light inside my heart.

It's the life of a timestar. These are the rewards of my fame.

"Dash, come on." Ryoko's voice teases me, as if catching her ought to be easy. Maybe she's right. After all, I'm a rooftop racer whose body is filled with technological enhancements. I could use my optics to track her down, but that would ruin the fun of the chase.

I turn a corner and catch a glimpse of her blue dress for a fleeting moment. She's just ahead of me.

I take a quick left around a thick hedge wall and find the center of the maze. Ryoko stands with her back to me in front of a fountain. She's admiring the sculpture—nymphs and winged horses springing up from the water to take flight. Torches surround the center of the garden. There are stone benches, but they're empty. We're alone. The sounds of the party are so faint, it's as if we've found our own little escape.

Ryoko looks over her shoulder at me, and emotion pulls me toward her. I walk slowly to savor the moment.

When I reach her, I lean forward and whisper, "I have more surprises for you." The jasmine fragrance of her hair catches me off guard. It takes all my strength to lead her away from the serenity of the fountain, but our night has only begun.

We return to the time platform and make another jump. Ramona is there again, waiting for us. She directs us to different dressing rooms, but across the hallway, I hear Ryoko giggle with excitement. Before this, I wondered if the different fashions and strange cultures would be too much for her. I can navigate them pretty well, but I grew up seeing images from various time periods, learning about them, experiencing them. I expected Ryoko to have a harder time adjusting.

Shows what I know.

I step out of my dressing room, wearing a tailored tuxedo, complete with a bow tie and shiny shoes. My hair is parted on the side and slicked back.

Ryoko walks out in a black sparkling dress with fringes that end just below her knees. The dress catches me off guard. It's nothing risqué by present standards, but I've never seen her in clothing that showed so much of her legs and arms.

But it's her hair that surprises me. She's wearing a blonde wig, bobbed a couple of inches above her shoulders. Her black headband sparkles as much as her dress. Her glowing smile completes the outfit, making it truly unforgettable. "Ramona said dancers in this time wore these outfits." Her smile widens. "Are we going dancing?"

"We are," I tell her. "Are you ready?"

She takes my arm, and we all but sprint out of the facility. When we get outside, we're in a dark alley, but the city in front of us is alive. Cars putt along the road. Headlights and marquees shine in the night.

Ryoko gapes as we stroll out into the street. "All the lights. How is it possible?"

"Electricity," I say, then realize that word means nothing to her. "In this time, people have learned to harness the power of lightning. To create it, even. We use it for light and other things."

"It's beautiful," she marvels. "It's like magic. Is this your home?"

"No. I'm from about two hundred years in the future, give or take." I'm praying she doesn't ask to visit the present. This has been the perfect day. I don't want to ruin it by explaining the time travel laws against bringing echoes to the present. That would involve defining a lot of terms that I would rather not define.

But Ryoko is watching the people passing by. They look at her as well. A man across the street comes to a full stop as we walk by. The woman with him—his wife, I assume—jerks on his arm, saying something that's obscured by the sounds of the busy street. From the look on her face, it wasn't nice.

I use my optics to guide us to the right place. The last thing I want is to seem lost in New York City. My visual display guides us down another alley. Ryoko seems disappointed as we duck into a small deli, which appears dull compared to the glittering lights of other buildings all around.

A large man behind the counter is busy wiping down his food preparation area. He waves his hand at us without looking up. "Sorry, kids. We're closed."

"Mr. Myrtrym said you'd be open," I say.

"It's okay, Dash," Ryoko says. She's speaking Japanese, so I'm sure the man can't understand her. "There are plenty of other places—"

The man's head snaps up, his eyes wide. He points to the freezer door to my right and nods. "Through there. Have fun."

When we walk through the freezer door, a blast of cold air hits us. To our left are shelves stacked with boxes of food, but another door lined with metal is to our right. We open it and walk into a warmer dark hallway, the cold of the freezer forgotten as music bounces off the walls. A single lightbulb shows the way.

We reach the end of the hall and turn right, finding a staircase that leads down into a club. Ryoko bobs in time with the music.

The club is crammed with people—men in tuxedos, women in sparkling dresses. Arching brick ceilings create almost a series of caverns around us. The bar is filled with people trying to get the bartender's attention. Most of the concrete floor is occupied by either a small wooden table or the shoes of a dancer.

A band plays in the far corner of the room. The musicians are nearly on top of each other—a large man banging away at a piano, a drummer behind him, and an upright bass player dancing with his instrument. The brass players stand in front of them, and in the center, a small woman with a big voice croons into a microphone. Ryoko asks me questions about the instruments, and I answer as best I can.

We spend several songs watching other people dance before we give it a try. Ryoko is a natural, picking up the steps quickly. As for me, I do my best. After a few numbers of dancing and laughing together, we plop down at an open table. A blonde woman with a tray saunters over and asks if we'd like to order a drink. We both ask for water.

"Have you been here before?" Ryoko almost has to shout for me to hear her over the music.

"Never." I lean in closer to her. "But I've seen it in pictures. Are you having fun?"

"Of course," she says, her gaze on the people all around us as if she's studying every move. "I like to dance."

"Of course," I say, "you dance all the time."

She pauses, thinking. "Not as much as I would like, though."

The server reappears with our waters. I thank her as we both take long drinks.

"I know you said you don't want to do kabuki," I say, "and I understand that, but I've been thinking. Maybe we could find other ways to make you more well-known in your time. You're such a magnificent dancer, Ryoko. You could really make a name for yourself."

"Maybe." The thought seems to pass her by as if I've asked whether she wants to sample a new candy, as if it's nothing important. Ryoko's disinterest in fame and success has baffled me since the moment I saw her. Becoming a timestar has been such a difficult journey for me, but dancing seems to come so effortlessly to her. I'm sure she's worked hard on it, but she never seems concerned with making it a living. Not that I know how to gain notoriety in feudal Japan, but I can't believe people would look at her and not see a star. And what more could she want?

As the room grows more crowded, pieces of our conversation are lost in the shouting, laughing, and music. I want to ask more, but it's too loud here. Our next stop will be quieter.

"Are you ready to go?" I shout over the music.

She nods, but as we stand from our table, the song changes. The drummer adopts a slow beat, and the clamor of the speakeasy dies down.

So instead, I lead Ryoko to the center of the dance floor and draw her close, placing my hand at the small of her back. She leans into me. The jasmine scent is gone—perhaps stifled by the blonde wig—but it is replaced by the smell of vanilla. It makes me wonder whether Ramona is behind the change in fragrances, perhaps trying different concoctions to urge me toward kissing Ryoko, as if I needed further temptation. I close my eyes as we sway to the music, neither of us speaking, but our bodies saying everything.

As the song ends, she looks up at me. A light from somewhere in the room sparkles in her eyes—another opportunity. And yet, the time still isn't right, not yet. I tell her so with my smile, and with a smile, she tells me she understands.

We whisk out the door and onto the streets of New York City. After turning down another alley and entering the door that leads to our time platform, the Dominus time scientists welcome us and direct us to the lily pad, telling us that our table is ready.

"Table?" Ryoko asks.

"One final surprise," I say as the light of the platform activates, enveloping us.

Ramona waits on the other side. She tells us we may choose whatever we want to wear. In this particular time period, Dominus has made their presence known; there is no concern about standing out. I opt to keep on my tuxedo, but I remove the tie. Ryoko puts on a long, flowing dress. It's the same shade of blue she wore when I met her, though it has stars and galaxies flowing around the bottom hem. She loses the blonde wig and styles her hair in loose curls.

We leave the facility, walking up stone steps toward a fading daylight sky. I smell the desert air. It feels healing, somehow, and the warmth embraces me.

At the top of the stairs is a platform of polished wood sitting on a large sand dune. In the distance, the sun hides behind three pyramids, its light shining around the one in the middle, the largest of the three.

In front of us, a table offers an array of fruits, meats, and cheeses. Champagne bubbles in cold glass flutes. I pick one up and hand it to her.

"Try it," I say. "It won't taste like any drink you've ever had."

Ryoko takes a sip. Her eyes go wide. I try to act like I've done this before, remembering the way heroes on the timenet look when drinking in tuxedos. When I swallow, the bubbles tickle my throat, and I cough, nearly spitting champagne all over our food.

Ryoko giggles. "Sip it," she says, mocking me with a quirked smile.

"Pull out her chair for her." It's Ramona speaking in my ear, taking the place of Mr. Myrtrym, though I have little doubt he's seeing this too. I almost thank her for reminding me as I ease Ryoko's chair away from the table and invite her to sit.

She accepts the gesture with a curious expression. "Do women from your time need help sitting down?"

"No." I sit across from her. "I think, at one time, it had to do with the dresses women wore, but it became customary after that. It's more like a compliment, I guess. You're doing me a favor by allowing me to pull out the chair for you, if that makes sense."

Ryoko doesn't tell me whether it makes sense or not, but she seems to appreciate the gesture. We sit and nibble on the food, but neither of us drinks much champagne. As daylight fades, colored lights embedded in the sand dunes shine on the pyramids, making them look mystical against the backdrop of stars, like they're magic relics floating in space.

I clear my throat. "You said something earlier about why you dance. I wanted to ask you more about that. You could be so famous, and that would let you dance more. Isn't that what you want?"

Ryoko thinks about the question as she takes a bite of a strawberry. "Dancing more, yes, but not so people will know my name. Not even really for the sake of dancing, I guess."

"Then why?"

She points in the direction of the pyramids. "When I look at this, I see not just the structures, but the sky. The way the sun looked when we first arrived, then the changing colors, the reveal of the moon and the stars, it makes me feel a certain way. It's beauty, but it's more than that. It makes me feel joyful, adventurous, wild. It's like a call to my heart."

Her words bring to mind the time I spent among the dinosaurs. I felt so at home there, but at the same time, it made me want to keep exploring, to discover what wonders lie beyond that valley.

"I think you know what I'm talking about," Ryoko says, looking into my eyes.

I nod. "It's hard to describe, but I always feel it when I'm sitting on the roof of my home, watching the sunset and seeing the moon while there is still some daylight left. It looks like another world beyond ours. It makes me want to chase it, I guess. Not the moon, exactly, but the adventure."

"That feeling," Ryoko muses, "if I could put it into words, I would be a poet. I feel glimmers of it when I dance. I want to share that feeling with other people. That's the best I could ever hope for."

I turn my eyes back to the night sky. My experiences over the past few months have changed how I think about the world. I can move through time, a feat man once thought impossible.

But maybe there's something more, something beyond the timestream, a well from which time flows and an energy that moves it along. It makes what I do seem insignificant, but sometimes I think I catch a glimpse of it.

"That feeling . . ." Ryoko says, drawing my attention back to her. She sparkles as if there are diamonds and stars inside her eyes. "Dash, I get that feeling when I'm with you. You make me believe anything is possible."

I take her hand, but not to dance. The smell of vanilla returns as she moves close to me, her eyes stirring everything wonderful in my soul.

She moves forward to the edge of her seat, and our lips meet. I close my eyes and feel as if I'm lifted off the ground.

Wherever I'm going—wherever this energy takes me—I don't want to go without her.

36

A LOUD BEEPING LIKE SOME

type of alarm wakes me the next morning. I shoot up in bed and look around. I'm alone in the cabin. The memories of yesterday come rushing back—the date through time with Ryoko, the kiss we shared at the pyramids. Where is she?

That's right. I took her back to the pagoda. Ryoko's been staying there since the death of her family. She still has nightmares about that day, but I think being in the pagoda makes her feel safe. I even left my sword with her, telling her it would protect her when I wasn't around.

The beeping is coming from downstairs. Once I'm confident the cabin is not on fire or under attack, I make my way down to find my communications monitor blaring. The face of a Dominus employee—a young man with red hair and a chubby face—appears on the monitor behind the words *Urgent call.*

"Good morning, Mr. Keane," he says.

Mr. Keane? Maybe I'm a real celebrity after all. I run a hand over my face, trying to massage away the sleepiness. "Good morning. Uh . . . what's up?"

His lips quiver like he's nervous to speak to me. "He's asked for you to come to Dominus Corporation's main offices in the present . . . Mr. Myrtrym, that is. Sorry. I should have said that first. Mr. Myrtrym would like you to travel through time to—"

"I got it," I interrupt, trying not to sound curt, but I'm pretty sure my annoyance shows. I'll need to work on that. I don't need Dominus interns jumping on the timenet to anonymously report that Dash Keane is a jerk in real life.

"Thanks," I say, trying to be more upbeat. "When should I get there?"

His mouth hangs open like I've asked an unbelievable question. His fingers run over the screen as if he's scrolling through information on his monitor. "It doesn't say. I didn't ask. I'm sorry, Mr. Keane. I can find out."

"Don't worry about it," I say. "Tell Mr. Myrtrym I'll be there this afternoon. I'd like to stop by my parents' house first. Haven't seen them in a while. Can you have a gravcar waiting outside the lily pad by the docks in an hour?"

"Uh, yes, sir," the kid says, but he doesn't sound sure. I could probably ask him for a kidney right now and he would agree out of fear of disappointing me.

I get ready, though not in a rush. I don't want to come off too eager, and besides, I'm conflicted about seeing my parents. It's been a while since I called Knox. The story I tell myself is that I've been busy, but deep down, the truth is I don't want to risk my parents answering the call. I've been sending them money since I started with Dominus. It hasn't been much, but I'm sure it helps. I know they're disappointed with the life I've chosen. I just haven't wanted to face it, to let it ruin my good mood or spoil this wild ride I've been on.

But ever since I dropped off Ryoko last night, I've wanted to see them. I even dreamt I was trying to get home but couldn't. Obstacles kept popping up—the platform in the cabin didn't work, Dominus sent me back to fight gladiators, then I got home and nobody was there. I woke up desperate several times and had to remind myself that it wasn't real.

I shower and dress in my modern clothes, including my jacket. I can't remember the last time I wore it. I eat a quick breakfast before stepping onto the lily pad, and in moments, I'm walking out of the docks facility in the present. A gravcar waits for me, the door opening as I approach. The intern came through.

Good for that kid. I'll have to mention him to Ramona. Maybe a favorable word from me will boost his standing in the company.

When I get in the car, I'm tempted to ask the driver to take me straight to Dominus Corporation, but I can't avoid my parents any longer. Besides, I'm excited to see my brother.

"Take me home, please," I say to the driver, taking a deep breath as the gravcar lifts into the air.

37

MY PARENTS HUG ME

the instant I step through the door, but the argument starts less than five minutes later.

To be fair, I'm the first one to get mad.

"You were supposed to use that money to make a better life for yourselves!"

"We used some to buy new leg braces for your brother." My father maintains a calm tone, but I can tell that I'm already pushing his limits. I don't care. Their refusal of my generosity is infuriating.

Knox sits on the threadbare couch. His new leg braces certainly fit him better, and there are no signs of rust, but they don't strike me as the least bit special either. I don't like seeing him living this way. My hopes were that the money would be used not only to help his condition, but also to improve our home. The apartment looks the same as it did when I left.

I didn't expect them to change their minds, though once or twice I dared to imagine them seeing me on the timenet and maybe trying to understand. I've thought about it a lot at the cabin when I had nothing but my thoughts to keep me company.

In my pride, I viewed myself like a bird born into a family of fish, trying to convince them that I should fly. Of course they wouldn't believe it until they saw me in the air.

But despite all my success, they still don't understand. The weight of it brings me crashing down onto the threadbare couch cushions. "I know you don't like what I'm doing, but you could have used that money for a better life, even if you didn't agree. What did you do with it, anyway?"

"All the credits are still in our account," my mother says, sitting in an easy chair on the other side of the room. "You should never have sent that to us, Dashiell."

"I wanted to help you. There are these treatments that could help Knox walk. Maybe even run, just like—"

"Like you?" Knox breaks in. "I don't need to run like you, Dash." He doesn't look angry, exactly. More like he's trying to make me understand. "You're a great big brother, but I don't need you to fix me, because I'm not broken."

"I didn't mean . . ." I place both hands over my face. Why are they making this so difficult?

"Dash," my father begins. "Son, why couldn't you have trusted me?"

I turn my attention to him. "I don't know what you're talking about."

He exchanges glances with my mother.

"Beckett," she says to him, "it's time to tell them."

"Tell us what?" Knox asks.

"The truth." My father clasps his hands in front of him and looks at us. "Dash, you're too young to remember this, but before Knox was born, I was a data scientist for a small company that specialized in researching the past. We studied the changes in nature over time. I was on assignment at P-200 when I . . ." His gaze drifts across the room to my mother, looking at her in a way I've never seen. "I met someone . . . not from the present."

My heart drops into my stomach. *Mom? No. It can't be true.*

"We got married," my father says. "I saved a lot of money and purchased the . . . rights." He grimaces as if the word is bile in his mouth. "We were married and made a life for ourselves in the past. Everything was great. The company took care of its employees, spouses, and children. We were happy."

Knox and I are both just staring at him. He continues.

"But when profits dropped, the company had to sell. We were bought by a larger corporation. They came in and said nothing would change, and then they got bought by somebody else."

"Dominus?" My mouth is so dry the words creak out.

"Intellenon actually, but what's the difference? My contracts were honored, and we thought everything would be fine. When we had you, Dash, we thought it was a turning point in our lives." He smiles slightly. "And it was."

"You were such a beautiful baby," my mother interjects. "You brought so much love into our family. We knew we wanted another child."

My father regards Knox. "We knew early on about your condition, son. Under my previous employer, you would have received all the benefits of a child from the present. But that was not the case with Intellenon. They weren't going to spend that kind of money . . ."

On echoes. He doesn't have to say it.

"Then how did we end up here?" I ask.

"I had to make a decision," he answers. "If we stayed in the past, Knox would have died in a few years. Even the free medical care available in the present was leaps and bounds ahead, enough to keep him alive. As a data scientist, I managed verification systems for people passing back and forth through time. I smuggled our DNA samples into the system, disguising us as vacationers. I knew that eventually what I had done would be discovered." He hesitates a moment. "So I made some deals I'm not proud of to cover our tracks. We moved here to start a new life."

I can't move. I can't breathe. "You're telling me that I'm half-echo?"

"You're a human being, Dash," my father says. "All of us are human beings, no matter what they say."

I look at Knox. His eyes are wide, but I get the feeling that somehow, he always knew.

Then a terrifying reality hits me. "If Dominus finds out about this . . ."

"It's why I tried to stop you." His eyes on me are stern but also sympathetic. "Dash, I understand this is devastating—"

"When were you going to tell me?" I blurt out. My confusion has given way to anger. I spit the words at him. It's not a question—we both know that. It's an accusation, and I'm glad I made it. How could they not tell me who—or what—I am? They're my parents. They're supposed to love me. I'm supposed to be able to trust them.

My mother's voice is quiet. "It would have been very soon."

I roll my eyes. "Right."

My father sits next to my mother. "We thought it best you finished school first, Dash. You didn't need this distraction. You didn't need to know until it was time to plan the rest of your life."

"And what kind of life would that be?" I demand. "One where nobody ever notices me? I would have to live my entire life under the radar." The anger is a hot coil wrapped around my stomach, tightening every second. I want to flip over the couch, hurl things across the room, and shatter them against the dingy walls.

But really, I want to go back in time. Maybe I could convince Dominus to send me back to fight somebody. *Bare-knuckle boxing.* I envision myself letting my opponent hit me a few times before I retaliate. It wouldn't be real, but it would sure give me a release.

Dominus. I'm not certain about the laws for half-breeds, but at the very least, I'm the offspring of criminals. This could ruin everything.

I need to get out of here before I get any angrier. I don't want Knox to see me lose it. "I'm leaving." I head for the door. My father jumps to his feet. "Dash!"

I round on him. "Don't you dare try to stop me. You know you can't, and if you try, I promise there will be lots of noise, lots of attention."

His nostrils flare, then his body seems to sag. "Be careful, son. Those corporations . . . you don't know who you're dealing with there."

"Seems like I don't know who I'm dealing with here either." The words are intended to cut deep. I curse the pang of guilt I feel inside me as I walk out the door.

The gravcar waits outside. I need to get to Dominus soon, but I need to cool down first.

I climb into the gravcar and slam the door. "Take me to Garon's."

38

"I COME HERE A LOT." GARON
sits on the concrete wall at the water's edge, his feet dangling over the side. I tried three different places before I found him here at the docks, not far from the Dominus facility.

I sit next to him, eyeing the water as images of the sea dinosaur flash in my mind, its predatorial eyes looking up at me from the murky depths. "Why's that?"

He shrugs. "I don't know. In case you need me, I guess. This is about as close to you as I can get lately."

Somehow that statement makes me feel better and worse at the same time. "Have you been watching?"

He laughs, breaking the uneasiness I've felt since I got here. "Of course I'm watching."

"What do you think?"

"The camera angles aren't great." I know it's a joke, but Garon delivers it as if he's dead serious.

"Nobody can shoot me as well as you," I tell him, not joking at all. "But do you like the show?"

The smile that crosses his face is sincere. "It's awesome, man. I'm happy for you, and Ryoko seems great. It looks like you're having a lot of fun. I wish I could've gone shooting with Duffy."

Duffy. The mention of his name makes me wince. *He would have liked Garon too.*

If he were still alive.

My gaze jumps back to the water, half-afraid that instead of a sea monster, I'll see the sheriff's body just below the surface, lifeless eyes fixed on me.

"So what's going on?" Garon asks.

"What do you mean?"

"C'mon, Dash. I've known you long enough to see when something's bothering you."

I let out a deep breath, procrastinating as long as I can before telling him the truth, but when I open the floodgates, everything my father told me pours out in sentence fragments and jumbled thoughts. I'm still trying to process it all. My mother is an echo. My brother and I are . . . half real?

Garon listens to the whole thing, not saying a word.

"I don't know what to do." My head is in my hands. "I can't give all of this up. I've worked so hard to get here."

He waits a moment before speaking. "That's probably what your father said, too, once upon a time. I mean, look at what he did. He risked everything for you."

"I guess." I avoid looking at him, trying not to become angry. Garon wants to help, but I'm not in the mood to sympathize with the people who lied to me for eighteen years.

Garon stares at the water. After a long moment, he speaks. "Why are you really doing this, Dash?"

I look at him in amazement. "Are you kidding me? I thought if anybody understood, it would be you." My skin heats up. He's trying to back me into a corner, and I don't like it.

Garon holds out a hand. "Humor me. Say it out loud."

"I want to build a better life for all of us, including you." I point my finger at him like I'm going to jab him with it. "You're as much a part of this timestar thing as you want to be."

His expression sobers. "It doesn't feel like I'm part of it."

My breath quickens. Shimizu Kaida would tell me to pause and focus, to feel the air coming in and out of my lungs. *Breath is the wind of life.*

"I have to help myself first. I'm building for the future. But once I'm a star, *really* a star, I'll have the leverage to bring you along. You and Knox. We'll be a team."

"We already were a team," Garon says. "The Red Dragon. It was you, of course, but it was also all of us."

I can't believe what I'm hearing. Does he seriously want me to give up all my success and go back to rooftop racing so he can feel like he's part of the team again? When did he get so selfish? "True. But I took all the risks, Garon, and I'm still taking all the risks. You've seen what I've done. I'm fighting lunatic warriors and running from monsters. Half the echoes I encounter are trying to kill me!"

"Exactly," Garon says pointedly. "Can you imagine what it would do to Knox to see you die on the timenet? Dominus will be sure to show your death."

Don't you dare bring my brother into this argument. I fight to keep my composure, but the fire in my gut is growing. "You're twisting this around."

"No, I'm not. It's the best thing they can hope for. They'll build you up as much as they can, then they'll broadcast your death in slow motion and from every angle all over the timenet."

"At least Knox will get some money out of it," I shoot back.

"I bet he'd rather have a brother." Garon looks at me. "I'd rather have my friend. I know it's tough to swallow what your dad did, but he sacrificed everything he had, and he did it because he loved all of you more than himself."

I jump to my feet, throwing my arms out. Any sense of control is gone. The words erupt out of me almost violently. "What do you want me to do? Quit? Walk away from all the work I've done? I don't think I could do that if I wanted to!"

Garon remains stoic. "Maybe we can help you."

"I can't believe this." I activate the card in my pocket, calling the gravcar to take me to the Dominus office. I thought I could count on Garon to be a friend who would listen. Instead, he's another person trying to keep me from achieving greatness because it reminds him that his life is miserable. "I've got to go."

Garon stands. I can hardly look at him, but his eyes are concerned. "I'm sorry. This is my fault. I watched the timenet for years, but I didn't realize what I was seeing until it was you on the screen. That made it more real. These corporations use people, and then they throw them away. I don't want that to happen to you, Dash."

"I won't let them," I say abruptly. "I'm better than that. I'm too valuable for them."

The gravcar lands in front of me. I open the door and give Garon one last look. Of all the people who could doubt me, I never thought it would be him. It's more than an insult.

It's betrayal.

But he's wrong. They're all wrong. Maybe they all liked me better when my life was as hopeless as theirs. I lift my sculpted chin and push out my enhanced chest to remind Garon that I'm not the scrawny guy rebounding for him anymore. I'm not that same poor kid from the Dregs.

"I'm Dash Keane," I proclaim, then climb into the gravcar.

39

WHEN I GET INSIDE THE GRAVCAR,
the driver rolls down the partition. "Good day, Mr. Keane."

I toss him a brief smile. After fighting with my family, arguing with my best friend, and discovering that my existence is a crime, it's the best I can manage. "Take me to the Dominus main office, please."

"I have instructions from Mr. Myrtrym to take you to the time platform," he informs me.

"Really?" I look out the window. We're still on the ground. The time platform is a short walk away, but Garon hasn't left yet. "Can you do me a favor then? Fly away and we can come back in a few minutes."

"Certainly, Mr. Keane."

The gravcar lifts, and within seconds, Garon is a speck far below me. Maybe he's done me a favor. If he doesn't want to be part of my team, I won't have to find a place for him. Convincing Dominus to bring on somebody so inexperienced would have been tough.

Now I don't even have to think about it. It's freeing, in a way. One more chance to leave the Dregs behind.

I try to relax and enjoy the view of the city as the gravcar circles the area. If I had more space inside the car, I would practice the kata that Kaida taught me. For now, I focus on my breath to calm down, to find my center.

By the time we're back at the docks, I don't see Garon. I head into the facility and get to the time platform as fast as possible. I can't wait to leave this time period. Reality is overrated. This isn't where I wanted to live. This isn't the family I thought it was. They lied to me, and now I'm the one who has to deal with the consequences. Who knows what other secrets they have kept from me? The injustice of it all is tearing me apart.

No more, I decide as the time platform lights up. *As soon as Dominus signs me to an extended contract, I'll be the master of my own life. I'll break the chains of my past.*

When the lights go down, I'm standing on a lily pad in a room of yellowish stone. There are a lot of time scientists around me, far more than I'm used to after a time jump.

"Welcome, Mr. Keane," one of them says with exuberance. The rest start cheering and applauding. I give them a short wave.

A woman awaits me at the end of the platform. She has tanned skin, dark hair, and is dressed in animal hide that reveals her legs, arms, and stomach. She's barefoot. Her face is beautiful, but her mouth curves down, and she bows her head as I approach. The woman holds up a tray with a single glass of champagne.

"Thank you." I take the glass.

She nods without looking at me, then motions for me to follow her down a narrow hallway toward a staircase. We pass a few dressing rooms. I expect her to direct me into one of them, perhaps to put on an outfit similar to what she's wearing. Even inside this facility, I can tell that the climate is very warm here. Maybe Ramona will have me play the bare-chested warrior. That could be fun. My physical enhancements and training have seriously changed my body. I have muscles in places I wouldn't have thought possible, and it's great. Maybe that's shallow, but right now, shallow doesn't sound too bad. I could use the ego boost.

But the woman ignores the dressing rooms. She stops at the bottom of the stairs and looks at me, as if asking a question with her eyes.

"You can speak to me," I say in English, hoping she understands. My translator won't work until she talks.

"They generally don't," says a familiar voice from above.

I look up to see Mr. Myrtrym at the top of the stairs. I would have expected to find him in a suit, but instead, he's hovering off the ground with gravboots, wearing a knee-length tunic of white and shimmering gold. On his wrists are golden bracelets with repulsors that extend over his palms to stabilize his flight.

"Come on up," he beckons with a smile.

I activate my gravboots, gliding above the stairs. When I reach the top and walk outside onto a balcony, it feels like I've stepped into another world. A city of stone stretches out in front of me, with gardens and buildings and temples that thrust high into a hazy golden sky. Complex water features run throughout the city, creating ornate fountains and streams, many of which are flanked by furniture that radiates luxury.

But I also see modern touches—holoscreens, a few steel buildings in the distance on the other side of a body of water, upon which is a yacht. Men and women all outfitted similarly to Mr. Myrtrym move about the scene, some walking, others flying. They're laughing, eating, and drinking. I see echoes, too, all of whom are dressed like the woman from the facility. They serve the people in gold.

But I don't see any cameras.

"What is this place?" I ask Mr. Myrtrym.

"Call it El Dorado," is his reply. "The Lost City of Gold."

"And these people?"

Mr. Myrtrym chuckles. "Dominus employees, at least most of them. This period of time is reserved for senior leadership in the corporation, influential guests, the wealthiest of—"

Another echo, a young man, appears before us and holds up a tray of champagne glasses. Mr. Myrtrym takes my glass and puts it on the tray. "Basically, very important people."

Important people. Like me.

Mr. Myrtrym begins to move away. "I'll show you around."

I use my gravboots to catch up with Mr. Myrtrym, and we glide down a stone staircase that leads to the heart of the city.

"What's with the gold outfits?" I ask. "Am I supposed to be wearing the same thing?"

"If you want," he replies. "It's all good fun. The corporation has chosen not to preserve historical accuracy in this time segment. Instead, we use it as a retreat. The gold clothes and the technology help the echoes here accept the . . . let's say the preferred dynamics between us and them."

"That we're from the future?" I see an older man lying on a red sofa in the middle of a garden as an echo woman rubs his shoulders with oil.

Mr. Myrtrym stops and looks at me. "That we're gods, Dash."

I freeze in disbelief. Maybe I heard him wrong. "What?"

"Well," he starts gliding again, picking his way through the gardens and fountains around us, "think about it from their perspective. We appear out of the air. We make their crops grow better. We control fire, lightning, wind, water. We harness the power of the sun. We heal their diseases. We fly through the sky, and that's just scratching the surface. How much more godlike could we be?"

I turn the question over in my mind as we move through the city. He's leading us toward a temple so large that it dwarfs the pyramids I saw with Ryoko. On the outside, it looks like a building from this time period, but I doubt it could have been built without present technology.

Echoes stare as I glide past, but every time I catch eyes with one of them, they look down. Many of them bow.

"It's strange," I say aloud.

"You get used to it," Mr. Myrtrym assures me. "It's better for everybody. We've improved their lives, and they feel blessed that their home is the chosen place of the gods."

The entrance to the temple is a massive archway, the Dominus logo carved into the stone at its crest. It leads to a long hallway lit by candles, casting flames against golden walls. As we move inside, piano music comes to life. There's a large open area in the center of the temple with no ceiling. A glittering pool of water is surrounded by men and women lounging around. Most of them are socializing, laughing the kind of laugh that tells you they have been drinking. Several seem to overly enjoy being served by the echoes. A queasiness forms in my stomach. Nobody is hurting anybody, but this still feels wrong.

"Why did you bring me here?" I ask Mr. Myrtrym. I doubt it was for the celebration.

Mr. Myrtrym looks around, studying the different pleasures in which the people—these golden gods—are partaking, then raises an eyebrow as he regards me. It's like he's evaluating me.

His expression shifts, alters as if he was hoping to find something in me but didn't. "I brought you here for a meeting, but it won't start for a few hours. We have a room set up for you. You should rest."

He leans in close with his most genuine smile yet. "This is the day you've been waiting for."

40

THE GRANDEUR OF THE THRONE

room is overwhelming. Everything is glittering gold. Even the servants wear shimmering paint on their sculpted bodies. They stand at attention like golden soldiers. An enormous chandelier hangs from the ceiling, figures of phoenixes, winged horses, gryphons, Minotaurs, and dragons filling the areas between flickering candles as if they're at war between the flames.

A long gold table sits on a dais in the center of the room, filled with food. The smell of meat makes my mouth water. As I approach, I also see fruits, breads, vegetables, and desserts. There's no way all this food came from this area. I see a plate of roasted duck surrounded by vegetables, reminding me of the restaurant in Paris. These aren't just foods from all over the world. They're from different time periods.

At the table, men and women—most of whom I recognize from my meetings at the Dominus main office—sit waiting for me.

I take my seat at one end of the table, and as usual, Mr. Myrtrym faces me from the other. "Dash." He lets my name echo in the room. "You've done it. Congratulations."

I briefly close my eyes and savor the feeling. All the hard work, all the time, all the blood and sweat. The moment is finally here. *I've done it. I'm on top.*

Of course I am. My confidence surprises me, but it shouldn't. I've accomplished more than any timestar ever has in such a short period, and I'm only eighteen. Of course Dominus wants to lock me down with a huge contract.

"You're the most popular timestar in the world," Mr. Myrtrym declares. "By any metric, you're number one. Frankly, it's not even close anymore."

"We'll negotiate a new contract soon. A long-term agreement." He looks approvingly at me like a proud father. "I don't want to spoil our celebration with too much business talk, but I can say with confidence that you are about to become an extremely wealthy young man."

The first thing I think of is Knox. Maybe I'll take him on adventures. Nothing dangerous—a mission that's easy and with lots of protection.

Then again, Knox probably won't want that. He doesn't care about the spotlight. He'll want to design costumes. I make a mental note to mention it in negotiations. Knox deserves a spot on my team. I might even give Garon a second chance.

"Thank you," I respond, catching eyes with as many people at the table as I can. "All of you. Thank you so much."

"We're all very excited." Mr. Myrtrym beams. "We have lots of ideas for your future. This team is committed to your success, and we're building some innovative story arc ideas."

"Really?" My grin stretches my face. "Can I hear some?"

"First, we're thinking of a team-up with other timestars," Mr. Myrtrym tells me. "We're going to recreate the Knights of the Round Table with you as the King Arthur figure."

I cock my head. "But I'd still be using my name, right?" I'm not eager to pretend I'm somebody else. I did that for long enough.

"Of course." Mr. Myrtrym gives a crisp nod. "Then we're thinking of stepping back from the combat for a little while to keep the audience guessing. Maybe a season in which you play for the New York Yankees alongside DiMaggio and Mantle. Do you like baseball?"

"Sure." The truth is, I'm not crazy about the sport. I'd rather play on a historic basketball team like the St. Louis Hawks, but I'm at the mercy of the current positions of lily pads in the timestream. Besides, I'm sure that when I hear the roar of the crowd after stepping up to the plate, I will learn to love it. Plus, I don't mind the idea of more running and less fighting for a change.

"But you're still a warrior first and foremost," Mr. Myrtrym continues emphatically. "So after that, we're considering putting you on a Viking ship to attack Europe. We're going to keep you busy. I hope you're ready for it."

"I am." I've never been so sure of anything in my life.

Mr. Myrtrym lifts his glass. "Then let's toast." Every Dominus person in the room raises their glass in perfect unison, and I realize they all have been waiting for this moment. This is the brain trust, I assume, but I get the feeling they weren't brought here for any reason other than to show me they were here.

A servant hands me a glass of red wine. I nod my thanks to her and hold it up.

"To Dashiell Keane and Dominus Corporation," Mr. Myrtrym proclaims.

Everyone drinks together, myself included. I've arrived.

The joy of it all pours over me. *I finally made it.*

"There is one thing I want to discuss," I say to Mr. Myrtrym from across the table. The others start to eat and talk amongst themselves.

He smiles at me. "Sure. What is it?"

"Ryoko," I say. The commotion at the table is growing louder.

"What?" Mr. Myrtrym leans forward, trying to hear me.

"Ryoko!" I don't mean to shout, but I do.

The table falls silent.

I lower my voice. "Everything you mentioned sounds great, but I'm hoping I can bring her with me."

Nobody says a word. Several look down at their plates while others gaze at Mr. Myrtrym.

"Not to be on camera," I say quickly, nervousness edging at me. Have I just screwed everything up? I scramble to try to make it okay. "You know, not on my show, unless that's what you want. I just thought it'd be nice to see her more when I'm not shooting."

The people trade glances with each other. As Mr. Myrtrym chuckles, they burst into laughter.

"What?" I ask, bewildered. "What's going on?"

Mr. Myrtrym stands while the rest of the table resumes their chatter, my request forgotten. "Come here for a second." Mr. Myrtrym beckons. "Let's look at the view."

He takes me to the far end of the room where large archways and golden pillars lead out onto a balcony with a view of the beach and the sky.

"Congratulations again." Mr. Myrtrym clinks his glass against mine. "I have a gift for you."

A servant appears, shirtless with bronze skin and dark hair. He holds out a golden platter with a small box on top of it.

I set my glass on the platter, take the box, and open it. When I see what's inside, my breath stops. "Your watch."

Mr. Myrtrym nods.

My mind jumps back to the day I stood in his office and he told me that gifts from wealthy men are more about implied debts than generosity. "This is too much," I say hesitantly. "I'm not sure I can accept this."

He shakes his head. "I know what you're thinking. You are learning, but there are no strings attached here. I want this to remind you of what you have accomplished. It's more than success, Dash." His eyes engage me. "You have real power now, and the question is what you will do with it. Some people exchange power for money. Some exchange it for recognition. Precious few, thank nature, hold on to it."

"What kind of power?" I put on the watch, taking a few moments to admire it. I'm wearing a timepiece on my wrist that probably costs more than my parents could make in a lifetime.

Mr. Myrtrym retrieves my glass of wine from the servant's platter and hands it back to me. "Nobody has ever become so famous so fast. You're a person of enormous influence now. You've ruined our metrics." He flashes a smile. "We're going to have to rethink all of our models."

"That's great," I say earnestly. "And I appreciate this, Mr. Myrtrym. I appreciate everything you've done for me. But about—"

"And I hope you're enjoying the fruits of your success." He lowers his voice, casting a glance back toward the room.

"Ryoko," I persist. "Mr. Myrtrym, you know she means a lot to me."

He lets out a deep breath. "Listen, Dash, the romantic angle played well, and it's to be expected that you would develop feelings for her. But that storyline's over. The audience will get bored with it, which means they'll get bored with you."

"So you don't want her on camera?" The idea is a relief. Ryoko never asked to be a timestar, and I would rather keep her out of the public eye.

"We're going to engineer a breakup."

"A b-breakup?" I stammer. "Why?"

"Because of this." He spreads his arms out toward the beach, the city, and the sky, but I know he's talking about more than the scenery, even more than the decadence of the temple. "Don't you want to be number one?"

"Of course, but—"

"Then this is the next step. Don't worry; it will be a tasteful breakup episode. We need to be conscious of how the public perceives you. You can't come off as the jerk, but it can't seem like she dumps you either. We'll make it more heroic, like you're doing the best thing for her. People will love it. They'll feel bad for you, but not sorry for you. Do you see the difference?"

He's avoiding what I'm saying. I grip my glass tight, trying to keep my cool. "Sure, but—"

"And we're thinking about the next one." He leans against the railing, now facing me. "We've got some good candidates lined up for future love interests, echoes from other time periods. It'll be a great experiment. The audience will root for one person or another, whoever they think is right for you. Of course, all the women will fall for you. You're Dashiell Keane!"

I feel my breath getting faster, my skin growing hot. "I really don't want—"

But Mr. Myrtrym keeps talking. "Plus, in our King Arthur story arc, one of our female timestars has agreed to do a romantic storyline with you. She'll play the Guinevere role, except she'll be much more fierce. Then, things will fall apart after her affair with the Lancelot figure. Now that I think about it, that could set up a great rivalry. The two of you could compete in—"

"Stop!" In frustration, I throw my glass against one of the pillars, and it shatters. "Listen to me. I'm your top timestar. I want to be with Ryoko. Find a way to make it happen."

Mr. Myrtrym shakes his head. "You don't know what you're talking about. Yes, you're valuable, but Ryoko is valuable too."

"Valuable how?"

He eyes me. "Look around you. How much money do you think we make off timenet programming? Do you have any idea? We lose money on every episode, but it's a means to an end. Among other things, it helps us sell experiences. *You* help us sell experiences. Ryoko is beautiful, charming, and a lot of wealthy people will pay well to meet her."

A wave of heat permeates my body. My mind races. How do I stop this? "I'll buy her rights," I state, thinking of what my father did for my mother. Surely my new contract will give me more than enough money to buy a single echo.

"She's not for sale, Dash."

"You can't mean that." I'm grasping for anything. "Name a price."

"It's not about how much she's worth." Mr. Myrtrym turns his glass in his fingers. "You don't get it, do you, Dash? It's what she represents. If we make her unavailable, the damage will be immeasurable. In many ways, she's the point of all this. Besides, even with your new contract, I don't think you could afford it. We've never had offers anywhere close to what we're getting for her."

I want to rip him apart with my bare hands, but what good would it do? There are countless suits in the room behind us, ready to take his place.

I try desperately to think of a solution.

"Listen." Mr. Myrtrym puts his hand on my shoulder. "I know you don't think I understand, but I do. You'll get used to this. It's like the killing—you have to get past the part of your brain that tells you this is real."

I push his arm away. I'm so angry I almost can't see straight. "Don't touch me."

The expression on Mr. Myrtrym's face changes from ally to enemy in an instant. His eyes narrow. The fake smile disappears. His lips part, revealing gritted teeth. "Don't do this, Dash. Don't do what I think you're going to do. You have everything you ever wanted in front of you, far more than you ever imagined. With my help, you could be a legend. An icon. But if you do this, there's no turning back."

I hear everything he's saying, but my mind is on Ryoko. If I leave now, how soon will it be before Dominus Corporation gets to her?

I eye the room behind me. The executives are no threat, and the guards are unarmed. I'm sure Dominus has weapons around here somewhere in case the people decide to rebel against their gods.

But they're not gods. Right now, they look more like demons. From the look on Mr. Myrtrym's face, he knows I've made my decision. "Pity. You could've been special, but I'll make a show of this yet. Tell you what, Dashiell Keane. I'll give you a head start, and then I'm coming after you with a fury you could never imagine. You have one last chance to save your own life." He extends his hand to me.

The half-second hesitation is not to think about what I'm going to do, but how I'm going to do it. The temple is filled with twists and turns, closed doors, obstacles. I don't even remember the fastest exit route.

Instead, I vault up onto the balcony railing and take a last look at the life of luxury before I leave it all behind.

I jump.

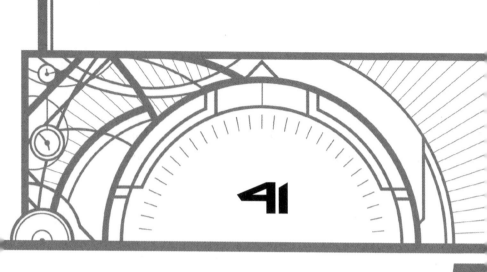

41

I PLUMMET OFF THE BALCONY

toward the beach below. My gravboots activate before I hit the sand, creating a cushion of air beneath my feet. I lean forward and increase the power, pushing the boots' thrusters to full speed as I zoom around the side of the temple. *How much of a head start will Myrtrym give me?* The question rattles my mind as I fly toward the facility. I can almost feel his hands right behind me, reaching for my throat.

But a colder reality grabs onto me as I arrive at the facility, deactivate my gravboots, and race down the stairs. Capturing me in this time period would be a wasted opportunity for him. There aren't enough cameras around, and he doesn't want people to see how Dominus treats echoes in this time segment.

I saw it in his eyes before I jumped, the wild thrill, the bloodlust, and the opportunity.

Myrtrym wants to hunt me, and he wants everybody to see it.

I expect the Dominus employees to try to stop me as I jump onto the time platform, but instead, one calls out, "Where to, Mr. Keane?"

I consider going to Ryoko first, but I left all my weapons in the cabin. *How much time do I have left?*

"My cabin." I kneel. Myrtrym will know where I'm going no matter what time I choose, and he will expect me to go for supplies. It makes for a better show—the illusion that I have a fighting chance.

The lights blind me. When they fade away, I'm in the cabin. I leap out of the tube and run to the armory.

It's empty except for my revolvers hanging from a hook on the wall. Myrtrym probably thinks it's funny to give me weapons that are hundreds of years old.

Still, I grab the revolvers, jump back into the tube, and set a new destination. Myrtrym must have sent people to the cabin before our meeting, disarming me in case I chose to rebel.

But if he can do that . . . my mind drifts to terrible realities. *Has he already gotten to Ryoko?*

In my frenzy, I enter the wrong numbers twice before punching in the correct temporal and geographic coordinates.

When I reach her time segment, none of the Dominus scientists say a word. They look at me as if I'm a ghost. Maybe I am.

I rush out of the facility, praying to find a horse outside, but I don't. I activate my gravboots again, unsure how much energy they have left. The fading daylight reminds me that the timestream never stops. My head start has probably run out by now. One way or another, Myrtrym is coming for me. *I have to get to Ryoko.*

I smell blood in the air the moment I reach Shimizu Kaida's home. Blood and gunpowder. No less than five bodies lie lifeless in front of the pagoda, their blood dripping into the stream that runs through the stone courtyard. All of them are dressed in samurai armor with the Dominus logo on their chests, swords and ancient rifles beside their bodies.

No! I run inside to find Shimizu Kaida lying on the floor, blood seeping through a wound on her side as one of her students tends to her. The bodies of more Dominus samurai litter the room. The other student sits slumped against a pillar, perfectly still, blood dripping from his mouth.

"What happened?" I ask as I drop to Kaida's side.

"She's been shot." The student glares at me. I can tell he thinks this is all my fault. He isn't wrong.

As guilty as I feel, as much as I owe Shimizu Kaida, I have only one question. "Where's Ryoko?"

Shimizu Kaida stirs and coughs, trying to force out words. "The . . . hill."

In a flash, I'm outside and sprinting toward the hill behind the pagoda, the place where Shimizu Kaida and I practiced kata, the place where Ryoko and I stared into the sky and talked about everything we wanted in life. The place where I first developed a deeper interest in her.

When I reach the bottom of the hill, a figure stands at the top, a silhouette against the setting sun and the red sky, holding a weeping sword. A body lies on the ground nearby.

I charge up the hill, terrified that I'm too late.

But a breeze blows, billowing the figure's robes, the light of dusk revealing a familiar shade of blue.

Ryoko.

"Dash!" Ryoko cries out as she drops the sword and runs to me. I throw my arms around her, burying my face in her shoulder as relief overwhelms me.

I pull away to look at her. Blood covers her blue robes, the same clothes she wore the first time I saw her when she danced with the demon.

"Are you hurt?"

Ryoko gazes at me blankly. I recognize the look. I saw it in the mirror after I killed the gunslinger. It's fear twisted around a dark disbelief over something she's done, something she would have never thought possible.

"The blood." Her voice quivers. "It isn't mine."

The man at her feet has a brutal slash across the neck. There are no other wounds, nor any signs of damage to her. A shudder runs through me. Ryoko has killed now. The memory of Myrtrym tries again to tell me it isn't real.

But the blood I see is real, as is the look in her eyes. She's crossed a line, lost a piece of herself that she can never regain. I might have expected her to be tearful after such a traumatic event, but despite her eyes, her face is strong, poised. Or maybe she hasn't had time to process it yet.

"We have to go," I say. "More will come, and soon. Grab your sword."

"Actually," Ryoko kneels to retrieve the weapon, "it's your sword."

My hand shakes as Ryoko passes me the sword with the red blade, the weapon I got from Dominus. I almost expect it to explode. Who knows what Dominus did to this thing before giving it to me?

But we need all the weapons we can get. I wipe off the blade, scoop the sheath off the ground, and shove the sword inside.

We hurry down the hill, and to my relief, we find Shimizu Kaida and her student waiting for us. Kaida is unsteady but standing, a bandage wrapped around her wound.

I stop before her. "Shimizu Kaida. Are you—"

"I am fine." She nods, then says, "Go. If more come, we will hold them off."

I consider telling them to come with us, but being in my presence is probably the most dangerous place in the timestream right now.

We take two of Kaida's horses and ride back to the facility. I keep my eyes on the sky, wondering what Dominus might do to track me. There must be cameras around. I want to scream out loud that I'm a real person, that Dominus is hunting a real person on the timenet. But Myrtrym would edit the whole thing out. He'll make me look like a criminal. I'm totally in his hands.

I draw my sword when we reach the facility. It feels like suicide, walking into a Dominus installation, but if we stay here, it's only a matter of time before we're found. We don't bother tying up the horses after we dismount. They'll make their way home to Shimizu Kaida, but I take time to thank my "powerful serenity" before I go inside.

The facility is deserted, but the equipment around the time platform appears to be active. Myrtrym could turn it off in an instant. He could send soldiers through time to intercept me right here, but everything looks almost like it's waiting for me.

He wants me to run.

One of the monitors that had been black turns on. My gaze locks onto the screen which has my own face staring back at me, Ryoko's picture beside it. Text scrolls across the bottom of the video.

Dash Keane: Fugitive

The broadcast cuts to Myrtrym walking out of Dominus headquarters, surrounded by microphones and hovercams. "We are fully aware of the unfortunate situation regarding Mr. Keane. Dominus security personnel are working in conjunction with law enforcement to detain him as soon as possible."

"Will you air the manhunt?" a reporter asks from off camera.

Myrtrym smirks and nods. "Yes. The public has a right to see justice be done."

Ryoko and I reappear on the monitor, running down the hill behind the pagoda. A man's voice speaks over the broadcast. "That's right, folks. It seems that our favorite timestar has gone off the rails. Dashiell Keane, also known on the illegal rooftop-racing circuit as 'the Red Dragon,' has violated the temporal laws by attempting to smuggle an echo into—"

I grab a chair and smash it into the screen before he can say anymore.

Ryoko stares at me in surprise. "What was that about?"

"I can't explain now." I turn my attention to the control console. It's more complicated than the interface in the cabin, but I think I can figure it out. "Get to the center of the platform," I instruct Ryoko as I punch in coordinates I never thought I would use. My finger pauses before beginning the activation sequence. I know Dominus has a lily pad over the time segment I have entered, but I've never seen a broadcast from that period, and for good reason. But it's the one place we might be able to hide.

When I press the button to activate the time jump, the console flashes red with an error message. *Restricted time segment. Insert manual override code.*

My muscles tense.

"Dash, what's happening?" Ryoko asks.

I don't respond, placing all my attention on the console. Maybe I did it wrong. I input the coordinates again, lying to myself that this time it will work.

It doesn't.

Of course it doesn't. Even Dominus wouldn't want people traveling to that time except under the most controlled circumstances.

"Dash!"

I look at Ryoko, guilt racking my body. They'll destroy her because of me. "I'm so sorry."

The sound of horses' hooves outside breach through the walls of the facility. The soldiers will be here soon. We have one sword and two six-shooters between us. No way we can fight them off.

Because I don't know what else to do, I enter the time coordinates again and slam my fist against the button.

A green confirmation blinks onto the screen. The platform lights up.

What?

My legs move before I know what's happening. I vault over the railing and onto the platform. The shouts of Dominus warriors ring out in the hallway.

I join Ryoko at the center of the platform as the lights activate, and I wrap my arms around her.

"Where are we going?" she says.

I want to say somewhere safe, but that isn't true. There's nothing safe about where we're going, but it's the one place that's as dangerous for Myrtrym's people as it is for us.

"It's called P-100," I say as the light blinds me. I pull the watch off my wrist and throw it into the light. "Stay close."

42

WHEN THE LIGHT FADES, Ryoko and I stand on a platform in a large, dank room. The monitors and control panels along the wall appear to be activated, but there is no sign of anybody. A chill runs down my spine. When I was a kid, we talked about this segment at school, all of us sharing ghost stories about the things that went on here. I assumed it was all made up, a competition amongst boys to outdo each other with grotesque details.

Now that I'm here, my palms are sweaty. I'm hoping none of it was true. Hoping this isn't the last time segment I ever see.

Ryoko pulls on my arm. "We can't stay here."

I follow her off the platform. As much as I don't want to go outside, she's right. Dominus knows where we jumped. The platform could reactivate any second.

We leave the room and find ourselves in an old industrial building. The floor is smooth concrete. The high ceiling is exposed steel, and there's a musty smell in the air. The narrow hallway is lined with drywall. Two rows of black doors run down the hall on either side of us.

A door on my left is ajar, so I poke my head inside. The drywall is cracked and crumbling. A thin carpet covers the floor, and a blue futon couch sits against one wall. Against the other wall is a dusty drum set, flanked by guitar amplifiers. "I've seen places like this. Bands used to practice music here."

The front of the building is separated into a few larger rooms with open doorways between them. Cracked windows reveal a gray, cloudy sky. We're in a large industrial complex, but there are no people, no cars, no signs of life.

"Where is everybody?" Ryoko wonders as we walk outside onto a loading dock.

I brace myself as I take in a breath of air. It's risky to be here, but we had no choice. I've heard there are a few habitable zones in this time segment, but I have no idea whether this is one of them.

"We need to run," I tell her. "I promise I'll answer your questions, but we have to get away from here as quickly as possible."

She gives a swift nod, and we take off. I set the pace, resisting the urge for an all-out sprint. We need to conserve energy. I have no idea how long it will be before we can rest, let alone find some food.

We run between buildings, my eyes darting from side to side, checking the windows, expecting to see the terrors from my childhood stories come to life—monsters hurling themselves through the glass panes, bloodthirsty and deranged, screaming for flesh. I try not to reveal my fear. I have to be strong for Ryoko. I have to be strong to survive.

When we reach the street, a traffic signal sways in the breeze at an intersection. An old building across the street has a caved-in roof. To my left lies a large city, decrepit skyscrapers piercing the clouds. *That's where they would be.*

"Let's go," I say to Ryoko, pulling her in the opposite direction of the city.

She resists firmly, staring at the buildings. To me, it's a corrupted picture of the past. But to her, it's a world she's never seen.

"Ryoko, we have to go."

We jog for an hour before I let us slow down, then we walk along an old highway and cross a bridge over a trickling stream. She peers over the side of the bridge. "Dash, what is this place?" I take a deep breath, still wondering about the quality of the air.

"A few decades ago," I say as we continue walking, "a few decades before my time period, that is, something happened. When people figured out how to travel through time, we didn't fully understand how the timestream worked. We didn't know that once you opened a portal, it stayed open but kept 'floating' down the timestream. Instead, we thought you had to open a new portal every time you wanted to go back. It was extremely expensive. Creating a portal requires a lot of power.

"So the corporations started buying up segments of time—years, decades, even whole generations. Two corporations owned pieces of time right next to each other. When one corporation created ripples—that's changes to the timestream—in one period, those ripples flowed down the timestream and eventually corrupted the other company's time segment."

"They didn't know that would happen?"

I shake my head. "Not at that point. It's part of how we came to understand the timestream. We knew that changes made to the past weren't affecting the present. Scientists thought that meant those changes didn't affect anything at all. They didn't realize that the changes never caught up because the present moves forward at the same speed as the ripples.

"But when one corporation's ripples started infringing on another's time period, which hurt their ability to make money off it, things got messy. They went to court, but the Time Laws said the government had no jurisdiction over the past. The politicians told the corporations to settle it on their own."

I stop at the center of the bridge and look at the river. The water disappears around a bend about fifty yards away. The riverbed is covered with large rocks and flanked by withered trees on both sides.

"They fought, didn't they?" Ryoko asks.

I nod. "People called it the Time Wars. The corporations started attacking each other's time periods. It was brutal. A lot of people from both sides were killed, not to mention the echoes . . . that is, the innocent civilians in the past."

Ryoko hesitates a moment. "Did they force the people of those time periods to fight for them?"

"I think they did," I say, remembering the samurai that attacked the pagoda. "At least, in certain time periods. But it ended here, in this time."

She looks around. "And what time period is this?"

A cold wind pushes over the river, chilling my bones. I start walking again, shoving my hands into my jacket pockets. "At this point in the timestream, the year is 2030. But it's been about twenty years since the wars ended."

I can see the understanding in her eyes. "So everything here died in . . ."

I nod again. "About 2010, but not everything is dead. After the war, this time segment became a wasteland. Nobody visits. Nobody wants to live or work here, but there are some survivable areas. The corporations leased those areas out for prison zones and . . . other things."

"What other things?"

"I'm not sure," I admit. "It's probably nothing, but I've heard stories that the government and corporations did experiments on people here, trying to create super soldiers."

The clouds stretch out endlessly in front of us like a thick blanket. I get a feeling that the sunlight hasn't touched the ground here in a very long time. Everything appears to be dead, or perhaps frozen.

We walk about a quarter mile and come upon another bridge, this one much larger. It runs over the top of an interstate. Rusty cars and trucks litter the lanes, pointing in all directions. One of them in particular catches my eye. It's a blue station wagon with the driver's door halfway open. The door sways back and forth in the cold wind, its rusty hinges creaking on the breeze.

We keep going. After we cross the interstate, Ryoko and I come to an old town—gas stations, fast-food restaurants, and more cars. I draw my sword. There are trees on both sides of the road, plenty of places for enemies to hide. I don't like being out in the open like this, but I don't want to go tromping through the woods either.

Ryoko glances at me nervously. "Are you using whatever it is in your eyes to look for danger?"

"No. I'm afraid to use my optics. Dominus can probably trace the signal."

Ryoko peeks inside a car as we walk past. "If they put all that equipment into you, wouldn't they include a device that would allow them to follow you anyway?"

She's right. For someone who spent her entire life in feudal Japan, her ability to grasp the concepts behind technology surprises me. We always assumed that echoes would never be able to understand what we could do, that trying to explain it to them would explode their brains or something. It was stupid pride. We thought ourselves superior because we were born in a later era than they were.

"Good point," I agree. The truth is I have no idea how they've always followed me. I figured that Dominus used satellites and cameras to achieve full coverage of the time segments they own, complete with facial recognition technology, thermal scanning, that sort of thing. But it also stands to reason that they wouldn't invest all this technology in my body without dropping in a few fail-safes.

My muscles tense as I prepare to activate my optics, knowing this might raise a huge digital flag. *Here I am, Myrtrym. Come get me.* But it's worth the risk. I don't know if the optics are equipped to measure radiation levels or air quality, but with a little luck, they might help us find a water source.

I activate the optics with a thought and turn in a slow circle. In my vision, energy pulses scan the entire area.

Red images pop up in the distance all around us, the closest one about a hundred yards away.

Threats detected.

I grab Ryoko's hand. "Run!" We sprint between the cars. A gruff male voice shouts an alert, and motorcycles roar to life. The engines sound like they're coming from multiple directions. My optics magnify the images—riders wearing thick black leather, gas masks, and hoods. Each holds a shotgun with one hand.

We reach an intersection where five roads come together, each bringing an enemy. I look around wildly. There's nowhere to run.

We're trapped.

I shove the sword into Ryoko's hand. She may not have my tech advantages, but in her heart, she's as fearless as I am.

I press my back against hers as the riders pull up, each with their shotgun trained on us. My optics outline the weapons in red. Since they haven't shot us already, they must want to take us alive. I'm terrified of what that might mean.

The marauders rev their engines to the point of deafening. It's a tactic meant to intimidate. It doesn't work.

Ryoko spins the sword in her hand and assumes a fighting position. *If I'm going to die here, I couldn't imagine a better person to have by my side.*

One by one, the riders kill their engines and step off their bikes. They circle us. The one in front of me pulls off his mask. Gnarled, burned skin covers his face. He bares black teeth that are sharpened to points.

"Been a while since we had fresh meat."

"We're not your dinner, friend." I challenge him with a smile. Everything they've done so far is an attempt to put fear into us—the engines, the masks, the teeth. But why?

My optics run a deeper scan of the shotgun held by the rider on my right. *No ammunition detected.*

"Maybe we can make some kind of arrangement," I say, trying to stall as I put my hand on Ryoko's side, pulling us back-to-back again. I tense my arm as I start to turn, leading her as if we're dancing face out. I need a good look at the other weapons. Ryoko keeps her back against mine as we rotate. By the time we're all the way around, I've scanned every weapon. Two have ammunition, the man speaking to me and the rider directly across from him.

"Arrangement?" the gunman scoffs. "Don't think you're in a position to make arrangements."

"Maybe I know things." I activate my armor with a squeeze of the button on my sleeve. I doubt the riders notice as the fabric of my shirt hardens beneath my jacket. I don't know if it can stop a shotgun blast at this range, but I'm about to find out.

The riders speak English, which means my translator isn't set to Japanese. If I can get Ryoko to speak, it will switch. I tap her on the side.

"I'm with you," she says in Japanese, as if reading my mind.

"When I draw," I say, "you dive and attack the man on your right."

"Hey!" The rider pumps his shotgun. "Talk English or you're both dead. Now what type of things do you know?" He steps closer and shows his rotting teeth again.

"And it better be good," he adds.

"It is." I smirk, part of me wishing there were cameras on me right now. "I know your friends' guns are empty."

His eyes go wide. The world moves in slow motion. Ryoko's back leaves mine. I turn, draw my revolvers, and take aim at the men on opposite sides of me. I pull the triggers.

Gunshots shatter the air. Pain slams into both sides of my torso. The men drop. The two in front of me charge, but I'm already pointing both guns straight ahead. My bullets rip through their chests.

I wheel in time to see Ryoko plunge the sword into the heart of the last rider. His shotgun lies in two pieces on the ground, and there's a huge gash on his leg. She pulls the sword from his chest, then wipes the blade on his shirt before he falls over.

The fight over, the pain of the shotgun blasts increases fast, burning both sides of my torso. My shirt took the brunt of it, but I'm still bleeding. My body crumples in on itself. I tumble to the ground.

"Dash!" Ryoko sheathes the blade and drops to both knees beside me. "Are you okay?" Her gentle hands inspect my chest as spots of blood seep through holes in my jacket.

"The shirt is armored," I say, coughing, trying to catch my breath. It's close enough to the truth, and I don't have time to explain. The wounds will need treatment, but I'm fine for now. "We need to hurry. More might be coming."

I lift my head and scan the surrounding area. No sign of immediate danger, but those shotgun blasts could be heard for miles. If there are other threats around, we could have company soon.

Ryoko helps me over to a motorcycle. I've never driven one before, but I've seen it on the timenet several times. Hopefully my implants will help.

I stretch out my arms to take hold of the handlebars, but the blinding pain in my side causes me to reel back.

"Let me drive it," Ryoko offers.

I grimace. "You've never even seen one of these things before."

"I saw them do it—it's like a mechanical horse," she says, urging me onto the back seat and taking the seat in front of me. "You tell me how to work it."

We manage to get the motorcycle started and move forward. After a few minutes, Ryoko gets the hang of it. We double back and take the exit onto the interstate, hoping the open road will take us far away as fast as possible.

THE SKY BEGINS TO DARKEN

around the same time the needle teases the large *E* on the motorcycle's fuel gauge.

"We need to pull over soon," I shout into Ryoko's ear. I'm unsure how long we've been riding, and I'm concerned about my wounds. The fabric of my shirt is designed to provide a temporary bandage, but it's not a long-term solution. Dizziness is creeping in.

Ryoko nods her understanding.

A few miles have passed since I lost sight of the city behind us. Withered pine trees line both sides of the interstate. Many look like the slightest nudge could topple them over. Except for the occasional abandoned car, the road is clear.

"Turn here." I point to a blue exit sign that promises a gas station. Without electricity, the pumps will be useless. But if I can find a hose, maybe we can siphon gas from other cars.

Plus we need a place to stay for the night.

Ryoko slows the motorcycle as we pull off the exit and into a small town. Gas stations, restaurants, and a run-down strip mall surround us. Broken neon signs with missing letters adorn what's left of the stores. Most of the windows are busted. This area was probably looted a long time ago, but maybe we'll get lucky.

I try to scan the area, but my optics glitch as if there's some interference. *Maybe it has something to do with the air.* What happened in the Time Wars is not public record, but common knowledge is that the corporations used nuclear weapons. For all I know, the fallout could be causing some distortion. I'm not picking up any signs of life, but I don't know whether I can trust the readings.

We pull into a gas station, park the motorcycle, and head inside, stepping over broken glass as we push open the door. The shelves and coolers are bare except for empty potato chip bags, leaves, and scattered magazines. Ryoko searches the store while I inspect the area behind the counter. I crouch down to examine the shelf beneath the register, finding only a few broken bottles, empty food cans, and old newspapers.

"Nothing." I start to stand up. Dizziness hits me like a storm in my brain. I crouch back down, holding onto the counter to keep steady. Blackness creeps around the edges of my vision. I take a deep breath and try to collect myself. I can't stop moving until we've checked the other stores. I pull my head up slowly.

Ryoko watches me from the other side of the counter, concern obvious on her face.

"I'm fine," I say, though I'm not sure it's actually true. "We've got to keep moving. It'll be dark soon."

When we walk back outside, I look toward the strip mall and let out a deliberate breath. *Keep it together, Dash.* The odds are slim that we will find anything useful, but we have to check all those stores, which means I can't pass out. Yet.

Do it for her, I remind myself as Ryoko and I walk to the motorcycle, her worried eyes still on me.

"Stop!" a voice calls out from behind us.

Ryoko and I whirl around.

Four people walk out from behind the corner of the

store–two men and two women. They're dressed like the riders we encountered before, except their faces aren't covered. Each holds a rifle, but they're not weapons from this time period. They're energy rifles. Modern tech.

Why didn't my optics pick them up? My hands go for my guns.

"Don't!" one of the women yells out, training her rifle on me. I stay perfectly still. Ryoko does the same. My optics scan again, but they're not detecting these people's weapons or thermal readings. *What is happening?*

"Well, what do you know?" one of the men says as they near us. "It's *him.*"

"Who?" the other man asks.

"The timestar," one of the women replies. "He's a soldier for Dominus."

"No." I raise my palms to show I haven't pulled my guns. "I'm no soldier."

"But you do work for Dominus," the first man says. "We've seen you on the timenet."

"I did." The dizziness returns. My body trembles, and cold sweat covers my skin. "Not anymore. They're hunting us."

"He's bleeding," one of the women notices.

I fight to keep standing, but my muscles all surrender at once, and I collapse. I feel arms encircle me on the way down. Ryoko tried to break my fall.

"Please," she says, but she's speaking Japanese. "Please help him."

They won't understand your language. I try to say it, but my lips won't cooperate. I fight the darkness taking over my vision, trying to stand again on sheer will, but it's no use.

The last thing I see is Ryoko's face before I slip away.

Strange visions surface in the darkness. First, I'm back in El Dorado, running from Myrtrym, but his cameras are everywhere, and I can't escape them. Golden soldiers block me at every turn. I'm powerless to save myself.

Then I'm looking up at Ryoko's face as clouds rush by. I try to call out to her, but my voice doesn't work. The riders surround us. I hear their shotgun blasts again, feel the pain erupt in my sides. It spreads over me, drowning out everything but a voice in my left ear.

The voice of Myrtrym. "There's no turning back."

Darkness again.

When I open my eyes, I'm lying in a hospital room. The walls are dingy white bricks and the open window to my left reveals a gray, cloudy sky. The stinging smell of antiseptic fills my nose. A white sheet covers everything below my chest. I pull it away and see bandages wrapping my ribs. The flesh is tender, but the pain is gone.

The pattern of footsteps draws my attention to the door, where I see a little girl with black hair wearing a pink T-shirt and jeans.

I close my eyes and run my hands over my face. When I look again, she's still there.

"Hi," I manage.

The child scampers away.

I swing my legs over the edge of the bed, surprised that I haven't been restrained. These people must not think I'm a threat. I don't see my boots, so I place my bare feet on the cold tile floor.

"Take it easy, timestar," a woman says.

My eyes flick up. A woman who looks to be in her early

twenties leans against the doorway, crossing her arms. Her black hair is shaved very short. Her pants are gray camouflage, and she wears a dark-green tank top that shows off slender but muscular arms. Matching snake tattoos run from her wrists to her shoulders. She's not holding any weapons.

"Where's Ryoko?" I test my body as I stand. The dizziness is gone. My strength is coming back.

"She's safe," the woman says. "In better shape than you, although that's some impressive tech you're rocking. It saved your life."

"Lucky me."

She laughs. "You must be hungry."

"Starving."

"Follow me." She straightens. "Your clothes are in the next room, then I'll take you to our cafeteria. Ryoko's there now."

The woman shows me into the next room, and I realize I'm not in a hospital after all. A thin carpet stretches out beneath rows of bunk beds. Old bulletin boards line the walls. There's a chalkboard at the far end of the room.

"This is a school?" My clothes lie folded on the first bunk.

"Used to be," the woman says. "Now, it's our home."

I inspect my jacket and shirt. A patchwork of fabrics covers the holes from the shotgun blasts. I have no idea if the armoring technology will still work. "I don't mean to be rude, but can you give me a second to change?"

"Sure." She points to a camera in the corner of the room. A red light shines beneath the lens. "Just know that you're still a celebrity around here."

After she leaves, I pull on my clothes and boots, then walk out the door to find her waiting outside. The smell of my leather jacket reminds me of home.

"Thank you for helping us." I extend my hand. "My name is . . ."

"Dashiell Keane," she says with a wry smile. "*The Red Dragon*.

Everybody here knows who you are. My name is Veira." When she shakes my hand, I notice the snake tattoos again.

"Nice ink."

Veira snorts. "You don't recognize me, do you? Makes sense. Ralf always made us cover our faces. Last time you saw me, I was dangling off the side of a building."

The memory of the Serpent comes rushing back. "No." I gape at her. "You can't be . . ."

"It's me." She strikes a quick pose. "And as always, it looks like I'm a few steps ahead of you."

I shake my head. "I . . . I can't believe it. What are you doing here? What is this place?"

"Come on. I'll show you."

Walking down the hallway, we pass rooms filled with beds, but others have been converted to workshops and equipment storage. A few still look like classrooms. People stare at me as I walk by.

"Are most of these people . . ." I consider the words before I speak, not wanting to insult the people who saved us.

"*Echoes*?" The way Veira says it tells me she finds the term disgusting. "No, we're all from the present."

"Prisoners then?"

"I guess you could say that, but we see ourselves as freedom fighters."

"Freedom from who?"

"More like freedom *for* whom," she states. "We fight for the people you call echoes, people like Ryoko."

The growing pain inside has nothing to do with my wounds. I want to explain why I've done the things I've done—but I keep silent. "So how did you get here?"

"Same as you, kind of." Veira pauses to smile and wave at a small group of kids scurrying down the hall. A young man chases after them with an old textbook in his hand. "I auditioned for Dominus too," Veira says, "but my tryout was in a different time period. Things went wrong. Really wrong. Dominus left me for dead, but the exiles saved me. I've been with them ever since, helping them with their mission."

I glance around. "Helping how?"

"Well, when this group first got together in the present," she says, "they tried protesting the way corporations were treating echoes by signing petitions and that sort of thing. But the government didn't care. The politicians are all in the corporations' pockets. So they started hacking the timenet technology, disrupting broadcasts, and so on. The corporations tracked them down, and the government officials turned a blind eye—no trial, no judge, no jury. The corporations sent them here and paid the government to keep quiet about it. But we still have some allies in the present. They do what they can to smuggle supplies to us—food, tech, weapons to defend ourselves."

"Tech?" I ask as we walk past one of the workshops at the end of the hallway. The room is a mess of wires and steel. A man hunches over a table, wearing a welding mask and gloves, inspecting some gadget I don't recognize. "Is that why my optics didn't pick you up when I scanned the area?"

Veira winks. "One of our little tricks. We had to get pretty good at jamming signals. Helps us hide."

When we walk outside, we're in a large open space surrounded by trailers. In front of us is a huge garden with lamps hanging from wires over the plants. Through the small gaps between the trailers, I see a massive fence constructed from scrap that creates an outer perimeter. An engine rumbles somewhere nearby, which I assume is powering the lights.

Interesting. "You can grow food here? I thought this time segment was too radioactive."

"For a while, it was," Veira says as we stroll toward the garden. "But they kept trying. A couple of years ago, things finally started to grow."

"Unbelievable." Stretched out in front of me are rows of corn, peppers, tomatoes, cucumbers, and a handful of other plants.

"The planet seems to be healing itself," Veira remarks. "Best thing the corporations ever did was to leave this time segment alone. Things have a way of getting back to their natural state when we stop trying to bend them to our will."

"And your people are just . . . living here now?"

"It's not as bad as you think," she responds with a brief smile. "Sure, there are things we would change. It would be nice if the clouds would break so we could see the sky once in a while. We could stop using lamps to grow food. But all things considered, it's peaceful. We have to protect ourselves, of course."

"I imagine so. We had a run-in with some people that I assume were prisoners."

Veira nods. "They've tested our walls a few times, but we've been able to fight them off. Don't get me wrong. There are some twisted forms of humanity roaming this time segment. I've seen things I'll never be able to unsee, but the darkest creatures moved on a long time ago."

I look at her. "Almost sounds like you *want* to live here."

She frowns as if thinking about it, as if this wasteland isn't a prison sentence. "Not much more we could ask for," she finally says. "We have food, water, peace. A lot of us feel more free here than we did in the present. The most dangerous thing that could happen to us would be if Dominus or the other corporations took an interest in this time period again. That's why we were cautious with you. We've seen what you've done."

"You have the timenet here?"

Veira resumes walking toward a large trailer that occupies the corner of the courtyard. "Some of the best technological and scientific minds of the present are on our side. Many of them helped develop tech the corporations still use today. We can hack into their signals and watch the timenet. Normally our people find better things to do, living their own lives and such."

The comment is like a pinprick—it doesn't do any real damage, but it hurts.

"Certain programs get flagged," she goes on. "Especially if it's highly popular."

I put on a smile, trying to salvage any dignity I can. "Did you enjoy my stuff?"

Veira stops walking and destroys my attempt at showing off with a single look. "You still don't understand. The people of the past are being abused on a massive scale every day by the corporations."

I wipe the smile off my face, replacing it with a stiff jaw. "I didn't kill anybody who didn't attack me first. Some of them did terrible things. I don't know how much Dominus edited out, but I've seen horrible stuff too."

"Fair enough, but maybe you shouldn't have been there in the first place. And I'm not unrealistic. What you did was a drop in the bucket compared to the carnage Dominus has executed against those people."

"But they're not . . ." I stop myself. *They're not real.* Is there a part of me that still believes that? If it's true, my mother isn't real, and I don't even know what it means about my brother and me. "But they're not breaking any laws."

"Depends on your laws," she responds. She looks up toward the clouds, but her eyes glimmer as if looking past the unending dreariness toward something brighter, something more powerful. "Regardless, it's not as much about what you did. It's what you represented. The timenet hurts everybody. Not only is it killing the people in the past and destroying their home worlds, but it's corrupting the minds of people in the present. It reinforces the worst parts of us. You've seen both the past and the present firsthand. Do you think humanity has improved because of this technology?"

I look away. I know I'm wrong, but that doesn't mean I'm not upset.

Veira brings me back with a hand on my shoulder to draw my focus. "We're still fighting. There are some among us, one man, really, who believes we can make a difference. He was a part of the breakthrough that achieved time travel."

"He must be pretty ancient," I say.

Veira smiles. "He's very old, but his spirit is strong. Having a reason to live will do wonders, especially when that reason has to do with helping other people." We start walking toward the large trailer again. It must be the cafeteria. I can hear lots of voices and clinking dishes inside.

"Can I meet him?" I ask hopefully.

"No," Veira says. "He's . . . not here. We provide him a safe space to work. If he can do what he thinks he can, it might give us a shot to help many more people than we ever have before."

She doesn't trust me. I can't say I blame her. "Thank you for taking us in." Despite all the jabs I've taken on this walk, I mean it.

"You're welcome," she replies. "You and Ryoko can stay here as long as you want. I have to admit, there are a lot of people who were very excited to meet her after seeing her on the timenet. We found an old, dusty translator mic and headset that our tech managed to get working, so she's using it to talk to her adoring fans." Veira chuckles as we come up to the cafeteria.

The words hit me like a sledgehammer. I've never explained to Ryoko what the timenet is, how it works, or the fact that our entire relationship has been broadcast to millions of people. I'm shaken to the core as I realize I might be too late. *Maybe she doesn't know yet. Maybe they haven't mentioned it to her.*

But any possibility of that melts away when I see her standing in the doorway, holding the headset in her hand. Her face says it all.

She knows.

44

"YOU LIED TO ME." RYOKO

punctuates each word as she walks past me.

Veira glances at me side-eyed before going into the cafeteria.

I hurry after Ryoko. I don't want to upset her any further, but I don't want her to leave either. "Please, let me explain. I was going to tell you."

She whirls around. "When, Dash? When were you going to tell me?"

The same question I asked my parents. The realization jolts my nerves. I look at the ground. "I tried so many times in the letters, but writing it out didn't seem like the best way to explain it. I wasn't sure if you would . . ."

"You didn't think I'd understand? Do you think I'm a fool, Dash? I couldn't possibly comprehend your technology, right? I'm just some stupid *echo* girl to you." She marches away.

I chase after her. "You know that's not—"

"Oh, I know that's not the real truth." Her words are clipped. "You knew I would understand everything. But you were too afraid to tell me."

My stomach is in knots at the thought of losing her. "You're right. I was afraid."

"You made me a joke." Ryoko's still moving, but she slows down a little. "The foolish girl from the past being led around by the nose, falling for the future boy. I bet your friends had a lot of fun with that."

"What? No," I protest. "It's not like that at all."

"It's exactly like that. Entertainment, right? That's why you're here, it's why I'm here, and it's why my village burned down. It's why the pagoda was attacked. It's why I lost my parents. And it's why you took me on that ridiculous date."

That comment hurts the most. Deep down, I've always known the attack on the village had something to do with me, and I've felt a lot of guilt because of it.

But the date through time was special. My feelings were real.

"It hurts, doesn't it?" Ryoko prods. "Did you believe I didn't know you were keeping things from me? You must think I'm stupid. Maybe I am. I knew you were hiding a secret, but I thought it was trivial, an insecurity, so I trusted you. You asked me to trust you, Dash, so many times, and then you do this to me."

"Ryoko, please," I beg, "can we sit and talk about this?"

She stops and hangs her head, closing her eyes. Ryoko never cries, not even after the death of her parents. She's steeling herself, I realize, compartmentalizing the pain I caused her.

When she looks at me, it's like she's looking at a stranger. "No. I'm leaving. I can't be around you anymore."

"Ryoko, that's suicide. You'll never make it out there."

"I don't need you to protect me. All that you've done is torn my life apart."

"Then I'll leave," I say. "Myrtrym isn't going to stop looking for me. What these people have here is special. If I stick around, it'll all be destroyed. I can't live with that on my conscience too. I should be the one, not you."

The gray clouds darken overhead. It's difficult to tell the passage of time here, but it will be night soon.

"You'll leave tomorrow?"

"Tonight," I say.

"Alright. Fine." Before I can say anything else, Ryoko marches back to the cafeteria, leaving me alone.

45

WHEN I TELL VEIRA I'M LEAVING,
she doesn't try to talk me out of it. Her people have been kind
to us, but I don't need advanced optics to see the doubt in
their eyes when they look at me. She offers me one of their
motorcycles, which I accept.

A few exiles gather at the outer gate to see me off, maybe to
be sure that I'm gone. A woman hands me a pack of supplies,
telling me Veira suggested I don't open it until I'm an hour away
from their city. The request is odd, but I'm more distracted by
the fact that Ryoko is nowhere around.

A pair of black riding goggles hangs from the handlebar of
the motorcycle. The exiles offer me a helmet, but I decline.
I'm done hiding my face. If Dominus does monitor this time
period, I want them to see me ride away from these people. I
put on the goggles and start the engine.

A guard opens the gate, which is composed of large pieces
of sheet metal nailed together, reinforced with wood and tires,
and wrapped with barbed wire. One of them gives a nod as I
drive by. I pick up speed as soon as I'm through the gate, the
wind whipping at my jacket. The faster I get away from here,
the better. I fight the urge to look back, instead using my optics

to scan the road ahead.

The wind rushing past my ears is all-encompassing as I hit the interstate and head north. Mountains break the dark horizon in the distance. It seems as good a place to go as any.

It feels strange not to have a goal, no specific direction except *away*. How did I get here? Not even a year ago, I was a kid in high school, a faceless rooftop racer, but at least I had Garon and Knox.

Now, I'm a hundred years in the past, running from a powerful madman bent on broadcasting my death. I've alienated all the people who care about me and endangered my family in the process. At least they got some money out of this arrangement. I doubt that Dominus will attack them, not with the attention that would result from it. Myrtrym will come after me, making my death look like a part of the show—but they'll be safe.

I think of Ryoko. She's right. I've destroyed her life.

But I can't dwell on that right now. Too much guilt. Instead, I focus on the road—cracked pavement, broken yellow lines, debris leftover from a once-thriving population. My knuckles are white from grasping the handlebars so tightly.

As the mountains grow large in front of me, my thoughts drift to Veira's mysterious pack. I'm confident that an hour has passed, so I pull off the road next to a field. Large wheels of hay are scattered across the ground like sentinels. I scan the area, finding nothing, though I can't trust my optics. I doubt the marauders have the same signal-jamming technologies as the exiles, but I can't be sure.

Instead, I have to trust my actual eyes and my instincts.

I turn off the motorcycle and walk to the wood rail fence lining the field. I set the pack on the top of the fence, gazing out across the clouds and wishing I were someplace where I could see blue sky.

When I unzip the pack, I find that the bag is filled with vegetables, bread, and a canteen of water. The exiles gave me more than they should have. As I pick through the contents, I see a cylindric metal canister at the bottom of the pack. It looks like a thermos at first glance, but when I pull it out, I recognize it immediately.

A power cell.

This doesn't make any sense. Why would they spare such a valuable item?

A folded note is taped to the outside of the cell. I open it.

> *Dash,*
> *You know what to do with this. Dominus monitors energy readings from this period, but if our intel on the location of the lily pad is correct, the radiation in the area should be enough to mask it.*
>
> > *Godspeed,*
> > *Veira*

My muscles tense. I look around for cameras but see nothing. Nobody. Yet I can't help but feel like I'm still a puppet on a string. Am I being used again? A canary in a coal mine, sent out to determine how dangerous an area might be?

But Veira wouldn't have given me a power cell without a good reason. Maybe I have a worthwhile mission after all. For the first time in a long time, maybe I can help somebody else.

Maybe help Ryoko.

When I activate the power cell, the light shines toward the mountains, the same direction on which I had already decided, like I was being led the right way all along.

I find a roll of tape in the pack and use it to attach the power cell to the handlebars. Seconds later, I'm driving back down the road, hitting the accelerator to go as fast as I dare.

I'm not sure how much time I have left.

46

THE CAVE IS NESTLED IN

the side of a mountain, the entrance less than twenty feet off the ground in a place where the terrain levels off slightly.

I park the motorcycle in front of a collection of boulders at the base of the mountain. The light from the power cell shines directly on the mouth of the cave.

When I activate my gravboots, they lift me off the ground for a second, then I fall back down. I knew the power would run out soon. Lucky it happened now, I guess, and not while I was midair.

I don't need Dominus tech for this climb. I'm a rooftop racer. Plotting a course in my mind comes naturally—the way I'll rebound off each boulder, the places where I'll need to push myself extra hard to reach the next landing spot.

I stow the power cell in the pack and take a few steps backward so I can get a running start before I jump. The motions come back like an old friend, the feel of hitting solid ground, tapping it with my body's energy, feeling the surface give that energy back as I bound off it.

I've missed this feeling. The boulders are more like trampolines as I bounce from one to the next, never losing my balance, never lingering for more than a heartbeat on each surface. Forget gravboots; I need to do *this* more often. My optics could find the optimal course, interacting with my brain to know what I'm trying to do and help me do it better, but I don't want that anymore. If I could, I would tear the tech out of my eyes and leave it behind.

I feel free.

My boots hit the last rock, and I spring into the air, propelling myself higher than I need to, only because I want to experience the sensation of flying without thrusters. The instant I touch the ground, my knees give just as I want them to, slowing my fall enough that I can break into a roll.

I come up on one knee, feeling exuberant as I gaze into the darkness of the cavern. The memory of the island cave comes back to me. Most corporations probably have small lily pads hidden across time in caves and underground bunkers like my cabin. I wonder who built this one.

I pull the power cell out of the pack and use it as a torch, lighting my way into the darkness. The cave floor has a downward angle. After twenty steps, I hit a wall and turn right, following as the rock curves left. The dim light of the gray sky disappears behind me as I venture further into the cave, every step landing a bit lower than the last.

Dust fills my nose, but the cave grows warm as I go deeper. The ground levels out as I approach a glass door that looks like it was once motion-activated. I immediately regret using my hand to clean a section of the glass; my hand is covered in dirt.

It takes a few minutes to pry open the door. Inside is a large, cavernous area. The air is musty and stale. The light of the power cell reflects off the tube of the lily pad ahead of me, tucked against a rock wall. Even with the power cell, I'll be surprised if it works.

I walk slowly across the cavern, scanning the darkness for any signs of attack. When I reach the lily pad, I place the power cell into the chamber.

The room lights up. Not only the lily pad, but walls of monitors and machinery all around me. I pull my sword with one hand and draw my revolver with the other. Machines whir and buzz to life.

There's nobody around. I don't recognize any of the machines. The technology looks older than what I've seen in Dominus facilities. Doubtless some of this controls the lily pad, but there has to be more functionality here than just that.

I approach a large monitor on my left. Beneath it, a control station sits covered with dust. A small camera on top of the station blinks a red light, then emits a sheet of green energy that scans my entire body.

Red letters appear on the monitor. *User authenticated. Dashiell Keane. Beginning playback.*

"Playback?" I say out loud.

A video appears on the monitor. The description of the vid reads *Dash Keane Highlights—Including Unaired Footage!!!*

The first thing I see is the four-pointed, echoing star of the timenet. It shines bright for a few seconds, then the video begins. Onscreen, Shimizu Kaida and I ride horses in slow motion in the light of a setting sun while epic music plays. The sight of my teacher makes me smile. I learned so much from her.

But my enjoyment fades when the vid changes to the battle against Akinari. I watch myself carve through enemy samurai. The battle is intercut with scenes of the village burning, switching between combat and destruction. It's supposed to make me look like a hero.

But from this perspective, I don't see justice.

All I see is carnage.

The vid continues and I'm reliving it all. The gunfights, Duffy's murder, the death of the pirates—all of it mashed together and set to orchestral music like I'm some type of god. I can't take my eyes off it.

And the question I keep asking myself is *why?* All of these scenes were carefully crafted to entertain people while building me up as a strong and courageous hero.

It was all a lie.

The view counter on the vid is well into the hundreds of millions. The vid wasn't posted by Dominus. The owner is a person called JackBSweet. I've never seen my Dominus vids; I wonder if any of this footage really was unaired and, if so, how JackBSweet got his hands on it. *Must be a hacker.* Dominus probably realizes that this happens, but as long as the vids are supporting their product, they let the content stay online.

The monitor in front of me must use facial scanning technology, because the moment my eyes drift down to the comments, faces come to life, holographic images of people who viewed the vid and wanted to leave their thoughts.

A boy with shaggy hair. "Dude, D.K. is the baddest timestar ever!"

An older woman. "I don't care what anybody says. He's setting a good example."

A guy using a demonic clown face as an avatar. "People need to calm down. None of this is real. If you ask me, he should have killed more of them."

The comments continue, most of them praising me for the blood I've drawn. "Fake blood," they say. "Echo blood . . . not real . . . just a game." It's not only adults, but children too. Some comments are short videos of them emulating me as I fight. A few have crafted their own costumes, complete with the *K* logo that Knox designed.

It's all I've ever wanted, and the weight of it is crushing.

"Stop playback." I feel like my mind is about to snap. "Please."

The vid stops. I press my hands over my eyes, but I can't stop seeing the images, the fire, the blood. "I'm sorry," I whisper, maybe just to hear the words.

Another vid starts on its own. I lower my hands and look at the title.

Dash Keane's allies.

Shimizu Kaida practices kata alongside me on the hilltop. Sheriff Duffy talks to me about the best way to draw before blowing his nose. There's even Cameron Cooper, feeding leaves to a young triceratops.

And of course, there's a long section of Ryoko dancing. I sit on the floor of the cave and watch. Every time the vid is finished, I start it over. This one has fewer views, but I don't care. I don't even look at the comments.

Seeing these people is bittersweet. I miss all of them so much. I would give anything—all the views, all the fans—to be with them in real life again. To see Ryoko dance, train with Shimizu Kaida, drink horrible tea with Sheriff Duffy, or talk dinosaurs with Cooper.

And though he's not in the video, I think about Knox. I wish I could hug my brother.

The lily pad sits in front of me, powered by the cell given to me by the exiles. I could go see any of them with the push of a few buttons. The opportunity is right at my fingertips.

But I don't dare think about it any further. Myrtrym wouldn't hesitate to kill any echoes if he thought it would bring him closer to catching me.

So instead, I hide in this cavern, the most famous timestar in history.

Alone with my vids.

47

THE RUMBLE OF ENGINES

jars me awake. I jolt forward, realizing I fell asleep sitting with my back against the cave wall. On the monitor, the vid of my friends plays on a loop. I dreamt I was with them again, reliving all those memories.

Except in every dream, I tried to warn them to get away from me, but they couldn't hear my voice. They kept doing the same things they had done before. It was like I existed outside of the timestream, shouting at the past but unable to change it.

I jump up and make my way back to the mouth of the cave, the engines growing louder. When I step outside, the sound dominates the air. I can't see where it's coming from, so I climb to a vantage point where the mountain juts out. From here, I can see for miles around.

A cloud of dust rises in the distance. I use my optics to zoom in, finding a group of vehicles.

The marauders.

My first instinct is to duck back into the cave. If they know I'm here, running might be an option, but there's probably no better place to hide. The cave would force them into a bottleneck. I could take my chances fighting smaller numbers at a time. Also, it would be harder for them to use guns in such close quarters.

All these scenarios run through my mind, though each ends the same. The marauders overrun me, and sooner or later, I'm dead.

The marauders draw close, driving trucks with mounted machine guns in the beds. The vehicles are covered with sheet metal that makes them look like ramshackle tanks. Bones have been nailed into the chunks of metal, an obvious attempt at instilling fear in their enemies.

Judging by the rattle in my soul, it's working.

But the marauders don't slow down as they near my position, nor do they show any sign of heading toward me. I lie prostrate on the ground and watch them drive past. My optics can zoom close enough to see their teeth, but none of them look in my direction. A chilling realization grabs hold of me.

They're heading for the exiles.

I bolt up. I doubt they can see me anymore, but even if they can, I don't care. Any concern about my own well-being disappears as I imagine what the marauders will do if they reach the compound. The exiles have fought them off before, but I doubt they've faced a horde this size.

I rush back to the other side of the mountain and leap down the rocks, rebounding off the boulders as I did before, but no longer taking any joy in it. I'm moving for a purpose now.

The motorcycle is where I left it, stashed at the base of the mountain. I jump onto the seat, slide on the goggles, and hit the ignition. In seconds, I'm picking my way around the mountain, going as fast as I dare without toppling the bike.

My tires screech as I jerk onto the main road. The wheels spin for an instant—filling the air with the smell of hot rubber before the tires grab hold and propel me forward. I zoom in with my optics again, but even with my technology, the marauders are just a blip in the distance.

The motorcycle engine whines as I push it to top speed, wrestling with the bike as it kicks back and forth on the broken pavement. I wish I had my horse. This machine has no soul. The horse wasn't as fast, but it was real, created by a power greater than the hands of men.

All that men seem to do is take beautiful things and destroy them.

Like I have. I've destroyed everything that I've loved. I've pushed away my family, my friends, and Ryoko. And for what? For vid views? For fame and fortune?

My heart races with the engine and the rush of the wind. The red blips grow in front of me. I'm gaining on them, but I'm not sure it's fast enough. They'll reach the exiles soon, and there's no way for me to raise the alarm. Will Veira and the others see them coming? I wonder if they have any way of monitoring their perimeter.

I check the fuel gauge. Almost empty. I don't care. I'll push this bike to the max. Who knows how much life is left in either of us? Maybe the machine has a soul after all. If it does, I'm crying out to it, begging the spirit of pistons and gears to find something more than gasoline, to draw energy from a deeper source. *We need it, friend. I'm sorry for doubting you. Maybe I'm going crazy before death, but we'll die gloriously, our bodies covered in the dust of battle until the ripples of change wipe us from the timestream altogether.*

I'd rather die here than at the hands of Myrtrym anyway.

A streak of red appears as a bullet rips through the air by my head, so close that I swear I can feel the heat. They see me. So be it. I'll make myself known. I would rev the engine louder if I wasn't already pushing it to the breaking point. The fuel gauge is forgotten; we die when we die.

The rider in the rear truck swivels his mounted gun around and opens fire. Streaks of red blips form lines in my optics. I swerve right to avoid them, riding along the edge of the road. The line of bullets chases after me. I hit the brakes hard and jerk left. Gunfire tears into the pavement in front of me as I accelerate. I can't keep this up for long, but I'm closing in on them.

My motorcycle surges forward, charging the both of us into the mouth of the beast. The spray of bullets stops as the rider reloads. This is my opportunity.

I pull alongside the truck. The motorcycle is running on fumes, but its job is done. I grip the handlebars with both hands to keep the bike steady. I pull my feet up to stand on the seat, then draw my sword and launch myself into the air.

The truck veers away from me, but my blade pierces into the sheet metal on its side. My feet drag against the ground. The marauder leans over the edge of the truck bed and lifts a spiked bat high over his head.

I hold the handle of the sword with one hand and pull myself up with speed and strength he probably didn't expect. I grab his shirt and throw him over the side. His body goes tumbling along the ground. A brutal fall, but he'll live. I'm tired of killing.

I climb into the truck bed, my sword still embedded in the side. I reach over to wrench the weapon free, but I can't get it loose.

The truck swerves, and a red streak of gunfire appears on my optics. Another truck is firing on me with its mounted machine gun, pulling in closer so the marauders can get a better shot.

I duck behind the side of the truck, gunfire streaking overhead and pounding into the opposite side of the truck bed. How long until it's ripping through my skin? I activate the armor in my shirt. It isn't worth much anymore, especially with the patches, but I'll take what I can get.

I peek over the side. We're getting close to the other truck. Soon he'll have an angle on me.

When the gunfire pauses, I stand and put one foot on the lip of the truck bed. My truck goes hard left toward the other vehicle. I step over the side, my foot hitting the handle of the embedded sword. The weapon gives beneath my weight before the strength of the blade rebounds back up, lending me an extra boost as I propel myself high in the air.

My body flips as I extend my arms. My optics lock on the marauder's chest, but I aim for his leg, firing off a shot as I somersault over the top of him. The bullet hits his knee, and he falters. I grab his jacket and hurl him off the vehicle.

A large bump knocks me off my feet, and I crash into the tailgate. My shoulder explodes in pain. The driver leans out the window, the steering wheel forgotten as he levels a shotgun at me.

Before I can move, the truck hits a huge bump, sending it airborne for a brief moment. I fly forward but manage to land in the bed. The driver's head slams against the doorframe, knocking him out. He lurches forward onto the steering wheel. The truck swerves right.

I clamor to my feet and manage to grab the mounted gun for support.

This can't go on much longer, but I need to take out as many as I can. A glance in the distance tells me we're approaching the exiles. In one of the trucks ahead, a marauder pokes out of a hatch in the metal-domed bed, balancing a large weapon on his shoulder. My optics zoom in to identify it.

Ion cannon.

"No!" I pull the trigger, my mounted gun spitting fire like a dragon. The marauder ducks back in as bullets pound the side of the dome. *Where did they get an ion cannon this far in the past?*

Myrtrym. The god of destruction, reaching back from the present to place fire into the hands of monsters. It has to be him. Even now, I'm sure there are cameras capturing all this violence to entertain the masses.

When my machine gun runs out of ammo, I climb onto the

roof of the cab and slide in through the open window on the passenger side. The driver is still unconscious. I reach across, open his door, and kick him out of the seat.

I slide into the driver's seat and slam my foot on the gas pedal. The truck picks up speed, but I'm far behind the tank with the ion cannon. Gunfire bombards my vehicle from the other marauder trucks. I duck as much as I can while still watching the road.

A gunshot grazes my right arm. Blinding pain shoots through me, and blackness creeps around the edges of my vision, threatening to drag me into the dark. *Fight through it. Almost there.* I can't prevent the attack, but if I can stop the ion cannon, maybe that will be enough. Then I can die in a blaze of twisted metal. I don't care about how I look on camera anymore.

I only care that she lives. I send out a plea that my actions here and now to protect the innocent, to protect Ryoko, can be my atonement for bringing chaos into her world. For being part of a society that assumes we are entitled to consume, manipulate, and label the past. To label her an echo. Like my mom. Like Knox and me.

Gunshots hammer my truck like bloodthirsty demons pounding at the door, promising that no matter what I do, they'll find their way in.

I close in on the domed truck, swerving back and forth, fighting the dizziness and pain. My foot eases off the gas pedal. I'll get one chance at this. My timing must be perfect.

The marauder leans out the hatch again and aims the ion cannon. I can see the outer perimeter of the exile's compound in the distance ahead.

The window behind me erupts. A thousand glass shards carve into my skin, but I slam on the gas, giving it everything I've got.

My bumper rams into the back of the truck. The marauder with the cannon falters. A red streak curves into the sky, cutting into the clouds like a comet.

I keep the gas pedal down, feeling the truck hit something large.

The vehicle flips. Everything twists in my fading vision.

Metal screeches.

Glass shatters.

I lose the light.

48

"DASH."

Ryoko's voice echoes in the emptiness, calling out to me, but the darkness pulls as well. It feels like a choice, like I could easily slip away if I wanted, allowing the void to claim me.

I move toward her voice. Being near Ryoko is all I want.

The strain of opening my eyes is like pushing a car off myself, but I manage, and nothing could be more worthwhile. For a moment, there is only her, and everything is right.

As my vision clears, I realize I'm back in the same room of the exiles' compound. Bandages cover almost my entire body, including much of my face. My weapons lie on a table against the opposite wall.

"Are we . . ." I'm not sure how to ask it. My thoughts are jumbled and drowning in pain.

"We're safe, Dash," Ryoko says. She's wearing the headset, but it's her real voice I hear, not the digitized output of the translator. "The battle was overwhelming, but we stopped them."

She leans closer. "You saved us."

I close my eyes and pray she's right.

"But there's another matter."

I already know what she doesn't want to say. "Myrtrym."

"He's demanding to speak with you," Ryoko says, her voice soft. "I'm sorry you have to deal with this right now."

"No." I force myself up, pushing through the pain. "It's okay. Show me where."

I pull on clean clothes—jeans and a white t-shirt given to me by the exiles—then Ryoko helps me down the hallway to a large room where Veira waits along with a man sitting at a computer station. Monitors of various sizes cover one wall. The floor is a chaos of equipment and wires. The Dominus logo appears on the central monitor.

Veira turns her back to the monitor so she can face me. "He can see you."

He can always see me. I nod my understanding. Veira and the others clear the room. Ryoko helps me lean against a rack of servers, checking on me once more before she walks out. I assume my employer demanded that we speak alone.

When the door shuts, Myrtrym's face replaces the Dominus logo, the inner walls of the golden palace shining behind him.

He chuckles. "Dash Keane, you look like death, my friend."

I consider asking him what he wants, but it occurs to me that this conversation might be broadcast. If that's the case, I want to show strength. "You should see the other guy, Myrtrym, or maybe I should say the other guys. Are those twisted thugs the best you can do?"

"Just the opening act," Myrtrym quips. "But I'm delighted that you're eager for the main event."

I curse my own arrogance. Why am I encouraging him? "Your fight's with me. Leave these people alone. They're no threat to you."

He smirks. "We both know that isn't true. It is convenient, however, that all my enemies have consolidated themselves. I guess I have you to thank for that."

He probably expects me to plea for mercy, but I won't give

him the satisfaction. It would be worthless, anyway. "How many views do you think my vid will get?"

"What vid?"

"You know exactly what I'm talking about," I snap. "You know where I am, which means you have a camera on me. This must be hard for you—seeing me destroy your marauders almost entirely on my own, but I bet the footage was great."

He scoffs. "If you think I'm in this for ratings, Dash, if you think this is all about the ridiculous timenet, you haven't been paying attention."

I frown. I'm unsure what to say, but I have to keep talking, to keep exploring possibilities and pray that some good comes from it. It's a risk. Conversation is Myrtrym's game, not mine, though the experience does feel somewhat like rooftop racing—blindly leaping to the next thing, not sure where I'll land. "Still, good content is good content, right? If you don't use it, somebody will. How are Dominus security protocols lately? I've seen some leaked footage. What do you think will happen if more of this gets out?"

Anger flashes across his face before he smooths it away. I'm not sure I've ever seen him break character, the mask he shows the world, the face that hides a demon in the shadows. "All people will see is one group of prisoners fighting another."

I shrug. "Maybe. Seems risky, though, right? The longer you chase me, the more chances the public has to change its mind about what's happening here."

He gives a short laugh. "And how is my attacking you any different than your attacking echoes on the timenet for the past several months?"

"Because I'm . . ." I pause. *A real person? Is that still true? Was it ever?*

Myrtrym stares at me with a devil's grin, evil brimming in his eyes.

Does he know?

"The risk," he states, "is your choice. The longer you're with them, the more you endanger their lives, especially her."

I can't let this conversation go on any longer. I don't know what I'll say. My heart is racing. I don't bother to kill the feed as I turn and walk out of the room, Myrtrym's laughter following behind me.

49

THE MEETING ROOM FOR

the exiles' leaders looks nothing like the offices of Dominus Corporation. There are no flourishes, only stained white walls. There is no time window, just a chalkboard filled with complex equations that I can't begin to understand.

But there is a table filled with people, Veira among them. I sit on one end. Ryoko sits beside me. I don't bother to recount my conversation with Myrtrym. I'm sure the exile leaders saw the whole thing.

"Myrtrym's been holding back," I tell them, "trying to make a good show, but he won't lose. He'll attack again, and next time, it will be devastating."

"This group has been fighting the corporations for a long time," Veira says. "We know how to defend our position, and if we need to, we know how to escape."

I have no idea how they could possibly get out of here alive if Myrtrym unleashes the full power of Dominus, but it's better if I don't ask for details. Myrtrym can't pull information out of me that I don't have.

"Sure," I straighten up in my chair, fighting off the weariness, "but it's too dangerous if Ryoko and I stay. If you tell us the safest places we can go in this time segment, we'll leave."

"We can do better than that," says a man on my left with freckled skin and short red hair.

Veira nods. "You did us a great service when you came back, but you also refused a gift. Maybe now is a better time for you to accept it."

"The power cell?" I ask.

"Yes." Veira leans over the table. "That lily pad isn't enough to send all our people to another time. If it were, the energy signature would be so large that we might as well tell Dominus where we're going. But if the two of you use it, they likely wouldn't notice. As I said before, there's enough radiation in the atmosphere here that it might not register."

I catch Ryoko's eye. Maybe we *could* disappear in time together. Our lives would be spent constantly looking over our shoulders, lying low, but we could do it. If enough time passed, Dominus would probably pronounce me dead to avoid questions. My family might even get a payout. Even if Myrtrym does know I'm an echo, I doubt he wants that information getting to the public. Maybe Ryoko and I could be free.

"But there is something we would need first," Veira adds.

"What is it?" I ask.

The exiles exchange glances, having a conversation with their eyes. They don't fully trust me. Or at least, they have no idea what Dominus might have done to me. I can't blame them. Their signal-jamming tech is impressive, but for all I know, I'm broadcasting all of this straight to Myrtrym's office.

"This is nothing Dominus doesn't already know," Veira says. "You've heard of Dr. Suvea?"

I nod, stifling a sardonic laugh. Suvea. That word represented everything I wanted for so many years.

"Not long after he discovered how to temporarily negate the energy of the timestream and open portals," Veira says, "Dr. Suvea realized he had made a terrible mistake. He had been so consumed by his work, trying so hard to achieve his goal, that he hadn't considered the implications until it was too late. He spent several years trying to undo what he had done."

"I thought Suvea died shortly after his breakthrough." It's what I've been taught since I was a kid. Teachers always glorified this as some grand example of somebody hard at work for the good of humanity, that he probably would have died much sooner if he hadn't been so driven. And after he finally reached his triumphant achievement, Suvea rested.

"That made for a better story than the truth," Veira replies. "He was one of the first among our people, really. He spoke out against meddling with time and started working on new technologies. Instead of just stopping the timestream, Suvea believed we could harness the energy of the timestream itself to open more portals."

"If he was against time travel, why would he want that?"

"He didn't," Veira says, "but we didn't have much choice. The government did nothing to help us. Before long, the corporations controlled everything in the timestream. The people see nothing beyond what the corporations want them to see. We can hijack the signal, but we don't have the resources or the power to do any damage for long before they shut us down.

"But Dr. Suvea believed that the timestream has limitless power. He said that it isn't like power at all, not in the way that we think of it. He said that calling the energy of the timestream 'power' is like calling a faint shadow 'light.' In his writings, he likened it to an exploding star that could last forever. He called it the Echo Nova."

In an instant, my memories take me back to Myrtrym's office, watching him play the piano, searching for the right notes to compose his great piece of music that would "live forever." *Echo Nova.* This is what he's been searching for.

I glance at the dingy white ceiling and picture the timestream running between the fluorescent lights, trying to imagine the energy pushing it forward. "But if we can harness it—"

"There's no limit to what we can do," Veira finishes my thought. "Powering all our tech is just scratching the surface. We could open portals throughout time, broadcast the terrible things the corporations are doing, gather allies, move echoes from one place to another while increasing our signal-jamming tech. The corporations would be powerless to stop us, especially if we could get public opinion on our side."

The unmistakable feeling of hope fills the room. Veira is nothing if not a talented speaker. It's no surprise these people follow her, despite her being younger than most of them. "What does any of this have to do with me?"

"Suvea needs help," she says. "His expertise was always more theoretical, but the available technology has surpassed his expertise. We need somebody to translate his theories into modern technology."

I know what she's going to ask for before she says it. My skin grows warm. "You can't be serious."

"We need a data scientist, Dash, and if our intel is right, your father is one of the best."

"*Was* one of the best." I put both hands on the table. "He's been doing menial work in a factory for decades."

Veira raises her chin. "It's our best option." Her mind is made up. "We don't need much from him, and we're confident we can keep your whole family safe."

I shake my head. "He won't agree to this. His entire life is about lying low. My parents were furious when I became a timestar. He doesn't want to fight the corporations. He wants to—"

"He wants to protect his family!" Veira pounds a fist on the table. The room falls silent. Nobody around the table dares to breathe.

"Myrtrym will go after them, Dash. Maybe not now—there's too much attention. But the public will quickly forget about you, and when they do, Dominus will come for your family, and they'll do it quietly. If you bring them here, we'll keep them safe."

My eyes drift to the door. The last time I felt this cornered, I ran, but this is different.

"Think about it," Veira urges. "Take the night."

I draw in a deep breath, then nod. "Alright."

50

THE SINGING VOICES OF THE

gathered exiles resound in harmony off the walls of the old dormitory. Between the polished wood panels, black wrought iron fixtures, and dim lanterns on the walls, a few people strum guitars while others clap their hands. Ryoko and I sit on a bench on the bottom floor, craning our necks to look up. The building is four stories high. At each story, exiles lean over the wood rails into the open atrium area, singing and celebrating.

Ryoko and I sit shoulder to shoulder, leaning against a wall. She knows what I must do, and she knows she can't come with me. I'm grateful that she didn't argue. Tomorrow, I'm going on a suicide mission. If tonight is my last night with her, I'm glad to spend it like this, not fighting over what may come, but enjoying what is now.

I sneak a glance at her. She's not wearing her translator headset, but the smile on her face tells me she doesn't need to know the language to discern the message.

It's a song of celebration, that much is obvious. There's defiance in the tone of the music, but not anger. Rather, it is the sound of people who have chosen to smile and sing in the face of darkness.

This is what the people in the present need to see, I think to myself.

One of the exiles gestures Ryoko and me toward one of the two elevators that runs up the center of the old dormitory. Each elevator sits in a metal frame that looks like a cage climbing to the top of the building. I take her hand as we walk into the lift. The door shuts behind us, the elevator moves up, and we're surrounded by the music as we ascend.

Ryoko stands close to me. I put my arms around her, and suddenly we're moving together. The music swells as we dance, lifting us higher every second. I gaze into the light that lives only in her eyes. This might be the last night that I ever see it.

I lean in and whisper into her ear the three words that I finally learned how to say in her language.

She smiles and leans back so I can see her face.

"I love you too, Dash."

51

THE INSTANT THE LIGHT

fades on the lily pad, I break into a full sprint. Dominus time scientists shout at me as I jump off the platform. They didn't know I was coming, but in minutes, Dominus security will no doubt flood the room.

When I land, I roll along the floor before popping up and darting down the hallway. My optics recognize the guard at the end of the corridor. He raises his energy rifle and opens fire.

I jump to the metal wall. Accelerometers activate the magnetics in my gravboots—a modification from the exiles. A wild thrill rushes through me as I run up the side of the wall.

The guard panics, adjusts his aim, and shoots again. I launch myself to the opposite wall and barrel toward him at a downward angle.

Before he can adjust, I dive and tackle him. The energy rifle falls out of his hands.

"Thanks!" I move away from him and pick up the weapon. He shouts as I burst out the door.

The gravcar is right where Veira said it would be. Our contacts in the present must have received the message. I jump into the driver's seat and hit the ignition.

Dominus sirens fill the air as the car lifts into the sky. I look in the rearview mirror and see gravcycles swarming in the distance.

"Come and get me." My foot slams on the accelerator. The force of the gravcar pushes me back in the seat. Whoever dropped off the car had loud music playing. Pounding drumbeats. Loud guitar riffs. Soaring vocals. I zoom through the air, weaving in and out of the buildings, my optics helping me chart a path.

I lose sight of the gravcycles as I leave the docks and head for the Dregs. *Maybe I lost them.*

Minutes later, I land in front of my family's apartment. I climb out of the car, leaving the energy rifle in the passenger seat. Garon and my father rush out the door, carrying Knox between them, my mother close behind.

"Dash!" My mother runs forward and throws her arms around me.

All I want in the world is to simply enjoy this hug. It kills me to pull away from her, but Dominus will be here soon.

Garon helps Knox into the back of the car, followed by my mother.

"Did you receive the directions?" I ask my father, but my focus is on the sky. Nothing yet, but we've got seconds at most.

"Yes," he answers. "But why can't you just take us to the hidden lily pad yourself?"

I shake my head. "I'm not coming with you."

"What? You have to—"

"Dad, I can't come with you."

My father pauses before wrapping his arms around me. "I'm proud of you, son. I'm so proud."

A lump forms in my throat as we hold onto one another. "I'll meet you there. I just have to take another path." I pull back and force a cocky smile. "Don't worry. They can never catch me."

We both know I'm lying.

Knox reaches out his hand. I grasp it firmly, and I'm surprised at how strong my brother has become. When I left, he was a kid, but not anymore.

My voice catches a little when I speak. "I'm sorry, Knox. I'm sorry that I put you through all this. The whole timestar thing didn't go as planned."

My brother smiles. "At least you looked good."

I laugh. "Got that right."

I release my brother's hand and shoot a look at Garon.

"I'll take care of them," he says as he climbs into the car. He always knows what I'm thinking. I realize how much I've missed him.

But now, I have to keep moving. I turn and rush down the road. Gravcycles appear in the air over the surrounding buildings. My optics zoom in. I nearly stop in my tracks.

They're not Dominus gravcycles. They're police.

"Dashiell Keane!" says a digitized voice in the sky. "Freeze. You are under arrest for violations of the temporal governance laws."

I don't slow down. I don't know how, but this is Myrtrym's doing.

I glance over my shoulder. The gravcar is already in the sky, flying in the opposite direction. I need to keep the police focused on me, so I decide to do what I do best.

Make a spectacle of myself.

The gravboots and repulsor gloves activate, lifting me high into the air. It takes all my available power to lift me to the top of the nearest building. The boots give out the moment I touch the roof.

"Freeze!" the police repeat, their speaker so loud it shakes the roof. "We will fire!"

My boots pound against the rooftop. I reach the edge and jump, clearing the distance between the buildings with ease. In midair, I catch sight of people on the street below, all looking up at me.

"Dash!" a young kid shouts. "Run, Dash!"

I hit the next rooftop. The police open fire. Energy rounds rip through the sky, hammering into the building.

More people flood the streets as I race across the rooftops, dodging and swerving in erratic directions, keeping the police busy as long as I can. Below, I hear laughing and cheering. A few onlookers hold signs with my scribbled name on them, obviously made in a hurry before they rushed outside. Some wear jackets that have been made to look like mine. A handful wear Ryoko's blue dress. Several people jump up and down, waving their arms as they search the sky for cameras, hoping that they'll be on the timenet too.

They think it's a show. They think this whole thing is a game.

I reach a roof with a large canopy that hides me from the gravcycles overhead for a few seconds. The police stop shooting, possibly because they know they're on the timenet, too, or because of the hundreds of spectators gathered below.

I change direction under the canopy, hoping that they can't see me. How long have I been running? I try to remember the amount of time Veira estimated it would take my family to reach the exiles' hidden lily pad. Five minutes? Ten? Nobody told me where it was located, which means I can't tell anybody else if they catch me.

A door leading to the rooftop bursts open. I whip my head around to look, expecting to see police pouring out the door.

Instead, it's a group of teenagers. Some are kids from my school.

"Dash!" One of the guys laughs. "Run, man! They're coming!"

"Take us with you," another guy says, jogging toward me. He takes an awkward step and stumbles close to the edge of the roof.

My body reacts. I leap for him as he falls over the edge. My hand shoots out and grabs his leg. He screams in terror, but I know I've got him, my enhanced fingers gripping him above the ankle.

I also know he's sealed my fate.

Gravcycles circle the roof as I pull him up. There are more police now, hovering on all sides of me. The faces of the teenagers go ghost white as they watch the police, all of whom use their rifles to let us know this isn't a race, it isn't a game.

"They're helping him escape!" one of the police calls out.

"No!" I push the guy back toward his friends and hold up both of my hands. "No, they were trying to stop me. They're just stupid kids."

Like me.

I move to the center of the roof, my arms above my head, and drop to my knees.

One of the officers drives his gravcycle beneath the canopy and lands on the roof. He sneers as he walks toward me. He wears a holographic shield on his chest with a name and badge number.

The badge flickers, then changes color and shape.

A Dominus logo.

Then he hits me so hard with the butt of his rifle that I black out.

52

A BRIGHT LIGHT BURNS IN

the center of the darkness, growing stronger, stretching out and consuming the black until there is only the light.

Then, it fades.

I pull myself up onto my elbows. Two Dominus guards—both dressed in full armor, including the helmets—stand near me. Steel cuffs bind my hands behind my back.

One of the guards pulls me up and jabs me in the ribs with his rifle. "Walk."

Normally I would fire back with some quip to let him know that no matter how bleak this may look, they haven't beaten me. Growing up in the Dregs will do that to a kid. Society has spent too much time kicking dirt in our faces and demanding that we thank them for it. Telling the elites what they can do with their money, their weapons, and their fancy tech is a vital part of life.

There's none of that left in me right now, nor does there need to be. Running from Dominus' fake police left me with only a few scrapes and bruises, plus they stripped me of everything but my jeans and a tattered white T-shirt. They didn't want me to have any tech when I came here. One guard told me they would have carved out my eyes if Myrtrym didn't want me to see everything that's coming, but I'm not sure I believe him. Putting a blade into a human being requires a certain mix of fortitude and insanity. These guys don't have the stomach for it.

The guards lead me off the lily pad, down the corridor, out the doors, and into El Dorado.

The pounding of drums fills the air with tense energy. As I approach the city, I keep expecting more music to join in, some type of melody from voices or instruments.

But it is only the drums, marching me forward. The music is so different, so much less alive than what I heard in the exile camp. I'm not surprised. These people are incapable of creating that same spirit. There are too many lone wolves here, looking out only for themselves.

A deep red sky, hazy with a fog that obscures the sun into a faint yellow orb, casts dim light over the city, but the temple shimmers like sparkling gold. My optics zoom in on the top of the temple, where Myrtrym waits. He looks like something between a god and a pharaoh, wearing white, loose-fitting pants underneath a gold belt encrusted with jewels. His chest is bare except for a golden mantle on his shoulders, and he wears gold bands along his arms. Behind him sit two large pieces of stone that form the shape of an X.

He's in better shape than I realized. It's a strange thought, but I'm doing anything I can to take my mind off what is to come.

As I walk through the city, cameras buzz around me. Slaves stand at attention on both sides of the path. Many catch my gaze, empathy in their expressions, but they say nothing. If they had witnessed the atrocities I have committed against other echoes, they might spit on me. They might curse me in their own tongue, banishing me to the underworld, praying that I have an eternal soul so that my torment might be without end.

But as it is, I see pain in their eyes. One of them—a large man with broad shoulders—dares to mouth a single word at me as I walk by, a word that reminds me to lift my chin and push back my shoulders.

Brother.

When we reach the other side of the city, the drums grow louder. The slaves lining my path are replaced by Dominus employees hovering in the air. They laugh at me, hurling insults I can't quite hear over the drums

I'm led to a stone staircase running up the side of the temple. Myrtrym waits at the top, a camera hovering above him, no doubt capturing the perfect angle. Two guards stand next to him, both bare chested and wearing black masks that look like jaguars. He knows how to make a good show.

I take my time climbing the steps, the guards no longer with me. I use every last bit of strength to not look defeated. He might be taking my life, but what's left of my dignity, I will hold onto with everything I have.

When I reach the top, I gaze out over the city. All of them—slaves and slavers—look up at us. The hazy red light makes it look as if time has frozen, or perhaps has forgotten this cursed moment altogether, casting us into a red abyss.

The jaguar guards remove my handcuffs and rip the shirt from my chest. One punches me in the gut. The other holds a shock baton in both hands.

They push me over to the stone *X* and force me onto my knees. I obey; there isn't much point in fighting anymore. When I'm down, the guards kick my legs so that my feet go into the opening at the bottom of the *X*. The movement scrapes my knees. I can feel blood dripping down. It won't be the last.

They tie my hands to the stones so that they're outstretched above my head. I look into the camera's lens. Would Myrtrym *dare* to broadcast this? I want anyone watching to feel like I'm looking directly at them.

Finally, Myrtrym looms before me, looking at me the same way he did in Rooftop Ralf's office. It seems so long ago, but when I see that predatory grin, I'm back there again, almost like nothing has changed.

Myrtrym squats down to my eye level. "Have you figured it out yet?"

More games. I might as well play along. "Figured what out?"

"What you are, Dash. Have you figured out what you are?"

I swallow. There must be some answer I haven't considered. "Why don't you tell me?"

Myrtrym lowers his voice. "My one regret is this can't be broadcast. These cameras operate on a closed circuit. The footage will be private, for Dominus employees only, though it might prove useful with the next timestar who gets out of line."

He stands and turns around. As if on cue, a guard hands him a sword with a golden handle. The blade is silver in color, but I would bet it's made from the same materials as my red sword, which I left with Ryoko. *I hope she never has to use it again.* Myrtrym holds the sword high above his head.

The people cheer. The shouting of the Dominus employees calling for my blood sounds genuine, but the applause of the echoes rings false, dutiful.

My optics zoom over the crowd. A few of the slaves refuse to join in the forced celebration, and when that happens, Dominus guards hit them with shock batons that cause them to fall over, alive but in extreme pain. I grit my teeth. The people of the present need to see what's happening. Maybe if they could, they would finally understand.

Myrtrym steps in front of me again and drags the tip of his sword along the center of my chest, drawing a thin line of blood. He avoids my neck—perhaps because he doesn't want me to die too soon—and lifts my chin with the tip of the sword.

"You never understood." He leans in so close I smell the wine on his breath, likely the same vintage we drank together in Paris. "But how could you? How could even the best cog understand the complex inner workings of a finely crafted timepiece? Only the maker understands, Dash."

"You talk like a god," I say, trying to sound as bold as I can manage. "You might be powerful, Myrtrym, but you're no god."

"Maybe not." Myrtrym swipes the sword away, slicing a bit of skin off my chin. "That depends on your perspective, and it also depends on time. Soon I'll have what I've been seeking, and when I do, my power will be indistinguishable from a god."

Blood trickles from my chin down to my neck. "People won't allow it."

He gives me a mocking smile. "Won't they? The people of the present have made their choice, though I suppose I helped them. You helped too. That's your purpose. It's all evolution. They need simple things to keep them entertained. That's where you came in. You distracted them while I did the things they cannot."

"They?" I scoff. "Like you're something special?"

"I'm something necessary," Myrtrym says with a disturbing calm in his voice. "There are differences between me and the rest of you. The vast majority of people carry certain weaknesses that would have destroyed humanity if not for those like me who do what must be done. The truth is, I pity your kind. You don't know any better. You can't help it. You trade all your power to me—gladly, willingly—in exchange for the slightest taste of fame and when it runs dry, you beg for more."

He seems more than content to keep talking, so I'm content to keep trying to appease him. "And what does your kind do with that power that's so noble?" I ask.

"What must be done!" Myrtrym's voice hardens as if he's offended that I would ask. "The greatest advancements in history have been made by those the weak considered brutal, the ones who did things most people can't stomach." His eyes glint. There's a realness about him in this moment. He's no longer the well-dressed businessman I knew before. The mask is gone. What lies beneath is more primal—a creature that sweats, a beast whose mouth waters at the sight of prey, who savors the moment before the kill.

True evil.

"This world would have perished long ago if not for men like me," he continues. "The human race survives by exploiting the timestream. Otherwise, we would have blown ourselves up, one way or another, or run out of energy or food or water. The earth would be a lifeless husk floating along the timestream. The past must be ravaged to save the present. People like me, people who lack weakness, are a product of nature."

"You mean psychopaths?" I look at him sideways. "You can't be serious."

He smirks. "Not everyone who receives the gift uses it correctly, I suppose. That's the price sheep pay for living in the same world as wolves. But the wolves are necessary." He flicks the sword. "Look around you, Dashiell Keane. The people of this time worship me as a god, and I'm not just talking about the echoes. Are they so wrong? What am I, if not a god? I exist outside of time. I move power from one place to another."

"You're no god," I say with scorn. "You're a madman."

In a lightning movement, Myrtrym punches me across the face. Then he unleashes a stream of curses as he grabs his hand in obvious pain.

I laugh at him through bloody teeth. The punch left me reeling, but there's no way I'm letting him know that. "Some god. Do you think all divine beings break their hands punching mere mortals?"

Something flits by Myrtrym's head as he draws himself up, glaring at me. It looks like an insect, but through the dizziness and the sweat, I can't tell for sure. My head throbs in pain, my thoughts are sluggish, jumbled. "Why don't you just kill me?" I ask. "What is all this about?"

"Because the greatest leaders understand the balance between mercy and fear." He bends over and lowers his face close to mine. "I will grant you the mercy of death, but this is about your audience." He casts a glance toward the gathered masses. The slaves continue to watch us.

"They saw you run, Dash," Myrtrym says, still looking at them. "They saw you run from *me*. If they believe it possible to defy us, they may dare the same. You never understood your role, your responsibility, but I understand mine. If they rebel, they will be destroyed. Don't you see? This is necessary."

Myrtrym runs the sword over my shoulder, carving into my skin. I cry out from the pain, trying to fight it back and failing. He slices the top of my thigh, an expert cut that opens a trail of blood. The dizziness increases. Tendrils of pain wrap around my body.

"I tried to help you." Myrtrym studies my blood on the blade as if it's fascinating. "I thought I saw potential in you, so I tried to bring you with me, but you wouldn't listen."

Something buzzes by his head again. The arc of its flight seems too controlled, too deliberate for an insect. I try to focus on it, but the pain blurs everything.

I close my eyes and think of what Shimizu Kaida taught me on the hill. *Breathe.* I acknowledge the pain and allow the depths of my mind to swallow it, to set it aside. It is only my body telling me that something is wrong.

Instead, I focus on the wind at my back, pushing in from the east, cooling my sweaty, bloody skin. My spirit lifts as I dwell on Ryoko, my parents, my friends, and Knox. Despite the pain, the blood loss, I feel peace as I think about them. Myrtrym can't get what he wants out of me.

I only have one thing left to do.

"There's something you should know." I open my eyes.

Myrtrym's face lights up. He has the look of a fox that's cornered its prey. "Go on."

His expression tells me he thinks I'm speaking to him, but I'm not. I'm staring past him at the tiny device, so small it's beyond his notice and that of his guards.

I raise my voice as much as I can so Garon's camera will pick up every word, so that all the people listening in the present will hear me. It's comforting to know he's filming. Nobody can make me look as good on camera as Garon. "My name is Dashiell Keane, and I'm an echo."

Awareness blooms in Myrtrym's eyes. He turns to see Garon's camera and swipes at it with his sword. The camera hovers out of his reach. He roars in anger, then whirls and levels his blade at me.

A boom—like the air ripping apart—shakes the temple as Myrtrym lunges for my heart.

53

MYRTRYM IS KNOCKED

off-balance. He gathers himself, and his eyes dart in every direction.

The world explodes into chaos as bright white portals open around us.

A million emotions flood my mind. *They did it. Somehow, they did it.*

Exiles pour out of the portals in droves. To my left, a group of them drive marauder trucks straight for the temple, firing energy rifles. Dominus employees run in the opposite direction, only to crash into a swarm of samurai on horseback emerging from another portal of light, Shimizu Kaida leading the charge.

Myrtrym's guards turn circles, not knowing what to do, but the look on Myrtrym's face is not fear. His eyes spark with discovery and opportunity.

"Suvea," he says to himself. He drops the sword and runs toward the steps. "Trace the signal!"

When he reaches the steps, Myrtrym turns and points a finger at me. "And kill him!"

One of the guards grabs the sword and starts toward me. With all the strength I can gather, I push down with both feet, launching myself upward. My bonds keep my hands pinned against the stone cross, but my feet swing out and kick the sword out of his hands. With a desperate flail, my other foot connects with a guard's face, knocking him to the ground.

The other guard hits me with a shock baton. My muscles seize at the electricity, and I cry out in anguish.

He raises the baton to strike me again. I brace for the pain.

The strike never comes.

Instead, a red blade pierces his flesh.

Ryoko.

The guard falls. My love stands before me, her warrior's robes of deep blue billowing in the winds. The sounds of battle fill the ground below us, but for a moment, there is only her and me, frozen in time.

She cuts my bonds and helps me to my feet.

"How?" is all I can manage, allowing her to support my weight.

"Your father," Ryoko says. "He helped Suvea complete the formula. The turbine uses the timestream's energy to open portals anywhere."

I stumble to the edge of the temple. On the ground, Dominus guards fight against exiles and samurai. A posse of gunslingers rides in on horseback, John among them, firing revolvers and rifles at the enemy. Filling in the gaps between them are the Mayans themselves. They fight with rocks and tools and courage, slaying their cruel, false gods.

"And Garon's camera?" I ask.

"The signal got through," Ryoko says. "Everyone saw what Dominus has been doing to these people, and they heard every word Myrtrym said."

Myrtrym.

I hurry down the steps as fast as I can, Ryoko close behind. My body protests every movement, blood dripping from my wounds. *He said trace the signal. Isn't that what he said?* If Myrtrym can follow the signal from the portals, that will lead him to Suvea.

The fighting continues inside the temple, a cacophony of golden guards, exiles, samurai, Mayans, and gunslingers. Many Dominus employees have given up fighting and try to loot the golden artifacts, as if they would have any value. Some scream for mercy. Others just run.

The tide is turning in the favor of the exiles, but I don't see Myrtrym anywhere.

"Dash!" a voice calls out.

I turn my head in the direction of my name. A slave runs toward me.

"The time platform," she says breathlessly.

I dodge back and forth between the fighting, my heart pounding as I rush down the hallway toward the stairs that lead to the lily pad. Ryoko keeps pace behind me, sword in hand.

We rush into the room with the time platform, the lights of the lily pad brightening as Myrtrym prepares to jump. Two scientists step in front of us, but we burst through them. Ryoko and I vault onto the platform as the light reaches its peak.

Myrtrym stands in the middle, appearing to disintegrate as he begins the jump.

I leap toward him, stretching out my arms, hoping to knock him off the platform.

My hands grasp nothing, and I fall into a bottomless pit of light.

54

AS THE LIGHT FADES, I FIND

that I'm lying on a time platform in a small, dark room, Ryoko kneeling beside me. Computer monitors and keyboards cover the gray stone walls.

"Dash," Ryoko asks, brushing my hair out of my face. "Dash, are you alright?"

I grunt my response, trying to pull myself up.

"Extraordinary," Myrtrym says from the other side of the room. He stands in front of the monitors as if he's in awe, as if the secrets of the universe have been revealed to him.

"Give me the sword," I whisper to Ryoko. She passes it to me as I come to my feet.

"No." Myrtrym reveals an energy pistol in his left hand. "You're good with that blade, Dash. But I don't think you're good enough to kill me before I fire."

My body freezes. I'm not afraid to die here, except that I would be leaving Ryoko behind. If I thought I could destroy Myrtrym and sacrifice only my own life, I would make that exchange a thousand times. The exiles would find and rescue her soon enough.

But Myrtrym's weapon isn't pointed at me.

"Step off the lily pad," Myrtrym orders, his pistol trained on Ryoko while his other hand punches buttons on the keyboard in front of him. The barrel of his weapon follows us as we move off the platform toward the wall on the other side of the cave.

"Now, toss the sword away, and I mean *away.*"

I throw the sword far to my left. The blade clangs against the wall, landing a few feet from the time platform.

Myrtrym presses more buttons. A loud beep confirms he's done something significant. "There," he pronounces and turns around, squaring off to us.

I glance around. "What did you do?"

"This technology is incredible." His voice is almost exuberant. "I've disabled the lily pad so we won't be interrupted, but that's only the beginning of the power right here in front of me. At long last. Suvea . . . just remarkable."

I look around the room again, expecting to see somebody else, but finding no one. Perhaps Dr. Suvea managed to escape. Good.

"You still don't understand." Myrtrym looks down his nose at me. "I don't suppose you would." He waves the pistol toward the monitors. "This is Suvea."

My jaw drops open as realization sinks in.

Myrtrym laughs at my expression. "You didn't seriously believe that the man who finally unlocked the timestream could still be alive, did you? At least, not in human form."

"You're saying . . ." I fumble for the words. "That he uploaded his consciousness?"

Myrtrym shakes his head. "Not nearly that interesting, I'm afraid. He uploaded his formulas and theories into this software. It's been collecting data ever since, though it looks as though some of the algorithms have been updated." His teeth gleam at me. "I suppose I have you to thank for that."

My father. The guilt is like hot coals in my stomach. All he ever wanted was to keep us hidden. When I stepped into the limelight, that was bad enough. When I brought my family into this, I doomed everyone.

I swallow. "So this is . . . ?"

"The turbine." Myrtrym's voice rings proud. Boastful. "A technology that can tap into the Echo Nova itself. It's how your friends managed to open multiple portals at once in El Dorado. A power surge that big was easy enough to trace. I was hoping they would take the bait."

"You knew they were watching?"

"Of course I knew." Myrtrym smirks. "And bravo to you, Dash. This is who we are together. We make a good show, don't we? A great team."

Ryoko looks at me with wide eyes. Without her translator, I don't think she can understand his words, but she seems to know what he's saying.

"We're not a team," I say.

He smiles that demon's smile. "Ah, but we should be. I'm going to make you an incredible offer. Most people would think I ought to kill you, but the fact remains that you're still the most popular star on the timenet."

Myrtrym waves his gun haphazardly as he talks. "Now I suppose I could find another dumb kid with more talent than intelligence, throw them some shiny toys, and soon enough, nobody would remember your name. But like I said, we're a different species from each other. I can't blame you for that. You did what you did for her." Myrtrym points the gun at Ryoko again.

I step in front of her.

Myrtrym snorts. "Exactly. Well, people still need their distractions, and it's useful for me too. I have all the control now. With a few keystrokes, I can open time portals wherever I want. I've already encrypted Suvea to my unique biochemistry. The full energy of the timestream is at my control. I alone can harness the Echo Nova, but you may reap the benefits as well.

Resume your place as my number one timestar. With this power at my disposal, your fame will be limitless. Money means nothing to me anymore; you will be the highest-paid employee in the history of Dominus Corporation. There will be nowhere you can't go, no limit to the technologies you can use. Your family's secret will be forever safe, and your brother will have all he could ever want. Time will be your playground."

Myrtrym gestures toward Ryoko with a flick of his chin. "I'll even let you keep her all to yourself. The only price will be a few more modifications to ensure you never try to bite your master's hand again."

I look straight at him. "I will never join you."

Myrtrym frowns a little, his expression trivial, as if he just found out it's going to rain on a day he planned to take a stroll. "I thought as much."

He swivels the gun to me and fires.

Before I know what's happening, I am pushed away by Ryoko. I hit the ground as the energy round slams into her chest.

I scream in desperation as I scramble over to her.

Smoke lifts from the singed flesh above her heart. I take her in my arms, fighting back tears.

She's already dead.

When I look up, Myrtrym is preparing to fire again. Any fear I have is gone as I leap up and lunge for him. Surprise flashes on his face. He didn't expect me to attack so quickly.

His shot is erratic, and I dodge to the side, his blast grazing my arm. I don't care.

I tackle Myrtrym, leading with my shoulder, hitting him hard in the gut. The energy pistol falls from his hands as he tumbles back into the monitors.

I grab the pistol and point it at him. My optics target his heart, reading my thoughts, showing me the kill shot.

I fire.

An instant later, his body slumps against the technology.

I let the pistol fall, my mind racing to take everything in. It feels surreal, this moment in time. My focus shifts from Ryoko to Myrtrym, then back again. *It can't end like this. There must be some way to save her.*

But there isn't.

I collapse onto the concrete floor. I'm bleeding, the weakness rushing back in, the dizziness, the disorientation. But my grief is more painful still. Darkness pushes in around the edges of my vision, a void waiting to claim me. I could choose to die now.

"Dash!"

My head lifts to see my father's face on one of the monitors. "Dad . . ."

"Son." He exhales a deep breath. "You're alive."

I stare at him dully. "She's dead. I don't know what to do. She's . . . dead."

His expression softens. "I can help you, son," he says. I see my mother in the background on one side of him, Knox on the other. "Get to the keyboard, and hurry. The interface is still open, but it will time out soon without Myrtrym in front of it."

I force myself up and stagger to the computer array. "What do I do?"

My father purses his lips, then takes a steadying breath. "I don't want you to do this, son, but you may have to. Dominus data scientists and guards will be there soon. Suvea's technology doesn't merely harness the power of the timestream. It can reverse it."

"Reverse it?"

He nods. "Just for a few seconds, probably. It would be like dropping a dam into the timestream. The energy will reverse on itself, then build up until it bursts. The past will keep coming, the ripples of change overtaking the time you're in now."

"But don't the exiles need this tech?"

"We have what we need," he assures me. "Your broadcast is all over the timenet. The uprisings in the present have begun.

People are marching in the streets. You did it, son. There is a long way to go, but the change has started. For now, you have to save her."

Hope flickers in my soul. "Tell me how to do it."

My father runs me through the steps to program the machine. It's simpler than I would have expected, as if Suvea might have foreseen this moment long ago when he first designed the turbine technology.

When the protocol is complete, the one thing left to do is execute the command.

"You don't have much time," my father warns. "They'll be there soon."

I hesitate. "What will happen to this time segment?" I ask. "If the ripples of the past overwrite this time segment, what will become of it?"

He struggles to speak. "I don't know, Dash. You have to have faith. We're so proud of you. We knew better than anyone that you had a different kind of greatness inside you. We love you."

I take a final look at the monitor, at the familiar faces of my father, mother, and Knox. "I love you," I say, one last time.

I press the button.

55

MY BODY MOVES WITHOUT

my thoughts, without my control. My fingers are typing on the keyboard again. I'm falling to my knees. I'm shooting at Myrtrym.

It's all moving in reverse. Everything is being turned back by time; only my thoughts move forward. And even in the confusion of it all, I realize how strange it is that my soul somehow exists beyond the reverse motion of the timestream. Perhaps there is something more after all, a state of being that is beyond all of this.

That idea gives me hope.

Seconds later, Myrtrym is standing and pointing his gun at Ryoko. She's alive. Joyous relief sweeps over me. The time reversal stops. I see the surprise on Myrtrym's face as he realizes what's happened.

"No!" he bellows. He fires, but I pull Ryoko down. The blasts hit the wall. The walls tremble as the technology overloads.

Alarms blare. Lights flash. I throw myself over Ryoko to protect her.

Myrtrym pounds on the keyboard. He turns and sprints toward the time platform. The instant he reaches the lily pad, it disappears along with all the other technology. Even the brick walls and concrete floor vanish, replaced by rock and dirt. The gun dissipates from his hand.

The shaking stops, and there are only the three of us—Myrtrym, Ryoko, and me.

And the sword.

Myrtrym and I spot it at the same time. He rushes for it. I do the same, but I'm faster than him, much faster. I reach the weapon a half second before him, diving into a roll and grabbing the blade.

But Myrtrym doesn't stop moving. He runs into a dark tunnel leading out of the cave.

Ryoko and I chase after him, sprinting up a short, narrow passage that feeds into the daylight. Ahead of us, Myrtrym disappears in the light at the opening of the tunnel.

When we reach the opening, the sunlight is so bright that it blinds me for a second, but I hear Myrtrym scream out in pain and curse loudly.

My eyes adjust. Myrtrym lies on the grass next to a large rock, clutching his foot.

The sun shines in a clear blue sky. The air tastes sweet and fresh as a warm breeze welcomes me. Aside from Myrtrym's moaning, the wind is the only sound. Everything looks new, untouched. Large creatures fly between cliffs and mountains in the distance. It reminds me of when I met Cameron Cooper, but somehow I know this isn't the same time period.

We're here alone.

Myrtrym grunts, trying to crawl away as I walk toward him, flipping the sword in my hand. He rolls over to face me, sweat pouring down his forehead and into his eyes. He spits at me as I approach.

"Do it!" he cries out. "Kill me!"

Ryoko steps up beside me and lays her hand on my shoulder. She says nothing. The choice is mine. It would be so easy; one swipe of the sword to sever the serpent's head. I don't know where or when we are, but with Myrtrym, we have brought the first stain of evil to this untouched land. If I let him live, who knows how much the evil will grow?

But if I kill him, the evil will take hold of me.

I lower my sword.

"Go," I say to him, gesturing into the distance. "That way. Never let me see you again."

Myrtrym tries to stand, but his foot falters, and he crashes back to his knees. He manages a sinister grin that I know is a dare, or perhaps a vow for vengeance.

Then, slowly, he crawls away.

I watch him leave as Ryoko takes my shirt, rips it into bandages, and wraps my wounds. Soon, Myrtrym disappears in the rolling hills to my right. I wonder if I *will* ever see him again.

As Ryoko finishes applying my bandages, I notice something like an insect buzzing toward me. My heart begins to pound as it comes closer, recognition sending my spirit soaring. Painted on the side of the device is the letter K, tilting back and colored with my shade of red. I don't know how they did it.

"Garon," I say into the camera. "I don't know if this signal will get through, if we're even still in the timestream or somewhere else altogether. All technology seems to have been wiped away by the time loop caused by the turbine, everything except this camera." I smile at him. For him. "I don't know how that's possible either."

I take Ryoko's hand in mine. "But if we are in the timestream, if you can see this, don't send anybody back. We're safe here. This is the best place for us now, and we can't let Myrtrym return. Tell my parents I love them and appreciate everything they've done for me. Tell Knox that he has always been the more talented of the two of us, that I love him, and that my only regret is not seeing the great things he'll do to make history of his own. Thank you, my friend, for everything."

The camera continues to hover as I turn and face west.

In the distance, a waterfall cascades down the side of the mountain, the mist rising into the afternoon sky to form a rainbow. My soul lifts at the sight, the openness in front of us, a new world filled with adventure. With spirit. I am with Ryoko, and I can feel the energy that created this place.

Maybe now, without the cameras, without begging the world to watch as I try to prove myself worthy of love, I can focus on that energy. I can learn more about it. I can breathe it in.

"What do we do now?" Ryoko asks.

I gaze at her and smile.

"We live."

ACKNOWLEDGMENTS

Anything and everything good comes from God. If there is anything good in this story, it is by His hand, not mine.

God often works through the people He places around us. With this in mind, I'm so grateful for those who have helped make this book a reality.

To my wife, Stefanie—Thank you for your endless love, support, and partnership. You have always been my first reader, my first editor, the smartest person I know, and the best person for discussing story ideas over truffle parmesan popcorn. I love you so much. You are the best thing that ever happened to me.

To my sons—I am so proud to be your father. This book is dedicated to both of you. Know that despite the allures of fame, fortune, and success, the most important parts of your lives will always be relationships—with God, and with others.

To my family—Thank you to my parents, who worked so hard to give me opportunities for a wonderful life. Thank you to my sister, Amy, who always taught me to be strong, most recently by beating stage 4 cancer. Thank you to Lynn for sharing your wisdom, love, and joyful selflessness with Stefanie, our sons, and me.

Thank you to the O'Connors, the Browns, and the Burkes for accepting me into your families as well and treating me like your own. Thank you to Tyler, Kari, and Eathan for being my first and biggest fans.

To Nadine Brandes—Of everyone in the publishing industry, no one has impacted my career more than you. Thank you for your support, encouragement, guidance, and friendship.

To Steve and Lisa Laube—Once again, you've taken a chance on one of my strange ideas and made it so much better. Thank you for helping me craft this into what God wants it to be.

To the authors who have supported me—Sara Ella, John Hartness, Diane T. Ashley, Caroline George, Brett Brooks, The Inspiriters, The Fireside Critique Group, everyone at Realm Makers and ACFW—Thank you for always being there with good conversation and helpful advice.

To my street team a.k.a Team Boom Release—You have made this experience so incredibly special and ridiculously fun. Thank you all so much for coming along with me to tell people about these stories.

To my teachers—Joy Carroll, Paula Gillispie, Joanne Dirring— Thank you for giving me the confidence and support to become a writer. Each of you made a huge impact on my life.

To my friends—Jack, Mike, Graham, Amanda, Skip, Trent—Thank you for the countless times you encouraged my writing, mourned with me during my setbacks, and celebrated with me when the right opportunities came along. You are lifelong friends.

To my music family—Myles, Brooke, Hector, Megan, Jered, Joanna, Milton, Ryan, Chase, Carey, Drew, Trent, AB—Thank you for always listening to, praying with, and cheering for me as I take this journey.

To everyone who worked to bring this book to life—Lindsay Franklin, Kirk DouPonce, Trissina Kear, Jamie Foley, Sarah Grimm, Megan Gerig, and the rest of the Enclave team—Your work makes a difference in the world. Thank you for allowing me to be a part of it.

ABOUT THE AUTHOR

Clint Hall is an author, speaker, and podcast host with a degree in communications from the University of Georgia. He has been writing stories since middle school, where he spent most of his time in English class creating comic books. (Fortunately, his teacher not only allowed it—she also bought every issue.)

Known for narratives that instill a sense of hope, wonder, and adventure, Clint's debut novel, Steal Fire from the Gods, was published by Enclave Publishing/Oasis Family Media in November 2023. Echo Nova is Clint's second novel.

You can find him moderating panels at conventions, online at ClintHall.com, on Instagram at @clinthall, or hosting The Experience: Conversations with Creatives podcast, available on all major platforms.

Clint Hall lives in Atlanta with his wife, Stefanie, and their two sons.